I0670765

Goliath

a novel by
Ray Holland

GOLIATH

© Copyright 1995, 2009 by Ray Holland

A different version of *Goliath* was e-published in 1995 by Spectrum Press. This version is much, much better. Trust me.

ISBN-10: 061527918X
ISBN-13: 978-0-615-27918-3

Published by Great Big Dog
P.O. Box 161272
Louisville, KY 40256
www.greatbigdog.com

This novel is a work of fiction. Any resemblance of the characters depicted in the story to actual persons, living or dead, or of events described here to actual events, is unintended and entirely coincidental.

You can contact the author at greatbigdog@gmail.com with comments, suggestions, questions, or whatever. I can't promise to reply to all e-mail, but I'll read everything.

—RH

Table of Contents

1. The Story Starts Here

Meanwhile, in another part of town, Roger Glass Door Knob was sitting down to get his hair cut in one of those fancy styling salons. He had come to this place a few times before, always making his appointment with the same stylist, Emma Lou Josephine Vernacular Bloobus Rebecca French Fry Snuffy McTelephone Etta Hortense Wingding Tifferson Hortense P. Barnacle. Yes, Hortense is in there twice. Her parents liked it too much to use it just once. And since they thought she had a long name, her friends called her Emma Lou Josephine Vernacular Hortense Hortense P. Barnacle. It didn't flow off the tongue easily, though. She felt the whole thing would have been much more poetic sounding if they were to leave Wingding in. Roger would have called her that—the Wingding version, that is—if he were ever to get an opportunity. He wanted to get friendly with her. She was very pleasant and agreeable to be around, and pretty besides.

But he didn't call her anything at all because he was extremely shy and scared senseless at the mere notion of talking to her. It was traumatic to ask her to cut his hair. Ask her out to the movies on Friday night? Holy smoke! She might as well be Satan's own evil, fire-breathing pet raccoon!

He had a girlfriend, a schoolteacher, but things weren't going very well with her. She wouldn't marry him because he didn't have a good enough job. He sold charcoal for Schurk Enterprises, out on the street corner in the rich people's neighborhood. He had himself a place on the sidewalk where he sat on a big, tall stool, like the kind they have in bars, except taller and not in a bar. It was customary for charcoal vendors to sit on tall stools so prospective customers could see them better. And he sold his wares out of a big ol' canvas bag to people who stopped at the red light.

She, the girlfriend, that is, said that selling charcoal wasn't a job for a real man. She said it was a dead-end job for a boring, underachieving loser kind of guy who had no talent, imagination, or ambition, no offense intended.

And of course he took no offense, but still, he liked the job. He liked being outdoors and passing the time of day with the rich people. He made enough money to pay the bills and even had enough left over to indulge in a little (don't tell anyone) diuretic paint thinner every other weekend.

He wasn't living the high life like some wealthy guy who was rich, or even like some rich guy who was wealthy, but life was good. Well, that is, it was good enough. Sort of. At least he had a better job than his cousin Sylvester, who worked as a television antenna at a nursing home. It seemed to Roger that it would be terribly boring to stand perfectly still all day, but Sylvester liked to point out that it took a special person to do a job like that. He took pride in his work. And that was what Roger admired about him.

Anyway, Roger had been thinking that maybe he should break up with his girlfriend and move on. He was sure there were plenty of women out in the world who could appreciate him for the man that he was. There were plenty of women who could appreciate him even if he couldn't afford a car or bus fare or clothes or food every day or toilet paper. Sure, all that stuff would be kinda nice, Roger had to admit, but really, to *expect* it was nothing more—or less—than decadent.

Emma Lou Josephine Vernacular Hortense Hortense P. Barnacle seemed like a woman who could appreciate him. And yes, he could appreciate her, too, for the woman that she was, whoever that might be (and if he could bring himself to talk to her, he might find out). They could get married and live in a big house, like with seven bathrooms and a tennis court in the closet. How could they afford such a house on a charcoal vendor's pay? She would inspire him to achieve greater and greater heights of charcoal sales, that was how. If you sell enough of *anything*, no matter what, you'll make a lot of money.

When he looked at it that way, it seemed so elegant, so simple and elegant.

But sadly, in reality, "I'd like a haircut" was all he could say around her, and he could barely say that. It came out in a croaky voice that sounded like a television set with bad reception showing a horror movie that has reached the big exorcism scene, while three guys with jackhammers are pounding away at the floor behind you (some would say four, but in my opinion that's overdoing it). You might not even be sure poor ol' Roger was speaking English if you were an impartial observer. But Emma Lou Josephine

Vernacular Hortense Hortense P. Barnacle knew what
he was saying. Hey, he was sitting in a barber chair in
front of her. What else *could* he be saying?

And not having the slightest clue how sick in love
Roger was, what else would Emma Lou Josephine
Vernacular Hortense Hortense P. Barnacle say except
"Of course"? So she said it and began cutting Roger's
hair. She clipped and snipped and trimmed and…well,
she cut Roger's hair. They didn't talk because Roger
couldn't, and Emma Lou Josephine Vernacular Hortense Hortense P. Barnacle just thought he was the quiet type who liked to relax quietly and enjoy haircuts.

After a few minutes, Roger suddenly remembered
he had left his wallet at home. Oh, pooh stains! He sat
in the chair, getting his hair cut, listening to Emma
Lou Josephine Vernacular Hortense Hortense P. Barnacle whistle the theme song from *The Many Loves of
Dobie Gillis*, and he had in his mind this vivid—terribly vivid—picture of the wallet lying on top of his stack
of Burl Ives Fan Club newsletters, right there by the
phone. At the very moment Roger was leaving home,
the commander of the Swedish army had called to invite him to a party. The call distracted Roger, and he
forgot his wallet.

(It's worth mentioning here that Emma Lou Josephine Vernacular Hortense Hortense P. Barnacle was
the president of the local chapter of the Burl Ives fan
club. If only Roger could have mentioned Burl Ives,
Emma Lou Josephine Vernacular Hortense Hortense
P. Barnacle would immediately have become interested in him. But it was not to be. Now, how could they
both belong to the club without her finding out about
his love of Burl? He never went to the meetings. As far

as the club was concerned, he was nothing more than some guy who sent them a check every year to pay his dues—and the chairperson of the membership committee was the only one who knew *that* much.)

Now, in the barber chair, Roger fought back a wave of panic. He wouldn't be able to pay for the haircut! And worse, he'd have to suffer the embarrassment, the humiliation, the mortification, the shame of having to tell Emma Lou Josephine Vernacular Hortense Hortense P. Barnacle he didn't have any money. Not just a barber, not just a hair stylist, but the woman he loved. Or, that is to say, the woman he *would* love if he knew what to do about it.

What would she think?

What COULD she think?

Would he even be able to tell her why he wasn't handing her any money?

What torment! But there was one way out: he could die. He could haul off and die right there in the barber chair, and then no one would be concerned about the money.

It wasn't a decision a guy could rush into, but she would be finished pretty soon. He had to think quickly. What else could he do?

Uh, well, he could pull that potato milk shake out of his pocket and pour it over her head.

No, wait. That would make things worse.

Okay, so dying was the only thing he could do. Too bad it had to come to this. And he almost had enough money to get the air compressor out of layaway at the pawnshop. It would have been really nice to have that machine to clean his teeth in the morning before work—not that he understand how to use it for that,

but the pawnshop guy had assured him that the daggone thing was the *future* of dental hygiene—but on
the other hand, he wouldn't be going to work anymore.
And he wouldn't be doing anything to get his teeth
dirty anymore. Ready, everybody over there Wherever
It Is That People Go When They Die? Okay, here goes.

Roger died.

Emma Lou Josephine Vernacular Hortense Hortense P. Barnacle thought Roger had fallen asleep. She
kept on haircutting as if nothing were wrong. As far as
she knew, nothing was, indeed, wrong. She finished the
haircut and nudged Roger.

"Wake up. I'm finished."

Roger didn't wake up.

Emma Lou Josephine Vernacular Hortense Hortense P. Barnacle nudged him harder. This time Roger
fell over and banged his head on a small antique wood-
en table. The banging didn't hurt Roger because he was
dead, but it broke the table.

"Jeepers," Emma Lou Josephine Vernacular Hortense Hortense P. Barnacle said. She wondered, oh-so-
briefly, if she should make him pay for the table. But
it had clearly been an accident and, for that matter,
partially her fault for nudging him (although she really
didn't think she had nudged him that hard).

At that moment Roger's roommate, Cato Kierkegaard, walked into the barbershop with a wallet-sized
object in his hand. He was waving this mysterious object around as if to show it to whoever happened to be
there. And this object was wallet-sized because it was,
in fact, a wallet. It was Roger's wallet.

"Roger," Cato said, "I saw this on top of your Burl
Ives Fan Club newsletters, and I knew you were going

to be here, so I brought it to you." He held the wallet out at arm's length.

After a minute, Cato realized that Roger probably wasn't going to take the wallet. "Roger," Cato said, with lots of concern packed into his voice, so much that it was like sardines packed into their little can, "why are you on the floor?"

Then he saw Emma Lou Josephine Vernacular Hortense Hortense P. Barnacle. "Hi," he said, smiling. "My name's Cato."

***

"All right," Miss Cranberry said, "who can work this problem?" She wrote 123 + 89 on the chalkboard and turned to look at the bright faces of her class, some of the brightest faces she'd ever taught. She had even received a special commendation from the school board for energy conservation because she didn't have to turn on the lights in her classroom.

The usual handraising kids raised their hands. It's always the same ones; every teacher learns that early on, and it's never the ones who need the practice, although it's understandable that you're not likely to volunteer to do something in front of the whole class if you think you're going to be a miserable failure and crash in a humiliating ball of flames.

But it was precisely the ones who needed the practice that Miss Cranberry would rather have at the chalkboard. And one in particular—yes, there he was, that little rascal, trying to hide behind Big Willie Fubar, which was no mean feat for somebody who sat four seats over from Big Willie and in the front row.

"Goliath," Miss Cranberry cooed, "would you like to try?"

Goliath looked as if his pants had fallen down. They couldn't have, though, because he was sitting down. "Uh, no, ma'am, I wouldn't."

She held the chalk out toward him. "Come on, Goliath. Give it a try."

"Can't I stay here and talk you through it?"

"I'm afraid that wouldn't work. Come up here."

Over by the window, Eunice Mae watched Goliath drag his feet up to the front. She leaned across to her friend Alma. "That Goliath, he sure is cute." She said that because she thought Goliath was cute. She had images in her head of the two of them getting married and living in a big house, like with seven bathrooms and a tennis court in the closet. That would be the way to live, oh, yeah.

Alma nodded. She liked her men big and rugged and muscular, which Goliath wasn't, but she agreed because Eunice Mae was her friend. Alma was careful not to agree too vigorously, though. She didn't want Eunice Mae to think she was going to try to ace her out.

Up front, Miss Cranberry gave the chalk to Goliath. He looked forlorn, much worse than he had looked when his pet snail broke its leg. She couldn't understand it, his problem with arithmetic. He seemed to be able to do everything else so well.

He was popular in school, little Goliath was. He could play ball well—one day at recess, she had seen him run to first base!—and he laughed at the other kids' jokes and told a few of his own, and he watched all the right TV shows and talked about how cool they were in school the next day.

In the classroom, Goliath did well in history and English, and, for that matter, all his other subjects, but, obviously, not arithmetic. He knew the names of all the presidents and could say them in chronological and alphabetical order, and in order of how tall they were and even in order of hair color, from lightest to darkest. He knew all about adverbs and Louis Pasteur, and barometric pressure and water clocks. He knew about the United States government's system of checks and balances, and all about Eisenstein's *Film Form,* and how radio, television, and the internal combustion engine work, and how the battle of San Juan Hill developed, and how diamonds are formed, and all the things Alexander the Great did. He knew both the additive and the subtractive color processes and the gestation periods of most mammals, and all about Brownian motion and red shift. He knew how they got steel and silver and red paint and paper and babies. He knew all that stuff and more, much more. Not bad for a third grader. But the kid could not add two and two together, even if you gave him a hammer and nails and a staple gun and two tubes of Stur-D-Glu, which is strong enough to glue a passenger jet to the ground, assuming you have some reason to do such a thing. He didn't have it in him—arithmetic, that is. (He had other stuff in him, though.)

And Miss Cranberry, his teacher, thought Goliath was cute, too. She didn't think he was cute in the way that Eunice Mae did because she was a grownup, Miss Cranberry was, and he was a little kid, but she thought he was generally little-kid-type cute. He would have been her pet, but Miss Cranberry didn't believe in teachers' pets because as a kid she had been one. She knew firsthand how rough a time the other kids give teachers' pets. One day, when Miss Cranberry was in the third grade, some bullies made her eat a whole bag of rusty washers. Yuck! She didn't want to inflict that on anyone.

But she was glad to see Goliath do well, which he almost always did, except in arithmetic.

And Goliath, now at the chalkboard with some arithmetic in front of him, began thinking of something else entirely, like nothing at all, because the pressure up in front of the class and the teacher and anybody who happened to be looking in through the window was much worse than it was when he did his homework with no one watching, and—well, let's face it—he wasn't real swift with the homework. Not in arithmetic. So he stood there for a few minutes thinking about nothing, and then about charcoal, and then he thought about fermentation a little bit, and then he wrote the number 17 on the chalkboard. He turned to Miss Cranberry.

"How did you get seventeen?" Miss Cranberry asked. She knew how he had gotten it, which was at random, and she was dismayed.

And Goliath was distraught.

"Goliath, what's three plus nine?"

Goliath broke out in a cold sweat. He trembled. He looked around, hoping someone would give him the answer. He picked a number at random. "Twelve?"

"Very good, Goliath!" Miss Cranberry was happy, almost as happy as she had been when she won the Miss Wholesome contest at the state fair five years earlier. "Now write two up there."

Twelve? Two? What? If the answer was twelve, why write two? What's the deal here? If Miss Cranberry

wasn't so nice, Goliath would think she was mislead-
ing him on purpose, just for fun. Someday, when he got
rich and famous, he would make them change arithmetic so he could understand it more easily. He'd show
that ol' arithmetic. But in the meantime, he'd have to
put up with it. He wrote 2. Goliath knew it was unwise
to antagonize the teacher. The teacher and the dentist.
Always make sure both of them like you, and life is
much better.

"Now write one up there above your two in one
hundred twenty-three," Miss Cranberry said, "because
you're carrying ten."

This is getting ridiculous, Goliath thought. Why
write one if you're carrying ten? And did he need a bas-
ket to carry the ten in? It was too much to think about,
so he dropped the chalk. It hit the floor with a little
"clack" sound, and a tiny cloud of chalk dust poofed up.
He blinked at Miss Cranberry.

She sighed. "Goliath, what am I ever going to do
with you?" Miss Cranberry frequently had these little
fits of despair. It was beyond her comprehension how
anyone could be so smart at so many other things but
so inept at arithmetic.

That's what she was thinking, but what she said
was this: "I hope you don't go into any line of work
where you'll need to know arithmetic."

Well, that was a really good one; Goliath, little Goliath, already had a job. He worked for Mr. Antwerp,
who competed with Roger Glass Door Knob's employer,
Mr. Schurk, in the charcoal game. Mr. Antwerp left a
hundred-pound bag of charcoal on Goliath's corner every day a few minutes before school let out, and Goliath
came along and sat on his tall stool and sold it. (That is

to say, he sold the charcoal, not the stool.) He was the only vendor in the downtown area, and he made big piles of money. He knew all the arithmetic he needed to know, too. He sold the charcoal at a handful-and-a-half handfuls of money a pound, and Mr. Antwerp gave him half. Mr. Antwerp had shown Goliath how that worked out to five handfuls of money for selling the whole hundred pounds. So he was doing okay. But he had to because he was supporting his whole family.

It was an unfortunate tragedy, or a tragic unfortune, but the rest of Goliath's family had been stricken with a rare disease, a disease so rare it didn't have a name. (Really, it's just that I don't want to bother with trying to think of a name for it. Thinking is hard!) This disease, this bad, bad mystery disease, seeped into their brains the way a flock of squirrels will seep into your bedroom and take over your bed and build a nice little playground and picnic area for themselves on it. (That really is a common occurrence, isn't it? It would be disturbing to think I'm the only one it ever happens to.) And once there—the disease, that is, in their brains—it embarked on a complex biochemical adventure that polarized the lining of the submolecular structures of their hemotonic membranes. If you don't know what that does to the unlucky victims, let me tell you: it disrupts their thought patterns and memories in unpredictable ways. Symptoms vary from person to person depending on age, weight, diet (especially the amount of citrus consumed), length of fingernails, and number of Robert Frost poems the patient has read. But that's enough of that. We don't want our story to turn into a medical textbook. Look it up on the Internet if you're interested.

Anyway, poor Goliath's father's symptom was that he came down with a case of spontaneous amnesia, like in the movies. He wandered away from home, although not having the slightest clue where home was, he didn't know he was wandering away from it.

He ended up living in a closet in a radiator factory in Denver. It was a nice place to live because the factory had a snack machine and a men's room, and it was close to a discount store where he could go watch TV during the day. Down the street and around the corner and up three blocks and around another corner, there was a tavern where the men gathered at night and talked about sports and the influence of *The Art of War* on biochemical research. It was quite a life, it really was.

Now, Denver was far, far away from whatever city our story takes place in. In fact, it was in a different time zone. So one day when he, Goliath's father, stepped off the sidewalk to cross the street, he didn't realize it was dangerous to walk out in front of the oncoming Rocky Mountain Stagnant Air Company truck. He thought he was still living on Midwest Time, and therefore the truck wasn't really going to be driving by for another hour! Tragically, he was kinda sorta right, but he hadn't accounted for the switch to Daylight Saving Time, which threw all his carefully calculated calculations out of whack. So he got clobbered anyway and ended up going Wherever It Is That People Go When They Die. In fact, he and Roger Glass Door Knob became good friends after Roger got there.

Goliath's mother, whose name was Cleopatra, used to make a very good living as a wasteful packaging designer. But when the disease struck, it made her completely lose interest in her career. She was upset about it. "I don't like it," she once said. But what could she do? You can't fake an interest in wasteful packaging, no matter how hard you try. She also believed now that she had been twenty-three years old at birth. "My parents did that on purpose," she told people. "They didn't want to deal with the hassle of raising a child, so they skipped over that part." Sometimes Cleopatra liked to go to services at different churches and then write fan letters to the priests and ministers. Sometimes her letters were extremely clever.

And there was Othello, Goliath's sister. His older sister, that is, and she liked to cook and write poems. Her poems were okay; some were good, but you can't make any money with poetry these days, even though her poems rhymed and everything, unless you write greeting cards (a line of work she didn't know about). The best talent she had, that she could make money with, was that she could mix paint and match colors. If she could have gotten such a job, she would have been a valuable employee at a paint store or a printing shop. Her boss would say something like, "Othello, mix me up a gallon of Gang-Green Number Five," and Othello would have it mixed up in less time than it would take to throw up after eating a moldy peach. But she couldn't because she was blind. Of course, no one had any way of knowing that—that she could mix colors— but it was true. In addition to all that, she went to the school for blind people, where they taught her how to do stuff that's hard to do if you can't see. The teachers were nice people, and she was a good student.

So Othello had fun writing poems and trying to

cook, although nobody liked it when she cooked. That was no fun at all. Cleopatra, their mother, always made Goliath eat some of whatever Othello "cooked" because, after all, the girl was blind and they had to be extra nice to her. Goliath didn't see the connection. Figuring it out was like trying to add numbers. And as we've seen, *that* was as big a disaster as Othello's cooking. Sometimes Goliath thought that if he didn't have to eat so much bad cooking he would do better with his arithmetic. He had heard somewhere that proper nutrition was important if you wanted to be able to think well. Maybe the way Othello abused the food destroyed all the nutritional value for the part of the brain that worked arithmetic. After all, he never noticed Othello or his mom do much arithmetic. He said so one night and got smacked, but such is the life of a nine-year-old boy.

And such were the people he had to work to support.

(You may be asking yourself, Why didn't Goliath get this disease, this horrible mystery disease that would have disrupted his thought processes? Simple. He was wearing a hat that day.)

Back in the classroom, Miss Cranberry was saying, "Sit down, Goliath." Goliath, trying to look invisible (and if he'd been thinking clearly, he'd have realized that you can't look invisible because if you're invisible, you don't look like anything), went back to his seat.

Miss Cranberry turned to the rest of the class. "Who can work the problem?"

Eunice Mae waved her hand enthusiastically. "I can, Miss Cranberry, I can!" This was her chance to show Goliath how they complemented each other perfectly as a couple. She could work all the arithmetic, and he could do other stuff.

"All right, Eunice Mae. Show us how to do it."

But Goliath wasn't paying attention. He was sulking because he'd been embarrassed in front of the class.

2. The Neuralgia Sisters

Let's visit with the Neuralgia Sisters, the notorious Neuralgia Sisters, Norma and Nancy, for a while. They were twins, and Goliath was soon to start having problems with them—much bigger problems than the problems he had with arithmetic.

Norma and Nancy did lots of stuff before they started causing trouble for little Goliath and his friends. Nancy was writing a biography of Woody Woodpecker. She had the upstairs of their house crammed with binders full of notes and three-by-five index cards, and books and DVDs of cartoons, and reels and reels of film and projectors, and TV sets, and a photocopy machine and dozens of pencils and six typewriters and a computer, and file cabinets, and a Magic Eight-Ball, and other general sorts of research and writing materials.

Norma was trying to develop a method of boiling water without using heat. She had the downstairs filled up with pans of water and wires and transistors and pipes and tubes and nine-volt batteries and egg timers and stacks of pornographic magazines, and all kinds of crazy things. She even had an autographed picture of Captain Ahab! She also had a big book full of blank pages where she wrote down all the stuff she did in her experiments. "That's the way the big-time, hot-shot scientists do it," she said. "That way, they can look at it later and figure out what they did wrong." Norma must have been planning to do a lot of wrong stuff because she sure did have a thick book.

It was a mess, and they couldn't let people in the house because it took a considerable amount of skill and grace, not to mention excellent balance and coordination, as well as incredible powers of concentration, to walk around without stepping on something and messing it all up, or tripping over something else and falling down and breaking your wrist and then suing them for a whole bunch of money. None of that would have been good, Nancy and Norma agreed.

The Neuralgia Sisters didn't always have their own house. When they were children—little girls, that is—their family was poor. They were so poor that Nancy and Norma thought the reason they were twins was that their parents couldn't afford a different face for each of them. Nonetheless, a lot of folks had quite strong opinions as to which sister was prettier, and they had lots of fights about it. Who knows what they were thinking, because most people couldn't tell a bit of difference to look at them, and the smart ones wouldn't have said anything about thinking one was prettier (even if they thought so) for fear of making the other mad, so what that means is that the people who got into fights about it were dumb, and if they were *that* daggone dumb, their opinions were pretty worthless.

And back then, when the Neuralgia Sisters were children, they lived in a hollowed-out dictionary, the whole family did, in front of other people's houses. Usually they showed up at the front door and said,

"Here we are," and put the dictionary under a tree so it wouldn't get rained on too much. Then they ran an extension cord through a window and plugged it in, somewhere in the house, so they could have electricity. That part was pretty well pointless because they didn't have any electrical appliances, but it made their father, Mr. Neuralgia, feel as though things weren't quite so bad— after all, they had electricity! Anyway, whenever they wanted to cook food or take a bath, they went into the house and did it. It usually worked well for a week or so, and then the people who honest-to-gosh lived in the house would get fed up and kick them out or call the police or organize the neighbors into a vigilante mob to run them out. Then the Neuralgia family had to move on and find another houseful of saps to take advantage of.

Sometimes the other family was so wimpy that the Neuralgias ended up using their car and watching their TV. Mr. Neuralgia especially loved *The Many Loves of Dobie Gillis.* "That Max Shulman sure is a television genius," he used to say. He insisted on watching it no matter what the other family wanted to watch, although often the other family turned out to be enthusiastic Dobie fans as well.

One time the Neuralgias moved in on a family and made really good friends with the people. They set themselves up in the basement and had the run of the house and the kitchen and all the food in the refrigerator. The other family let them make long distance phone calls for free. The two families had cookouts in the backyard together, went to the mall together, and started a traveling circus complete with robot trapeze artists and juggling chipmunks. But it turned out that the other family wasn't the real owners of the house. The real owners were on vacation, touring Valhalla, and they were *reeeeally* mad when they came back home and found all those strange people and robots and chipmunks living in their house, people and robots and chipmunks they didn't know and had never seen before, so they called the police. (It was the robots that were the last straw. They leaked oil all over the carpet.) The Neuralgias and the other family almost got thrown into jail, and indeed would have if they hadn't been able to pack up and move out before the cops could get there. It doesn't take long to move when all you have to do is pick up a hollowed-out dictionary.

So Nancy and Norma Neuralgia grew up learning to take whatever they wanted and not think about how anyone else felt about it. For example, they knew a couple of big guys who were really mean, and they got these guys to intimidate everyone at school to vote for Nancy's boyfriend as The Guy Who Most Looks Like a Member of Duran Duran. He was elected unanimously. Even the other candidates voted for him. But to be fair, he did look a lot like a member of Duran Duran. Heck, he had taken a couple of piano lessons when he was younger.

The girls got into blackmail, too, a little bit. But they did it the lazy way. They sent all the teachers at their school notes that said, "We know what you do on weekends. Leave a bag containing a handful of money under the Elmo Lincoln Memorial Bridge every Saturday night if you don't want us to tell anyone." Out of twenty-five teachers, twenty-one paid the money faithfully. They must have been doing *something*.

And they, the Neuralgia Sisters, always took a jarful

of moths to the movies with them, and if they didn't like the movie, if it was a real stinker, they opened the jar. The moths would fly into the light from the projector and mess up the picture. The showing would be ruined, and they could not only get their money back but also have a little fun and give themselves something to chuckle about on the way home. Did I say chuckle? No, they giggled like little girls. The only thing was, their friends never wanted to go to the movies with them because they were afraid Nancy and Norma would moth it.

And then there was the time when they made a girl in their class—they didn't even know her name— eat a bag full of rusty washers just because she looked wholesome.

One day—in fact, the day after Roger Glass Door Knob's unfortunate haircut episode—they saw a notice stapled to a telephone pole. It said, "Charcoal Vendor needed for the rich people's neighborhood. Call Mr. Schurk." And it gave the phone number. Yes, Schurk Enterprises needed to replace Roger, poor unfortunate Roger, ASAP. The rich people's neighborhood was too lucrative a territory to leave untended one instant longer than necessary. Those rich people were *desperate* to find stuff to spend their money on. Even if they didn't need charcoal, they would pay top dollar if a vendor happened to be nearby when they came to a red light.

"What's a vendor?" Nancy asked.

"I think it's a mechanism on a lifeboat that keeps the oars in the water," Norma said. The sisters were really pretty smart in the sense that they had high-quality, state-of-the-art, MVP, Grade A, USDA Prime brains, but they hadn't learned much school stuff like vocabulary because they were busy being mean all the time.

"That doesn't make any sense," Nancy said.

"Let's call the number and find out," Norma said. "It sounds like a good business opportunity."

Right then a little boy—not Goliath but a different one—came walking down the street. Norma and Nancy stopped him and took a quarter of a handful of money coin away from him so they could make the call at a nearby pay phone.

Mr. Schurk's secretary, Miss Spikenhammer, answered. "Good afternoon, Schurk Enterprises."

"My name is Nancy Neuralgia," Nancy said; she was the one making the call. "Me and my sister Norma, we saw your notice on the telephone pole here, and we were wondering what a vendor is."

"It's somebody who sells something," Miss Spikenhammer said. "Are you interested in selling charcoal?"

"I don't know," Nancy said. "It sounds awful dirty. And not the fun kind of dirty, but just dirty."

"You can make a whole lot of money, especially in the rich people's neighborhood. And it's not dirty. And who's that I hear crying?"

"Oh, uh, some little boy who…uh, lost his mommy," Nancy said. Norma shooed him away. "So you say we can make a lot of money, eh?"

"Yeah. Big piles of it. As much as you can carry. Do you want to come in for an interview? We can work you in this afternoon."

"Do you want to go in for an interview?" Nancy asked Norma. "She says we can make big piles of money, as much as we can carry."

"Sure. I think we can carry a lot of money. And if it

turns out to be a waste of time, we can always throw someone out the window."

"Okay, we'd like an interview. What's your address?"

"We're at the Intolerance Building, thirteenth floor."

"One more thing. Does your office have a window?"

Mr. Schurk's office had a window, but nobody could throw him out of it because it was that kind that doesn't open. Anyway, Norma and Nancy went down there to the interview. They knew all about the Intolerance Building because they used to work there, on the fifth floor, for the management of a professional Russian roulette team. They were secretaries. Unfortunately, the team went out of business because the coach insisted on calling practices every day.

Outside the building, Nancy stopped and said, "Let's go in there and be real aggressive so we'll impress him. That way he'll know we really want the job."

"Yeah, that's a good idea," Norma said. "Employers like to see enthusiasm."

"They do. We'll show him so much enthusiasm that if enthusiasm were water, we would have enough to, like, put out the sun."

So they got in the elevator and tried to get their eyes to sparkle as they rode up. Unfortunately for them, your eyes don't sparkle very much when you're as mean as the Neuralgia Sisters. But they weren't worried. They could ace the interview without sparkling eyes.

At the thirteenth floor, they barged into Mr. Schurk's office, right past Miss Spikenhammer. "We're the Neuralgia Sisters, Norma and Nancy," Norma said.

Nancy was checking out the window, trying to figure out whether it would open.

"Which is which?" Mr. Schurk asked.

"Listen, afterbirth-breath, we want that job and we want it now, or we'll rip your pancreas out and tie it into a pretzel."

"Is that possible?"

Nancy leaned in close, nose-to-nose with him. "We'll figure it out," she said in a low voice, so low he could barely hear it. The lowness (lowosity?) made the threat all the more threatening. "We're in no hurry."

"I think you'll fit right into my organization."

"We'll be the judge of that," Nancy said.

"I have a special project you might be interested in," Mr. Schurk said. "It'll require a lot of ingenuity, villainy, cunning, and ingenuity."

"You said ingenuity twice."

"I know. I wanted to say four things, but I could only think of three. Anyway, that's for later. The special project, that is. It's the thing that's for later. Right now, I want you to sell some charcoal because, well, that's the job I'm interviewing you for. I have an opening in the rich people's neighborhood. Very good sales potential, very good tips."

"Do people tip charcoal vendors?" Norma asked.

"Yes," Mr. Schurk said. "These people are so rich, they'll give you a hundred-handfuls-of-money bill and not wait around to get their change."

"Sweet."

"So I want you to do that for a while. If you show me you have all four of the qualities I mentioned—"

"Three," Nancy said.

"What?"

"You only mentioned three qualities."

"But I wanted to mention four."

"But you didn't."

"Okay, so if you show me you have all the qualities I mentioned, however many there were, I'll promote you and let you take care of this special project. I already see you have the right attitude for the job. So now I need to see the aptitude."

"We led the charge up San Juan Hill," Nancy said. It hadn't required villainy, but she figured it would show bravery and a zest for adventure. Yeah, zest.

"Oh, really?"

"Yeah," Norma said. "Teddy Roosevelt paid us to let him take the credit."

"How do I know you're telling the truth?"

Nancy sighed. "You're trying my patience," she said. "If we're lying, don't you think that having the unmitigated audacity to tell you a story like that proves we have cunning and ingenuity?"

Mr. Schurk didn't think so, but he was kinda scared of these women. And that proved they had enough villainy, no doubt about it. "You sound good to me," he said. "You're hired."

***

Working for Mr. Schurk, the Neuralgia Sisters made lots of money. They quickly made enough money to buy themselves a house in the rich people's neighborhood. What about their parents? Pooh on them. Remember, Norma and Nancy were mean. They didn't care if their parents had to keep living in a hollowed-out dictionary.

Here's the kind of stuff they did, a typical day at

work for the Neuralgia Sisters after they had entered the exciting and challenging field of charcoal vending:

They reported for work at their corner, bright and early at nine o'clock in the morning. The charcoal was waiting for them in a big hundred-pound bag, the same way it had been for Roger Glass Door Knob and the same way it was for Goliath. They opened the bag and stood around on the corner looking seductive. It was one of their techniques, one that worked well with married guys whose wives wouldn't have anything to do with their tallywackers, and with young single guys like Cato, guys who liked women and all the things women can do.

On one particular morning, a morning that was special only because each day is special in its own way, Norma and Nancy started out with the seductive bit. A guy in a gray twenty-four-cylinder National Motors Leviathan stopped and rolled down his window. He was wearing a gray four-piece Rubella Brothers suit. This guy was Important and Busy. He had a job in which he spent most of his time talking on the phone. He wheeled and dealed. He owned the streets he drove on. A lot of people were scared of Norma and Nancy, but not this man. He didn't have time to waste being scared of the likes of the Neuralgia Sisters. He was in control of any situation that came along.

"Good day," he said. His words dripped gold dust. Nancy watched it twinkle softly through the window and flutter down to the street next to his car, and she wondered whether it might be possible to vacuum it up after the guy was gone. "Are you ladies the neighborhood charcoal vendors?"

"Yes, sir, we are, sir," Norma said.

"I would like to purchase a modicum of charcoal," the man said. "Specifically, four chunks."

"Yes, sir," Nancy said, and she counted out four chunks. It was important to be polite to these people. A rich guy like this could do some good for you sometime, if he liked you.

The man sorted through a bunch of credit cards. He had the Usury card, the Exorbitance card, the Gold Ostentatious card (issued to only a hundred people in all of the whole entire universe!), and a bunch of others. "Do you ladies take credit cards?" he asked.

"No, sir. Sorry," Norma said.

"Oh," the man said. He tightened his lips and looked through his wallet. Not that he had to tighten his lips to look through his wallet; it was a mannerism he had, one he had developed in the making of hundreds of millions-of-handfuls of money deals. His work was full of tension. Usually everything on his body was tense. Even his clothes. Finally, he found some money. "Can you break a one-hundred-handfuls bill?"

"No, sir. Sorry," Nancy said. She tried to think of some way to keep the guy talking so that more gold dust would accumulate on the street. She wanted to ask him to recite Hamlet's soliloquy, but he would undoubtedly be in a hurry.

The man handed her the bill. "Keep the change," he said. Wow, the Neuralgia Sisters thought. Mr. Schurk was right about these people!

Usually, the Neuralgia Sisters did what they did best. The next car that drove by was a Spartan Motors Clunker. "Hey," Nancy shouted. "Come here!"

The car stopped and backed up to them. The driver was obviously from the poor neighborhood. He hadn't had a haircut in ages. His clothes were three sizes too small. His tires were rubber bands stretched around the rims of garbage can lids, and the car had a model airplane engine instead of a car engine. (Once he had gotten too close to some children who were playing with a radio controlled toy airplane, and they made him drive zigzags through a playground.) This guy was in the rich people's neighborhood only because he worked there, polishing driveways. "Yes?" he said.

"What?"

"Sorry. I mean, yes, ma'am?"

"Buy some charcoal."

"Yes, ma'am." He got out of the car without bothering to turn it off. Nancy saw that he was standing on the rich guy's little pile of gold dust. She hoped he wasn't grinding it into the pavement with his shoes.

The poor guy took his wallet out; it was an old cardboard thing held together with dabs of chewing gum. "All I have is a third of a handful of money," he said.

Norma grabbed his wallet and looked through it. An expired driver's license, an expired library card, an expired insurance card, an expired video rental card, an expired Royal Order of the Golden Ferret membership card...and an ATM card that was going to expire the next day. "You can get more money out of the machine," Norma said.

"Oh, I can't do that. No, please," the guy said. "I only have seven handfuls of money in the bank, and my little girl needs new glasses, and my son needs orthopedic toenails."

Norma knew that orthopedic toenails were expensive, but she had a job to do. "Get the money and bring it back here," she said. "All of it."

"Yes, ma'am," the guy said, and got into his car. The car trembled as he drove away.

The Neuralgia Sisters chuckled to themselves and amongst themselves. They felt pleased.

A few minutes later, the guy came back. He drove up really fast and screeched to a stop. "Here you go," he said, sticking seven handfuls of money out the window at them.

Norma snatched the money from the guy and counted it. "It's all here," she said.

Nancy took some charcoal out of the bag and stuck it in the guy's hand. "Thank you," she said. "Come back."

Nervous, he dropped a chunk on the pavement. He pretended not to notice. He didn't want to stay there for the extra few precious seconds it would take to open the door and pick it up. "Oh, I will. I promise," the guy said. He stomped on the gas and drove away so fast that a ghostly image of the car lingered at the intersection for about thirty seconds after he was gone.

Nancy picked up the dropped piece of charcoal and put it back in the bag. Yeah, they could sell it again.

***

It didn't take the Neuralgia Sisters long to make a lot of money, enough money to buy a big house with seven bathrooms and a tennis court in the closet.

3. People in Love

Another person important in this story is Dexter Kroger. He was Miss Cranberry's boyfriend.

Dexter was a big guy, big and strong and athletic, and he had been an all-pro offensive guard on his college football team. He was offered a contract by the Kansas City Cowboys, which was a real professional football team from 1924 to 1926. Unfortunately, Dexter wasn't born until 1978, and by then the Kansas City Cowboys hadn't existed for forty-two years. Don't ask me to explain it. Of course, the Dallas Cowboys started up in 1960. And a team in the AFL called the Dallas Texans also started in 1960, and in 1963 they moved and became the Kansas City Chiefs. Small world. There was also an NFL team called the Dallas Texans, and they were only around for one year, 1952, which was still before Dexter Kroger was born. The 1952 Dallas Texans were the last pro football team to go belly-up. And then—get this—after the Houston Oilers moved to Nashville, Houston got a new team a couple years later, and it was called The Texans!

And he couldn't sign up with the Kansas City Cowboys because they were gone. If he had, though, they would have kicked him out of training camp for playing his Stan Kenton records too loud at night.

At any rate, Dexter worked for the Midwest Stagnant Air Company, which had been serving the stagnant air needs of the American Midwest since 1966, the year the Miami Dolphins started. Dexter drove a truck around and collected people's dryer lint and dust bunnies, and he took it all back to the plant where they infused it into the stale air tanks, which in turn were delivered to the customers, who used stagnant air for various industrial, medical, and (ahem) personal needs. Dexter liked his job; he felt useful. He had a brother named Earl, who was a ne'er-do-well. His parents believed he was being a ne'er-do-well just to irritate them, but he was a real, live, honest-to-gosh ne'er-do-well. Earl and Dexter both liked Peter Sellers.

And Miss Cranberry liked Dexter Kroger. She thought he was smart and witty and charming. She thought he was stylish and good-looking. She thought he had black hair, which was true.

***

Later on, "later" being a few days after Goliath had his little adventure at the chalkboard and a few weeks after the Neuralgia Sisters had begun their exciting and lucrative career in the charcoal business (and, I might add, the same day the sisters moved into their big, new house), Miss Cranberry and Dexter were watching TV. *Serve that Soup* was on, a reality show in which groups of successful pop music stars competed to serve soup to people in various places such as fine art galleries and auto assembly plants.

She told him about Goliath's problem with

arithmetic. Since the chalkboard adventure we saw earlier, he, Goliath, had muddled his way through two more chalkboard adventures and failed a quiz. "I just don't know how to get through to him," she said.

"You know what?" Dexter said. "I'm willing to bet that if he had a situation where he actually had to use arithmetic, it would all become clear to him, like a light switch flipping on. I bet he could do it."

Dexter really believed what he was saying. Miss Cranberry, however, wasn't so sure. He, Dexter, hadn't been there. He hadn't seen Goliath choke like a mosquito trying to suck the sap out of a tree (which happens more often than you would think).

But she didn't say anything. She merely sighed, grabbed his hand, and pulled his arm tighter around her shoulders. Both of them liked that.

***

Another person who's important in this story is Billy-Bob, also known as Billy-Bob Kierkegaard, if you want to know his full name. He was Cato Kierkegaard's younger brother, and he lived next door to Goliath and his family. He was a big kid, the biggest kid in school, like in high school or something. At any rate, he was older than Goliath, old enough that he should be finished with school altogether and working at a job and stuff, but he wasn't. He had flunked out a whole bunch of times and was far behind, several years behind other guys his age, and still not doing well anyway. He was dumb-looking and goofy and smelled like a mayonnaise jar full of rancid carrot wine mixed with sweat from a hockey goalie after an overtime game. Fortunately, the jar's lid is screwed down very, very tight, so you can't smell the odor unless you get all up close, but still, it's unpleasant.

And he wore things around his neck. Things like DVDs and light bulbs and paper punches and crayons. Things like plastic gargoyles and candy bars and rabbit-ear antennas and beer cans. He tied strings on these things so he could wear them around his neck, a different thing each day, and then he walked around where people could see him. One girl at school kept a spreadsheet to document all the stuff he wore, with the various objects cross-indexed by function, color, size, and shape.

All the girls thought Billy-Bob was creepy and icky. None of them would go out with him, and he asked them all. Many times. He was too awful, they said. Maybe if he had just one less bad thing about him, then maybe... no, not even then. No.

Eventually, Billy-Bob decided he had a crush on Goliath's sister Othello. Now, understand that Othello didn't get many dates because the guys didn't like trying to figure out how to act around someone who couldn't see. And to be honest, Billy-Bob was no different. For a long time, he kinda sorta avoided thinking about her. But after he finally came to understand that nothing was going to happen with any of the other girls he knew, he figured that maybe, just maybe Othello would go out with him because she...well, let's come right out and say it...she might be desperate. Yeah, hoping someone will date you out of desperation sounds pathetic, but he was okay with that (mostly because he didn't understand much about the concept of "pathetic").

So Billy-Bob pondered on all this stuff, and one day he was ready to make his move. "I'm gonna get me a girlfriend, har har," he said. But he had to make extra sure to do it right because Othello was his last chance, and he didn't want to mess it up.

He went to see his brother Cato. Cato was a real, live, authentic ladies' man. He didn't have to work because every day a big crowd of women wanted to buy him dinner and give him all kinds of gifts. One rich lady gave him a house and a car because she liked a joke he told her. I mean, yeah, sure, it was a pretty good joke, but imagine—just try to imagine—what kind of joke could be *that* good. That's right. No joke can be that good, but Cato could.

And although Cato was dating Emma Lou Josephine Vernacular Hortense Hortense P. Barnacle at the moment, he never dated one woman very long. No, because another one always came along to divert his attention.

So Billy-Bob went to Cato's house, the one from the rich lady, the one that until recently he had shared with his lifelong best buddy, poor Roger Glass Door Knob. And Billy-Bob asked Cato for some expert advice about women.

"Girls like presents," Cato said. "Give her a little present, and you're in like an abscessed wisdom tooth." He was pretty sure that was how the girl would feel about it.

"What kind of present?"

"Any kind of little thing. It doesn't have to be big or expensive. Or fancy. It's the gesture that counts. And send it to her anonymously. Let her think about it for a few days and wonder who her secret admirer is. Later, when you tell her you were the one who sent it, she'll do absolutely anything you want." Then Cato went back to reading *The Adventures of Hrobigothr the Troll*. He was afraid he had said too much. He didn't want to encourage a project that, no matter what, was doomed to total failure.

And Billy-Bob, well, he didn't know what gesture or anonymously or absolutely meant, but he got the idea. He got the idea that if a little present would do that well for him, a great big present would do much better. After all, he had such rotten luck with girls that he needed all the help he could get. And if it was a big enough present, she might be his slave for life! Gee whiz! He had heard about stuff like that. Then, when he got tired of her for a girlfriend, he could keep her around to shine his shoes and clean his room. Oh, boy! Maybe she would do his homework for him! This was going to be good!

Billy-Bob saved up his allowance and got a whole bunch of money, but he didn't know what to do with it. He didn't know what to get Othello or where to get it. He didn't want to ask Cato because Cato would think he was dumb if he asked too many questions. Yeah, you read that right.

So he took the bus downtown, Billy-Bob did. He got off at a street corner and walked around. After a few minutes he came to a pawnshop. He looked in the window and saw that they had a whole bunch of different stuff. They had jewelry and cameras and musical instruments and bicycles and a heart-lung machine. Hmmm...this might be a good place.

He walked in. The guy behind the counter looked up and said, "Can I help you, kid?"

"Uh, yeah, har, har," Billy-Bob said. "I'm looking for a present for a girl, har har. So she'll like me."

The guy paused a moment to size Billy-Bob up. You could hear the wheels turning in his head. You could hear them because they needed to be oiled. Maybe they could have used some of the oil those circus robots had leaked on the carpet. "I can see you're a man of discriminating taste," the pawnshop guy said. "Step over here."

He led Billy-Bob to an ornate display case designed by famous artist Augustus Paradine. It contained a wooden box, a little cube about six inches to a side. "You have to promise not to tell anyone I showed you this. Only special customers get to see it."

Wow, Billy-Bob was special. "Sure," he said. "Har, har."

"Yeah, okay." The pawnshop guy took out his key ring and opened the case. He picked up the wooden box and held it out for Billy-Bob to admire. "Do you know what's in here?" he asked.

"I've never seen it before. How would I know what's in it?"

"Good point. Well, check this out." The guy opened the lid. Inside, the box was lined with topaz-colored velvet. A little brown bean-shaped thing was resting on the bottom. It had a slight glow.

"Wow," Billy-Bob said, awestruck.

The pawnshop guy made a big show of looking around, as if to make sure no one was within earshot. "It's an imagination," he whispered.

"An imagination?"

The pawnshop guy grimaced and looked around again. "Not so loud," he hissed. He paused and looked intently at Billy-Bob to drive the point home, the point being that this was a highly important secret for a special customer. "Yes, an imagination. In prime condition, too. A woman brought it in about a month ago. We gave her a pretty good price on it, too, let me tell you."

"What would anyone do with an imagination?"

"Imagine things."

Of course, Billy-Bob didn't have enough imagination to understand how someone could use an imagination. Besides, it looked like a little, glowing bean. That wasn't much of a gift. "I don't think it's what I want," he said.

"Ah, I can see you're a sharp one." The pawnshop guy replaced the box in the display case. "Let me show you something else." He motioned for Billy-Bob to follow him across the room. "How about this heart-lung machine?" he said.

"What does it do?"

"Well, it...it...does heart and lung stuff. What do you think it does? Some kid brought it in. I don't know where he got it. Heck, I don't know how he managed to get it here, but here it is."

Billy-Bob could see that it was big, all right, and cool-looking, but he was pretty sure Othello already had a heart and some lungs. "I think, har har, I think I want to get something else, har, har."

"How much money you got, kid?"

Billy-Bob pulled his money out of his pocket. He had a big wad of bills all wadded up. "This much," he said.

The pawnshop guy gave the wad a casual glance so as not to appear too eager. "Yeah, I got just the thing. Come over here."

He went to the back corner and gestured toward some kind of funny-looking machine that was next to a life-sized ice sculpture of Michael J. Pollard. Billy-Bob studied the machine. It had a tank-looking thing laid down on its side, and some motor stuff, and dials and buttons and a round part that looked like a clock with only one hand. It was not quite knee-high, this funny machine, and it was painted a color like blue and grey mixed up together.

"What is it?" Billy-Bob asked. Maybe it was a time machine, he thought. That would be cool!

"It's an air compressor."

"What's it for?"

"It compresses air."

"Oh." Billy-Bob, of course, didn't know what that meant, but once again, he didn't want to ask too many questions because he was afraid it would make him look dumb. So he regarded the machine with what he hoped was a thoughtful look on his face, and he nodded slowly. "You think she would like it?" he asked.

"No doubt about it," the pawnshop guy said. "Girls *love* these things."

"How much?"

"Are you ever in luck," the guy said. "I can give you a good deal on this. No, not just a good deal. A *great* deal."

"Wow."

"Yeah. Some guy had it on layaway. He had only one payment left, and then he died."

"Aw."

"Yeah, aw. But since it's already mostly paid for, I can give you a good deal on it. I can sell it to you and have it delivered for what you got right there in your hand."

"Wow."

After Billy-Bob was gone, the pawnshop guy's co-worker shook his head slowly. "Irving, why did you tell him girls love air compressors?"

"Hey, man," Irving said. "Did you *see* that kid, all slouchy-looking and smelling funny and kind-of-but-not-quite-drooling on himself and wearing a dirty gym sock on a string around his neck? It doesn't matter what he gives her."

"How much did you get for it?"

Irving counted. "Thirty handfuls of money." Added to the fourteen handfuls of money that Roger Glass Door Knob had already paid, Irving reckoned he had gotten forty-four handfuls of money for a machine that had cost him only five. And the daggone thing didn't even work! He had played around with the wiring to see whether he could get it to turn on, but since he didn't know what the heck he was doing, had no luck. Oh, well.

He pulled the "15 handfuls of money" sign off the air compressor and replaced it with a sign that said "SOLD."

***

Billy-Bob went back to Cato and got him to write the card for Othello's air compressor. And Cato, good ol' Cato, he wrote the card in his best handwriting even though he didn't expect it to do any good on account of Billy-Bob was so creepy, but it might work. And if Billy-Bob got himself a girlfriend, she would keep him busy and out of Cato's way. Then Cato could bring girls home without having Billy-Bob show up at his swingin' bachelor pad at exactly the wrong time, as he always did, so it was worth two minutes to write out the card.

Of course, Cato didn't know what the gift was. He didn't care enough to ask, and it was unfortunate because he would have had Billy-Bob take the air compressor back and get some roses, which would actually have made Othello want to be Billy-Bob's lifelong love slave. (So often, it's the simple things that have the greatest effect.) Instead, the roses Billy-Bob would have bought, had he bought roses, were purchased by a middle-aged man who was in trouble with his wife after she found a strange pair of women's panties in the backseat of his car. Well, he was innocent of any wrongdoing. What happened was that another guy who had really been cheating on his wife was driving home from a date with his girlfriend and noticed that she had left her panties in his car. He figured he had better get rid of them, like, as quickly as possible, so he tossed them out the window. But then, see, our noncheating guy was driving by in the opposite direction, and the panties flew into his car through an open window, and he didn't notice. Uh-oh. So then, his wife found the panties the next day and a sort of nuclear fallout kind of scene ensued. He couldn't explain where the panties had come from. (And if he had known, how could he try to tell his wife a story like that?) So this guy, he bought the roses. That made the situation worse, though. The wife got all upset over the idea that he apparently believed he could buy his way out of cheating (which he hadn't really done anyway) with a handful of flowers that would be dead in a few days. And who was the cheating guy cheating with? The noncheating guy's wife's sister! Whoa!

Sometimes it amazes me how all this stuff works.

Anyway, Billy-Bob took the card to the pawnshop and taped it to the air compressor. The delivery people didn't know why someone would want an air compressor delivered to someone else's front door as a gift, complete with gift card, but they knew they were getting paid. So they made the delivery early the next morning.

Later, when Cleopatra tried to step out to get the newspaper, she couldn't get the door open more than a few inches. The air compressor was blocking it. She banged the door against it a couple times to see whether she could knock the obstacle, whatever it was, out of the way. No luck. The realization that she couldn't get out of the house struck her like a drunken troll falling into a mud puddle. Thoughts of starvation floated through her mind. Goodness, would they have to turn to cannibalism? And more pressing, would the door open wide enough to let air in?

Othello came into the living room. "What's for breakfast?" she asked.

"Breakfast? We're all going to starve!"

"Do you think we could starve tomorrow? *Willie the Incoherent Weasel* is on tonight, and it's a new episode. Willie meets Imogene the Fabulous Ferret, and they go on a spree of doing good deeds for puppies."

"I don't think we have a choice. We can't leave the house."

"Why not?"

"Something's blocking the door."

Othello ruminated for a moment. "Why don't you go out the window?"

"Yeah, I could do that." Cleopatra slid the window up. It was a small window, but she figured she could make it through. She had to; what was the alternative? She put her foot through the opening and then bent over and began laboriously working herself the rest of way out. After about ten minutes, she was standing on the porch.

And there was the...the thing. She saw the envelope on top, taped down neatly and marked "For Othello."

"Othello," she said, "there's something out here for you." She said "something" because she didn't know what it was. If she had known it was an air compressor, she would have said, "Othello, there's an air compressor out here for you." But she didn't.

"What is it?" Othello asked.

"I don't know."

"Maybe Goliath would know."

"Yes, go get him."

Othello went to Goliath's room and shook him awake. "Goliath, we need you to go look at this strange thing on the front porch."

Hmmm. Strange thing, Goliath thought. "Oh, it must be Billy-Bob."

"Yeah, I bet it is."

Othello went to the front-porch window. "Goliath says it must be Billy-Bob."

Cleopatra studied the air compressor. "No," she said. "I'm pretty sure it's something else."

Back to Goliath's room for Othello. "She's pretty sure it's not Billy-Bob."

Goliath roused himself.

"You can't go out the front door," Othello said. "That

strange thing is in the way, so it won't open."

"You're sure it's not Billy-Bob?"

"Yeah, pretty sure."

Goliath walked out the side door and around to the porch. Cleopatra was still standing there looking at the air compressor.

"Gosh, that sure is a funny-looking thing," Goliath said.

"I. beg. your. pardon," Cleopatra said, offended.

"The machine thing," Goliath said. Of course, he didn't know what it was. He thought it might be a great big can opener, but that didn't seem quite right.

"We'd better take it inside," Cleopatra said.

Goliath tried to pick it up, but it was too heavy for him. It was too heavy for all of them together. They tried.

"Let's leave it out here," Cleopatra said. It seemed like a good idea. She opened the envelope and looked at the card. "From your secret admirer," she read.

"Oh, I have a secret admirer," Othello said. "That's neat."

"If this thing's from an admirer, then it must be something that's good to have," Goliath said.

"We should try to find out what it is," Cleopatra said. "We'll call the public library. They can answer all kinds of questions. Come on, kids."

Goliath led the way in through the side door. Cleopatra looked up the number of the public library and dialed. "Hello, library? What's that thing out there on our front porch?"

"Don't ever call here again," the library person said, and hung up.

Just then Billy-Bob came to the front door. Although

Cato had told him to wait a few days, he couldn't, dag-gone it. He was too impatient. And Othello had not yet gotten around to wondering who the secret admirer might be. She was still wondering what the thing was.

"Hello, Othello?" Billy-Bob called.

"Billy-Bob," Goliath said, "can you push that big thing out of the way so we can open the door?"

"Sure thing, har har." Billy-Bob bent over, took a deep breath, and shoved the air compressor a couple feet away from the door.

"Oh, thank goodness," Cleopatra said. "I was sure we were going to suffocate in here."

"Maybe we should get Billy-Bob to bring it inside," Goliath said.

"I'm not sure about that," Othello said. "Maybe we want to find out what it is first, so we'll know where to put it."

Well, Goliath thought, if it was really a can opener, they would want to put it in the kitchen. But if it was something else, then...who knows?

"Can I come in?" Billy-Bob asked.

"Yes, of course," Cleopatra said.

Billy-Bob bounded into the house with youthful en-thusiasm and vigor, excited because this was the be-ginning of having a real girlfriend. He tried to tell them he was the secret admirer. "Hey, Othello," he said, "I'm me, har har."

"Hi, Billy-Bob," everyone said.

"How do you like my present?"

"It was you who sent it?" Cleopatra astutely guessed.

"Yeah, har har." Billy-Bob got all self-conscious and blushed a bright-red blush that wasn't quite like any color Goliath had ever seen on a person.

"Oh, thank you, Billy-Bob!" Othello said. Hey, maybe he wasn't such a creepy and icky and disgusting kinda guy after all! She rushed up to Cleopatra and hugged her and gave her a great big kiss. She was really aiming at Billy-Bob, but he was standing right next to Cleopatra, and Othello could only tell the general direction his voice came from.

"Aw, it wasn't nothing," Billy-Bob said. He didn't think that he might have been the real target of the hug. But Othello realized her mistake when he spoke. Cleopatra sort of didn't do anything. Othello moved over to Billy-Bob.

"You're real nice for a creepy guy," she said, and Billy-Bob blushed more.

"Gee, Othello, har har, would you like to, har har, go to the movie show, har har, Friday night, har har?"

"I'd love to," Othello said.

"What's the present?" Goliath asked. "What is that thing out there?"

"It's a...a..." Billy-Bob stopped and put his hand in his mouth for a few seconds, thinking. "Oh, I know," he said. "It's a tongue depressor."

"It'll be useful in case we get sick," Cleopatra said. "What a thoughtful boy you are."

Goliath thought that meant the thing, the tongue depressor, should rightfully be in the bathroom, in the medicine cabinet. But maybe not. It looked too big for that. Well, he figured it was all right out on the front porch for the time being, as long as it wasn't blocking the door.

***

And Billy-Bob, who almost never laughed, laughed a lot in the few days before Friday because he had him a real, honest-to-gosh date with a real, live, genuine girl. Har har. Now he would be just like Cato and all his friends. Wow! An actual girl! And Billy-Bob, he knew that girls were fun to take your clothes off with, and then you could do something real neat with them, although he wasn't clear on what it was, but he knew that once he got both of all their clothes off, he could figure it out, and then he could have a lot of fun with her, although a lot of people told him stuff like that was nasty and you shouldn't do it unless you were married, but he didn't care because most of the really fun stuff was nasty, stuff like playing in mud and eating tapioca pudding. So he knew if being naked with a girl was something nasty, he sure as heck wanted to try it. And what did any of that have to do with being married, anyway? Also, he could brag about it if he did naked stuff with Othello, and maybe people would start thinking he was cool and liking him.

***

Friday came, and Billy-Bob showed up at Othello's house early in the morning, before anybody was awake. Cleopatra stepped out to get the paper and saw him sitting on the air compressor. "I want to make sure I'm not late for my date with Othello," he explained.

"Oh," Cleopatra said, and took the paper in.

A little later, Othello and Goliath left for school. "No, I'm not going to school today," Billy-Bob told them. And he didn't. He sat on the porch all day, waiting. The truant officer drove by once and noticed him, but Billy-Bob was so big that the truant officer didn't think he was a kid. Later, Goliath and Othello came home from school and went inside. Billy-Bob kept sitting there. Finally, when he figured it was time, he knocked on the door. Cleopatra answered.

"Is Othello home?" he asked.

Othello came to the door. "You're late," she said. "I didn't think you were coming."

Billy-Bob didn't know what to say. "I'm not late," he said defiantly.

They went to a movie, *Wuthering Heights*. Billy-Bob didn't understand it, and truth be told, he got all impatient and fidgety after about a minute and a half, but he didn't care. He was having a date with a real live girl, and that was more important than having fun. He didn't have to fidget long, though. After about ten minutes, a whole bunch of moths started flying around in the light from the projector, making flickering shadows on the picture. A few rows down toward the front, two women stood up. They looked exactly alike, and they were giggling like little girls. They kept giggling as they ran up the aisle and out of the theater.

Billy-Bob didn't understand any of it. He just hoped a lot of people would see him with Othello, a lot of people he knew, but no one did—that is to say, no one he knew saw him. He was still having a date, though.

After the movie, Othello said she was hungry. Billy-Bob didn't know what to do because he didn't know how to count money, and he didn't know how much it would cost to eat. "Aw, you don't want to eat," he said.

"Yes, I do," Othello said.

"Let's take off all our clothes," Billy-Bob said.

"NO!" Othello sputtered.

"But we can do nasty things."

"I don't want to do nasty things!"

"You have to! I gave you a present! A big one!"

"Billy-Bob, shut your mouth!"

"My brother told me you would do anything I said. And he knows what he's talking about 'cause he gots lots of girlfriends."

"Take me home."

"You will, then?"

"No. Take me to my house. I'm going to stay there and you're not."

***

At this point, we'll note that it's a good thing Othello got all mad and stuff. If she had agreed to whatever Billy-Bob thought he wanted, he would have realized he didn't have the slightest clue how to go about, like, actually doing anything. It would have embarrassed him so much that he would have hitchhiked to Kansas and sat in the middle of a cornfield for the rest of his life, never to be heard from again.

No loss to humanity, you say? Read on, read on.

4. Eavesdropping

Billy-Bob took Othello home, to her home, and he didn't stay there. He went to Cato's house. He wanted to beat that daggone ol' Cato up for lying to him, but Cato wasn't home. He had a date with Emma Lou Josephine Vernacular Hortense Hortense P. Barnacle. Knowing that she was president of the local chapter of the Burl Ives Fan Club, he had been reading Roger's fan club newsletters so he could talk knowledgeably about Burl. Did you know he had six brothers and sisters?

Anyway, they spent the night at her house, Cato and Emma Lou Josephine Vernacular Hortense Hortense P. Barnacle, and in the morning she took him to the salon to do his hair for free. So Cato wasn't home at all that night. Billy-Bob sat on the front porch and waited for him. That Cato, he wasn't going to get away with this, nosireebob. (Yeah, Billy-Bob is racking up some serious porch-waiting time in this story, isn't he?)

Cato, though, he didn't know anything about Billy-Bob's catastrophe with Othello. He was too busy having fun with Emma Lou Josephine Vernacular Hortense Hortense P. Barnacle, being witty and charming and all kinds of stuff like that, stuff that Roger Glass Door Knob would have loved to do but couldn't. Cato was doing quite well for himself, and he had no intention of dying.

During his haircut, Miss Cranberry came in. She was with another schoolteacher friend, Miss Fluorine, who also wanted to get her hair done, and while they waited, they sat and talked about teaching and pupils and stuff like that. They talked about Billy-Bob, too. They had both had him in their classes, and he was an unusual case and interesting to talk about.

When Cato heard them mention Billy-Bob's name, he asked Emma Lou Josephine Vernacular Hortense Hortense P. Barnacle to be quiet so he could hear what they were saying. Partitions divided the place into little cubicles, so he couldn't see them, but he knew them, Miss Cranberry and Miss Fluorine, and he recognized their voices. And since they didn't know that Cato was there, they thought they could speak freely.

"I'm sure there must be something inside his head," Miss Cranberry said. "But in all the years I've known him I've never seen anything but a slob. A big, clumsy kid."

"It looks as though he drools his weight in saliva in a day's time. I wonder how he does it."

"When I had him, he stared at me a lot. It made me uncomfortable. The girls in the class, too. I had to rotate the seating so no one had to sit near him very much."

"The boys didn't like him, either. When he was in my class, they wouldn't let him play ball with them because he was too clumsy. He talked them into it once, and the whole time he stood around or ran the wrong way or threw the ball through a window. They kept yelling at him, and he finally got mad and hit somebody, and a big fight started."

Cato considered, oh so briefly, saying say hello to Miss Cranberry and Miss Fluorine. But he didn't for two reasons. One was that they would realize that he had heard them talk about his brother. It would be awkward, and everyone would end up standing around looking at the floor saying "uh..." and whatnot. The other reason was that Emma Lou Josephine Vernacular Hortense Hortense P. Barnacle might get jealous. You should never anger someone who's holding scissors close to your head.

So Cato listened quietly. He used to get upset when people talked that way about his brother. Even though Billy-Bob could be a major pain, and frequently embarrassed him, and sometimes broke his furniture, he was, after all, his brother. That counted for a lot. But Cato didn't get upset about such talk anymore. He couldn't because it happened so much that if he got upset about it every time, he would never have a chance to do anything else. It would be like getting upset every time that...oh, what's her name, you know, that blonde bimbo movie star who goes into rehab every six months...yeah, *her*...it would be like getting upset every time she says some stupid thing that shows how self-absorbed she is.

"By the way," Miss Cranberry said, "are you going to the diuretic paint thinner party tonight?"

"I hadn't heard about it. Where is it?"

"At Mr. Sigmoid's house."

"Who's going to be there?"

"Oh, lots of people. After all, it's a party. And you know who else? Billy-Bob's brother Cato."

"Hmmm...That's interesting. Miss Chinstrap—you

know her, I think, the third-grade teacher at Mixed Metaphor Memorial Middle School—she went out with Cato a couple of times," Miss Fluorine said. "She says he's real nice, in every way you can imagine and in three others you can't. I wouldn't mind dating him."

Cato noticed Emma Lou Josephine Vernacular Hortense Hortense P. Barnacle's snipping was getting noticeably slower. It occurred to him that maybe he should talk to her, so as to distract her, but he wanted to hear this. Now it was an ego thing.

"Weren't you dating that other guy? Roger...what was his name?"

"Roger Glass Door Knob. Yes, I was dating him for a while, but he died."

"Oh, that's terrible! What happened?"

"He died while he was getting a haircut. Right here in this salon. No one knows why."

The snipping stopped. Cato twisted around and looked up at Emma Lou Josephine Vernacular Hortense Hortense P. Barnacle. Her mouth was hanging open. He didn't want her to be reminded of that while he was there with her.

"I'm surprised that you would come back here, where he died."

"Oh, but they do such good work here. Roger looked really spiffy at his funeral."

"That's nice. He was the one who sold charcoal, right?"

"Yes, for Schurk Enterprises. He worked in the rich people's neighborhood." Miss Fluorine sighed. "He wanted me to marry him, but I wouldn't do it unless he got a better job. Selling charcoal is okay, like, if you're a little kid, but for a grown man...well, I appreciated him for the man that he was, and I really, really wanted to marry him. It's just that he could have accomplished so much more with his life." She paused. Cato felt a moment of sadness, thinking about Roger. He felt a little guilty about sitting in the chair where Roger had died, getting his hair cut just so as to get close to a beautiful woman.

Oh, but gosh, he *really* liked being close to her...

Then Miss Fluorine said, "He and Cato were roommates, you know."

"I saw Cato a couple days ago," Miss Cranberry said, "and he told me he wasn't dating anyone. You should go to the party. I bet the two of you would get along very well together."

ZAP! Emma Lou Josephine Vernacular Hortense Hortense P. Barnacle torpedoed Cato's earlobe with her scissors. He screeched like that funny noise your air conditioner makes when it stops working and zipped out the door as fast as he could, without saying anything to Miss Cranberry or Miss Fluorine. They sat with their eyes wide and mouths wider, not sure who (or what) the blur was that ran past them so quickly. What they were sure of, though, was that they weren't ready to get their hair done by an irate stylist right after someone ran out of the place screaming and leaving a trail of blood on the floor.

Cato went home, and was he ever in a foul mood. Billy-Bob was still on the front porch, waiting to beat the pooh out of him, but he had fallen asleep. He was piled up in front of the door, sort of like the air compressor on Goliath's porch, except that Billy-Bob was snoozing away, off in wherever it was he went when he slept, whereas the air compressor was more-or-less inanimate. Cato kicked him awake.

"Wake up, Billy-Bob," he said. "You look like a big trash bag full of mildew."

Billy-Bob drowsed around. As you might expect, it always took him a long time to wake up. Usually eight or ten hours or so. Of course, with a guy like Billy-Bob, you could never tell whether he was truly awake or sleepwalking or hypnotized or a zombie or what, so you had to judge by whether his eyes were open and how much he was moving around. Billy-Bob opened his eyes and saw Cato. He didn't move, at least not much. He had heard the word "mildew" and thought Cato was talking about Bruce Mildew, the famous TV actor who had starred in the long-running hit series *The Possum Twins Go to Town.*

"Get out of the way," Cato said. "I need to go in and put a bandage on my earlobe, and eat lunch, and go someplace and finish getting my hair cut, and then get ready and go to the diuretic paint thinner party at Mr. Sigmoid's house tonight. Miss Fluorine and Miss Cranberry are going to be there, and I want to see them."

"What about mildew?" Billy-Bob asked.

"Move," Cato insisted. "I have a lot to do." And now that Emma Lou Josephine Vernacular Hortense Hortense P. Barnacle had started thinking he was icky, it was of the utmost importance for him to go to that party, looking good, so he could see Miss Fluorine and Miss Cranberry.

"I don't care," Billy-Bob said. "You lied to me. You said if I got Othello a present, she'd do anything I wanted, and she didn't. I wanted to take off all our clothes, and she wanted to go home. You lied to me."

"No, I didn't lie," Cato said. "I just forgot to tell you

it wouldn't work for a guy who's a big a jerk as you are. Now get out of my way and let me in." Cato didn't usually talk to Billy-Bob like that. Normally, Cato would have sat down and had a little talk with Billy-Bob and explained things to him, but this time he didn't care what he said. He was mad about all the stuff that had happened at the hair salon and feeling anxious over the need to get all fixed up in time for the party.

Billy-Bob punched Cato in the knee. Cato fell down, and then he got up madder. He wasn't as big as Billy-Bob, but Billy-Bob was so clumsy that it was no advantage for him to be big. Cato knocked him down flat, at least as flat as he could get.

"Miss Cranberry was right," Cato said. "You're nothing but a slob and a big, clumsy kid." And he jumped right over Billy-Bob and went inside.

Gosh, Billy-Bob thought. Miss Cranberry, who had been his teacher six or four years ago or sometime or other, she said he was a big slob and a clumsy kid, and after he had spent all that time believing she was so good and nice and everything. Daggone her! Wasn't there a law against that? Well, he should teach her a lesson and show her he wasn't really a big, clumsy kid, or at least not clumsy, because he had to admit that he was big, which really wasn't such a bad thing, and he knew where to find her because Cato had said she was going to be at Mr. Sigmoid's party. Not bad thinking for Billy-Bob, eh? But that was the only time he could do any kind of real thinking—whenever he had a chance to cause trouble. Even then he almost always messed up, but at least he did some thinking.

***

As Cato was eating his lunch, Mr. Schurk was in his office—yes, on Saturday, because he was such a busy guy! Well, not really; it was just that he didn't like any of the current batch of Saturday morning cartoons, so why not come into the office? Anyway, he going over his records and evaluating the Neuralgia Sisters. Their job performance was impressive, so impressive that he hated to take them off the vendor job. Roger Glass Door Knob had been...well, he had been an average vendor, no problems...but these women...oh, boy! Sometimes they sold so much charcoal that he had trouble keeping them supplied. Yes, in a short time they had proven themselves, and he had promised them a promotion if they did well. Not that he was honorable enough to keep a promise, but he was scared of them, Norma and Nancy. So now, he called them into his office.

"I have a competitor I want run out of town," he told them. "Not many people know this, but two different companies sell charcoal on street corners in this city. First, there's me, of course, and I have vendors in the rich people's neighborhood, which you already know about because you're those people, and also in the poor people's neighborhood and the young professionals' neighborhood. I do good business in all those areas. And then there's my competitor. He's a guy named Antwerp. He has people in the downtown area, the redneck neighborhood, and the suburban neighborhood."

"Well, technically, I don't think you're really competitors if you stay in different territories," Norma said.

"Yeah, well, see, that's the point," Mr. Schurk said. "I want to move into his territory."

"And you need somebody to run him out of business,"

Nancy said.

"Exactly. If I can find the right person..." he trailed off and paused for dramatic effect, and then he raised his eyebrows (hoping they were forming the devilish arch he had practiced earlier), leaned close to the Neuralgia Sisters, and added in a low voice, "or *pair* of people..." he continued in his normal voice, "they can not only take over the whole city for me, but run things here while I concentrate on opening offices in other cities. I want to expand across the whole country. If you can do this job for me, you'll have important positions in what is about to become a Great Big Company, like the kind they write about in those business magazines." Norma and Nancy didn't read business magazines, so they didn't know what he was talking about. Nonetheless, they liked the sound of it. "You could each run operations for an entire state if you want," Mr. Schurk said.

"I want Nebraska," Nancy said.

"I'll take North Tendonitis," Norma said.

"No, take Ottawa, and we'll be right next door," Nancy said. Just as they hadn't gotten their job on the basis of vocabulary, they weren't getting this promotion on the basis of knowing geography.

"Or maybe the entire country," Mr. Schurk continued. "I have other businesses I'm involved in. I have some real estate, and I own a radiator factory in Denver, and some other stuff. So I could concentrate on building up these other businesses if I knew the charcoal business was in capable hands. And by capable I mean ruthless sociopaths who'll stop at nothing to eliminate the competition."

Well, that description fit Norma and Nancy to a T. Literally—they had once had T-shirts printed for themselves with those exact words on them.

"What I'm thinking," Mr. Schurk was saying, "is that if you can get rid of his vendors, I can replace them with my own people."

"Could be a tough job," Norma said.

"Do whatever you have to do."

"By tough I mean expensive."

"I understand. Effective immediately, I'll pay you a thousand handfuls of money a week."

A thousand a week! That was a lot more than they made selling charcoal, and they made a lot selling charcoal. Wow. Norma and Nancy didn't know how to think about that much money!

"I need you to keep selling charcoal until I can find someone to take over your corner," Mr. Schurk said. "In the meantime, start thinking of ways to eliminate Mr. Antwerp's vendors. Okay?"

"Yeah, you got it," Norma said. For a thousand handfuls of money a week, they would think about anything Mr. Schurk wanted.

The Neuralgia Sisters went back to their street corner to sell charcoal. But they weren't just selling charcoal. They were planning and plotting. Planning and plotting was almost as much fun as actually doing mean stuff.

"We could throw disappearing ink on one of them," Norma said. "Then no one will buy charcoal from him because they won't know he's there."

"Yes, yes," Nancy said. "You know, this sure is fun."

Norma and Nancy giggled like little girls.

***

It was getting dark, almost time for the party, and Cato was getting dressed. After lunch, he had stuck a dab of chewing gum on his ear to stop the bleeding. Useful stuff, chewing gum. Then he went to the Kaal Hair Salon, where a nice woman named Miss Foomfaddle fixed up his haircut. Cato thought she was attractive, and he tried to charm her with his wit. Unfortunately, she had lost her sense of humor four years earlier when she fell off a flagpole. When she hit the ground, it (her sense of humor) broke off and went rolling across the grass. She tried to get up and grab it, but a dog came running along and ate it.

Poor Miss Foomfaddle. And poor Roger Glass Door Knob. If he had gone to her for a haircut, he would have been able to talk to her. They would have fallen in love and gotten married.

Anyway, Cato was about to leave for the party, dressed in the height of diuretic paint thinner fashion—loose-fitting, semireticulated carbon-fiber pants coated with a special sneezium alloy that constantly hummed at a pitch of two Fs below middle C, with a metallic-gold-colored muscle shirt made of woven flea hair. (And I know what you're thinking. You're thinking it's amazing that the height of diuretic paint thinner fashion three thousand years ago when this story took place was exactly the same as it is today. Hey, some things are timeless.)

Yeah, these were some expensive, fancy duds. Cato was going to impress lots of women tonight.

He drove to Mr. Sigmoid's house in his red Universal Motors Scapegoat, the one from the rich lady, and Billy-Bob followed on his scooter. Cato didn't notice him because it would create an unwanted problem for me in plotting this part of the story. When they got there, Cato went in and Billy-Bob hid behind the bushes across the street.

Billy-Bob thought about how mad he was at Miss Cranberry. Oh, that Miss Cranberry, he thought. I'm mad at her! Clumsy kid? Yeah, right. He would show her. When she came out of that house, he would walk right up to her and start dancing. Yeah, because a clumsy kid can't dance, right?

He decided to practice. He did a few jerky moves, which was all he could do. If anyone had seen him, it wouldn't have looked as if he was dancing, or trying to dance, or trying to practice dancing. It would have looked as if a family of porcupines was dancing in his pants. Well, that is to say, except for the distinct lack of any porcupine-sized bulges in his pants.

After a few minutes, he got tired of "dancing" because he wasn't in very good shape, so he sat down and tried to catch his breath. He drooled on the front of his shirt. Daggone it. He hoped it would dry up before it was time for him to dance for Miss Cranberry. He didn't want her to see him with a drool-encrusted shirt.

5. The Big Commotion

At the party, Miss Cranberry was sniffing diuretic paint thinner. Yes, you might be thinking, if she was supposed to be all wholesome and stuff, why was she sniffing diuretic paint thinner? Well, she had bought a whole bunch of Wholesomeness Dispensation Credits, which were expensive, but they allowed people to do things like sniff diuretic paint thinner without taking any points off their Wholesomeness Index Rating. Miss Cranberry considered it a worthwhile investment.

Of course, as a teacher she wasn't supposed to sniff that stuff anyway, regardless of any question of wholesomeness, on account of it was against the school district rules. But it was all right. The superintendent was there, too, and he was a more avid diuretic paint thinner sniffer than Miss Cranberry. He was there because it was his house. Mr. Sigmoid was the school superintendent.

So Miss Cranberry sat there admiring the poison ivy plants hanging in the windows, and Dexter Kroger sat there admiring Miss Cranberry. "She's a fine, fine woman, with attractive eyebrows," he once told his friend, the legendary Russian film director Sergei Eisenstein. At the time, Sergei was fuming about the feebleminded cameraman the Soviet Film Bureau had stuck him with. The guy was so daffy that he would forget what he was doing about ten seconds into a shot and become distracted, or shoot the wrong thing, or wander away. Once they went in to look at the previous day's rushes and found they had a seventeen-minute shot of the fire extinguisher by the studio door and six minutes of the script girl's crotch. The script girl was embarrassed. Presumably she didn't want anyone to know she had a crotch. The fire extinguisher wasn't embarrassed. But then again, it didn't have a crotch.

Back at the party, Cato was a little disappointed to see that Miss Cranberry was with someone. He had schemed up a little scheme in his head, a wee bit of a hope, actually, that he might be able to hook up with both Miss Fluorine and Miss Cranberry at the same time. But still, Miss Fluorine by herself was pretty good. He walked over to her. "Hi," he said. "Remember last year when no one got anything for Christmas?"

"Yeah," Miss Fluorine said. "Everyone was so disappointed. Only a few people in Alaska got anything."

It had indeed been odd. The whole world buzzed about it for months afterward. No Christmas presents for anyone except a few people in Alaska. Something had obviously happened to Santa Claus, but no one ever found out what. Or if they did, they were keeping it secret.

"I heard from a trustworthy source what happened," Cato said.

"Yeah? What?"

"Well," he said, leaning in close and turning his head so that she wouldn't see the dab of chewing gum on his ear, "Santa got a few deliveries made, starting up there in Alaska, and then he ran across some guys in the middle of a dice game."

"You mean..."

"Yeah. He got into the game and lost it all."

"Oh, no, that's awful!"

And so, having impressed Miss Fluorine with his access to inside information, which he didn't really need to do because she was already impressed by him anyway for other reasons, but he had to have something to say to start talking to her, Cato was able to get her away from the party and off by themselves, at his house. He only hoped Billy-Bob wouldn't come slobbing over acting like Billy-Bob. It always happened at precisely the wrong time, like when women were there. Billy-Bob never showed up when Cato was trying to get rid of a noise purifier salesman.

And it was becoming clear that the party was going to be a full-blown, indisputable success. Mr. Sigmoid was circulating among his guests, making sure everyone had plenty of snacks and ice water and diuretic paint thinner. He was making sure the Duran Duran tunes continued to flow freely. Above all, he was making sure his Immanuel Kant coffee table book was clearly visible at all times so people would see how sophisticated he was. Things were going great, yes, indeed.

***

Outside and across the street and behind the bush, Billy-Bob kept on waiting for Miss Cranberry to come out. He thought about stuff while he waited and decided he was going to grow up to be Jimmy Page.

Of course, Jimmy Page would have to become someone else because two people couldn't be him, but that was Jimmy Page's problem. Maybe he could become George Bush. If that sounds like a preposterous thing to be thinking about, remember that Billy-Bob had precious little experience at thinking.

He decided to practice some more. Dancing, that is, not thinking. He felt all rested up from his first practice session, which hadn't gone well, so he figured it would be a good idea to try again. He stood up, made a few jerky moves like the first time, lost his balance, and fell down.

A few blocks over, little Goliath had just sold his last piece of charcoal for the day. The customer—the *consumer*—was a guy who wanted to conduct a blindfolded taste test with his friend, like on TV. He was going to feed his friend an order of Scraps-O-Chicken, the well-known and immensely popular deep-fried chicken scraps menu item at Hamburger Sty, and he was going to mix in lumps of charcoal with the chicken scraps. He wanted to see whether the friend could tell the difference. "I bet he can't," the customer said.

Goliath knew from experience that he couldn't tell the difference in the way Scraps-O-Chicken and a wet stuffed doll tasted. One time, he was hosing down the driveway, and Alma walked by with a little stuffed Andrew Jackson doll (from the Presidents Who Were Opposed to the Electoral College Series—collect 'em all!). Right at that moment, Goliath's mom called him, and he turned around without paying attention to the hose and sprayed Alma. She got mad and stuffed Andrew Jackson into his mouth. The next time he ate Scraps-O-Chicken, it reminded him of how Andrew Jackson had tasted. But no one had ever stuffed charcoal into his mouth, at least not that he could remember.

Anyway, back to the present, Goliath's last customer of the day handed him a half-a-handful of money bill and walked away without getting his change, so Goliath was ready to go home.

On his way, Goliath saw Billy-Bob behind the bushes in someone's front yard. He, Billy-Bob, was trying to get up from his little losing-his-balance fall, but it was hard because he had twisted his ankle. It looked to Goliath as if Billy-Bob were trying to do push-ups. The way he was flopping around didn't look the way it would look for most people doing push-ups, but remember, he was Billy-Bob.

On the other hand, this seemed like an awfully odd place to be doing push-ups—even in this story.

"Whatcha doing, Billy-Bob?" Goliath asked.

Billy-Bob splumbled around until he was sitting up. "I'll tell you," he said. "Miss Cranberry is in that house across the street. They're having a party. When she comes out, I'm gonna show her I'm not a big, clumsy kid. I'm gonna dance for her, har har. I'm getting ready."

Well, Goliath wasn't much of a dancer, but he knew enough about it to know the difference between bad push-ups and dancing. "It looks like you're doing push-ups," he said.

"Yeah, har, har. I'm practicing."

Goliath thought about that. Then he thought about how he knew where babies came from. And although he wasn't sure what it looked like when mommies and daddies do that thing they do to make babies, he had an idea that what the daddy was supposed to do looked kinda like doing push-ups. Well, that was what his friend Hoobabloobus had told him, anyway.

So Goliath was wondering why Billy-Bob might be doing push-ups and talking about dancing for Miss Cranberry across the street from a place where she was at a party. None of it made sense. Nothing he saw or heard in this little scene helped explain anything else he saw or heard. But it was clear to him, to Goliath, that something was wrong. He also knew that sometimes people did that baby-making thing not to make babies, but just because they liked doing the baby-making thing.

Was that what Billy-Bob wanted to do with Miss Cranberry?

No, couldn't be.

But then again, if Billy-Bob was practicing to do something, that sure seemed to be what it looked like, as far as Goliath could tell. He wished Hoobabloobus could be there to give his opinion.

Billy-Bob tried once again to stand. He flopped around a little and managed to end up, by accident, in the same sitting position he had just been in. Well, that would be good enough for now. His ankle hurt, and Miss Cranberry could come out of the house at any time. "Goliath," he said, "do you have any duct tape?" He knew you could fix things with duct tape. Why wouldn't it work on his ankle, right?

"No, I don't think so."

"But I need to be ready for when Miss Cranberry comes out of the house over there."

That confused Goliath more. Why did he need duct tape when Miss Cranberry came out of the house? "I don't understand," he said.

Billy-Bob got impatient. If Goliath couldn't help, he should get out of the way. "Aw, go home," Billy-Bob said. "You don't know anything."

Little Goliath picked his nose. Billy-Bob watched him carefully, as if he expected to pick up some of the finer points in regard to technique. So Goliath gave it a good long dig and swished his fingernail around up in there, giving it a nice stylistic flourish at the end. He looked at the result and then flicked it toward the bush. It landed on a butterfly. The butterfly didn't understand what was going on any more (or less) than Goliath did.

"I...well, I didn't know why you needed duct tape," Goliath said.

"Shut up and go away," Billy-Bob said, and punched Goliath in the knee. Goliath fell down. Then he got up and went away.

"Okay for you, Billy-Bob," he mumbled.

And okay for Billy-Bob, indeed. Because Goliath was walking away with the idea in his head that Billy-Bob was going to try to do the baby-making thing with Miss Cranberry. He was also pretty sure that Miss Cranberry wasn't going to like it. He was pretty sure it would be a miserable kind of experience for her.

Goliath figured there was enough misery in the world without people going around adding to it on purpose. Not that he knew how much misery was in the world, or how you would measure it, but he knew there was at least a little bit because there was a word for it. And this would add more. He should try to stop Billy-Bob, then, right? Miss Cranberry didn't deserve to be miserable. But if he stopped Billy-Bob, then wouldn't Billy-Bob be miserable? Gosh, what a pisser!

Goliath decided that Billy-Bob deserved to be miserable, since he wanted to make someone else miserable. After all, the Golden Rule, and stuff. So if Billy-Bob wanted to make someone else miserable, then it must mean that he wanted to be miserable himself. And then if Goliath stopped him, everyone would be happy. Or miserable. Or whatever. And anyway, he would rather see Billy-Bob miserable than Miss Cranberry. After all, Billy-Bob had hit him in the knee, and Miss Cranberry hadn't. Not once. Making him come up to the chalkboard had been bad, but not as bad as punching.

So what could Goliath do? He could warn Miss Cranberry. He could tell her all about what Billy-Bob had said, and then she could do something about it. Being a grown-up, she could handle Billy-Bob better than Goliath could.

Yeah.

So Goliath walked up to the front door of Mr. Sigmoid's house and rang the doorbell. A woman named Ann Onimous answered and exclaimed, "Oh, what a cute little boy!"

Goliath blushed, not because of the compliment but because he could smell the diuretic paint thinner. It caused a chemical reaction in his body. Ann Onimous saw the blush, and she assumed it was because of what she had said, and she started thinking he was cuter. She didn't want to expose Goliath to the adult things going on in the house, so she stepped out on the front porch and shut the door. "What can I do for you, big guy?" she asked.

Goliath was confused. Was he a little boy or a big guy? He didn't see how he could be both, although he had to allow as how this might be one of those things that kids don't understand. Or maybe this woman was confused. But that couldn't be, since she was a grownup, and grownups know more than children. But then again, Billy-Bob was older than Goliath, so it kind of stood to reason that Billy-Bob would know more about life than Goliath. And *that* sure didn't seem right. But then *again*, maybe he was thinking too much. The important thing was that Miss Cranberry shouldn't be miserable.

"Is Miss Cranberry in there?" he asked.

"Why, yes, she is," Ann Onimous said brightly. "Are you in her class at school?"

"Yes, ma'am, I am. Can I talk to her?"

"You mean, 'MAY I talk to her?' and I'll see if I can find her. Wait here." She disappeared inside, and Goliath waited on the front porch thinking about using the word "may" as opposed to "can." If "may" meant he had *permission* to do something, and "can" meant he had the *ability* to do it, then it seemed that "can" was really the right word for his question because he would be unable to talk to Miss Cranberry if someone didn't go get her.

Inside, Ann Onimous found Miss Cranberry. "One of your pupils is at the door, and he wants to talk to you. A really cute little boy."

"Must be Goliath," Miss Cranberry said, and got up. "I wonder what he wants."

Dexter Kroger didn't want her to get up, of course, because he was happy with things the way they were, the two of them sitting on the sofa, his arm around her, his other hand working its way up her leg, and so on. But he was a real sweetheart of a guy, so he got up and went to the door with her.

Meanwhile, Billy-Bob saw little Goliath at the door, and somehow he caught on that Goliath was trying to mess things up for him. As soon as Ann Onimous closed the door to get Miss Cranberry, Billy-Bob went running up to the porch. "Goliath, what are you doing here?" He was trying to be intimidating, but to Goliath he sounded confused. After all, that's what you automatically think when you think about Billy-Bob.

"I'm going to tell Miss Cranberry you want to do the baby-making thing to her," Goliath said.

"You better not," Billy-Bob said, and punched Goliath in the knee one more time. It was the same knee he had punched a couple minutes earlier, so it hurt worse this time. Goliath fell down, and Billy-Bob jumped on him. He grabbed Goliath's wrist and started squeezing. He had his eyes closed, so he thought he was choking Goliath, but he really wasn't. He was just being foolish. Goliath didn't breathe through his wrist.

The door opened, and Dexter Kroger and Miss Cranberry were standing there. Dexter reached down and grabbed Billy-Bob by his shirt collar and pulled him up. "What's going on here?" Dexter said. He was irritated over this interruption of a dandy party, and besides that, Billy-Bob's shirt felt unpleasantly damp.

"Miss Cranberry, Billy-Bob wants to do that baby-making thing to you!" Goliath shouted.

"I do not! I do not!" Billy-Bob shouted, louder. (And of course, you should remember that this was the truth.)

"Yes he does," Goliath insisted. "He even has duct tape. Show them the duct tape, Billy-Bob."

"I don't have any, remember?"

"You wanted some, and that's just as bad."

Dexter Kroger was confused by all this talk about making babies and duct tape, confused and irritated because he didn't like being confused, and he couldn't figure out how it could possibly make any difference anyway, since all he knew was that these two kids were causing a commotion on the front porch, and what reason could there possibly be for it considering that neither of them lived there, and if someone saw what was going on they might call the police, which would be really bad because although diuretic paint thinner wasn't illegal, the German stuff was, which was what they had, and it was illegal to sniff any of it anyway, so they could get sent to jail for a long time not only for that, but also for contributing to the delinquency of a minor, even if the kid *did* show up at the door unexpected and uninvited, so not only was this keeping him from enjoying himself (Dexter, that is), but the possibility of going to jail for a long time scared him because his brother had been in jail lots of times, his brother Earl, and he had told Dexter about it, and it didn't sound like a place where a fella could enjoy himself much, which was what he really wanted to do right at that moment but couldn't because a couple of kids were fighting on the front porch, and he couldn't see how any of what they were shouting could possibly make any sense, so he decided that he didn't want to hear any more of it.

Dexter summed up his feelings on the matter in one short sentence. "Shut up," he said.

"But Billy-Bob was going to get Miss Cranberry," Goliath pleaded.

Dexter yanked Billy-Bob up a couple more inches. Billy-Bob had an antique porcelain foot on a string around his neck, and the string had gotten all tangled and twisted, and Dexter Kroger had a handful of it, so Billy-Bob was kind of choking. The foot looked as if it were growing out of Billy-Bob's throat. Miss Cranberry was amused. Many years later, when she was an old woman, it would be the last thing she remembered before dying.

"Were you going to do something to Miss Cranberry?" Dexter demanded.

"No," Billy-Bob said. "It was Goliath. Goliath was going to get her. I was trying to stop him."

Dexter did some analyzing. The little one was obviously too young to want to get women. The other one looked as if he was probably old enough, and if he did want to get women, it was easy to believe that he was too stupid to do it right, and whatever he thought he was doing was obviously wrong, no matter what it was that he thought he was doing. But he looked too dumb to blame his screwups on other people, so something totally different was probably going on. "I don't believe you," Dexter said. Yeah, that was a good response, appropriate no matter what these boys were doing or why they were doing it.

Billy-Bob screamed. "You have to! I'm a kid! You have to believe me! It's the law!" It wasn't really the law, but Billy-Bob believed it was.

"Get out of here," Dexter said. "And don't you ever try to bother Miss Cranberry again, or you'll be sorry, oh so sorry. I'm big and tough. I used to be a football player. And Miss Cranberry is my friend, and I hang around with her a lot, so I'll know if you try anything."

"But I didn't do anything!" Billy-Bob screamed. The foot was wagging around. Goliath giggled, but no one noticed him. They were paying attention to Billy-Bob.

"Then keep it that way, and we won't have any problem. Now shove off. And quit being a miserable little puke."

Well, Billy-Bob didn't think he was a little puke, but he sure felt miserable. When Dexter let go of him, he kind of slunk away with his tail between his legs, metaphorically speaking, shuffling off looking at the ground. He didn't look back because all those people would be there. As it was, he could hear a lot of chattering behind him, and finally he heard the door slam shut and nothing but muffled music from inside the house. Well, they'd see. He'd get them. Daggone those daggone people anyway. And that Goliath—well, Billy-Bob didn't know whether he was miserable, but he sure was a puke, and a little one, too. It was all his fault.

Dexter Kroger and Miss Cranberry stayed out on the front porch with Goliath and talked about what they should do. Miss Cranberry was afraid that if they let Goliath go home by himself, Billy-Bob might be lurking around somewhere waiting to pounce on him. He had already punched Goliath and made his knee sore. But gee whiz, after this big commotion, who could say what else Billy-Bob might do if he got the chance? So they decided to drive Goliath home.

Dexter Kroger was glad about it. After they dropped Goliath off, it would be Miss Cranberry and him, all alone. The big commotion had ruined the party, as far as he was concerned, and he was thinking maybe he could get her to come home with him and play a little bouncy-bouncy. He couldn't blame the goofy kid for wanting to, if that was really the true poop, but he didn't have to be a creep. And how did Goliath get involved in all this? Dexter tried to ask about it on the way to Goliath's house, but Goliath's knee was hurt, and he was upset, so they didn't get much of a story from him.

6. Human Sacrifice

And while Goliath was getting dropped off at his house, Billy-Bob was home, at his own house, calling the police.

"Hello, Mr. Policeman," Billy-Bob said. He wanted to sound nice and extra polite so the police officer would listen to him and take him seriously. "I want to report a wild party, har har. They're real loud, and they've got drugs, har har." Billy-Bob didn't know they had drugs. He was making stuff up so it would sound as bad as possible.

"What kind of drugs?"

"Oh, uh…all kinds, har har. All kinds of drugs. And human sacrifice, too." Billy-Bob didn't know exactly what human sacrifice was, but he knew it was bad.

"What's the address?"

"It's at 451 Fahrenheit Lane, Mr. Sir, I mean, officer, Sir. Uh…Your Honor."

"All right. We'll send a car out."

"Thank you, sir, har har, thank you very much." Billy-Bob hung up, and he was pleased with himself, har har. He could indeed think okay when he had a chance to cause trouble. He remembered the address, and that was big-time brainwork for him.

***

The police went to Mr. Sigmoid's house. The door was standing open, and they had to shut it so they could bust in with a battering ram. They shouted and screamed and waved their guns around. "Yaaaagh!" one of the policemen shouted.

"Aaargh!" another shouted.

"Festoons!" yet another shouted.

And of course, one of the first things they saw were the containers of diuretic paint thinner, the illegal German stuff, sitting right out there on the coffee table in the middle of the living room.

"You're all under arrest," the lead officer said. "Who lives here?" The other officers started handcuffing people.

Mr. Sigmoid stepped forward. "This is my house."

"Where are the bodies?"

"Bodies? What bodies?" asked Mr. Sigmoid.

"We heard there were human sacrifices going on at this party," the officer said.

"There aren't any bodies here."

"You've eaten them! Hey, Henderson, add cannibalism to the charges."

"Yes, sir."

"Oh, no," Mr. Sigmoid said. "There were never any human sacrifices in the first place."

"Let us be the judge of that." And then the police officer, not believing a word Mr. Sigmoid had said because you can't trust those diuretic paint sniffers *or* those psycho human sacrificers, and especially not people who were both, told his friends to look for bodies.

"Look in the basement," he said. "That's where they usually do it." Of course, the only thing in Mr. Sigmoid's basement was his headache collection, but the police didn't know that. All they knew was that a polite-sounding voice that deserved to be taken seriously had called to report a wild party.

"Okay, burn down the house," the head policeman told his guys.

"You can't do that," Mr. Sigmoid said. "You don't have an arson warrant."

"All right, then, men. Glue carrots to the walls." The lead policeman turned to Mr. Sigmoid. "You know we can do that, don't you?"

Mr. Sigmoid hung his head. Yes, he knew they could do that. Daggone it.

***

And Dexter Kroger, Dexter and Miss Cranberry, they were at Dexter's house. Miss Cranberry had agreed to go there with him, and he was pleased because he liked her. When they got to his house he gave her a good, stiff drink of lemonade, and then he kissed her. "I like a woman who appreciates good lemonade," he said. Igor Stravinsky had taught him the finer points of making cold, refreshing drinks.

Dexter took Miss Cranberry into his bedroom, and they both took off all their clothes. At the very instant Dexter's shorts hit the floor, the phone rang. Dexter usually turned his phone off for this kind of stuff, but he hadn't gotten to it yet. "Hold on a minute," he said to Miss Cranberry. "I'll blow this geek off real quick and be right with you." He picked up the phone. "Hello.

This better be important because I have a beautiful woman here with me. And I'm not buying anything."

"This is Mr. Sigmoid. The police raided the party, and we've all been arrested."

"Oh, that sounds important," Dexter said.

"Yes, it's incredibly inconvenient."

After hanging up, Dexter said, "Miss Cranberry, the gang's been arrested."

"Oh, what a crazy bunch."

***

The next morning was Sunday, and Cleopatra went to a church service. It was a Catholic church, and the priest was the Reverend Willis O'Grotten. Cleopatra had picked this particular church at random, so she didn't know what to expect. But when she saw Father O'Grotten walk down the aisle and up to the altar, she knew this was going to be a good one.

Father O'Grotten was a big guy. Cleopatra liked big priests and ministers because that meant they had more God in them. And Father O'Grotten kind of reminded her of Tom Selleck on that TV show, except he was older, almost totally bald, and a bloated-looking kind of fat. Also, the tip of his nose drooped. Oh, yeah, and his ears stuck out. But otherwise, he was a dead ringer for Tom. Well, except for the eye patch. And the huge scar on his left cheek. And he was tremendously red all over. You might think he had just gotten off work at a foundry on a hundred-degree day. Well, actually, you probably wouldn't, but if someone else said so, you wouldn't argue about it.

Cleopatra listened, rapt. Father O'Grotten was

rough and gruff and...well, vulgar. He was a refreshing change of pace from clergymen who knew what priests and ministers were supposed to be like.

"For today's sermon," he growled, "I want to talk about loyalty." He paused to squint at the congregation. "I hate people who aren't loyal. People who aren't loyal are lowlife scumsucking warts on a flea's butt." Cleopatra thought fleas' butts were probably too small to have warts, but that was a minor detail. The big question was that she didn't know how a wart could suck scum, but this priest sounded as if he knew what he was talking about. Well, she could look it up on the Internet after she got home.

A few people tittered nervously.

"Who the hell did that?" Father O'Grotten demanded. "You think this is funny? Who's out there laughing?" He studied the congregation. "If there's one thing I hate worse than people who aren't loyal, it's people who laugh in church. Well, I hate communist vampires from Saturn worse than anything, but I also hate people who laugh in church. Who was laughing?"

No one said anything. Father O'Grotten sighed. "All right, I'll let it pass this time. But next time, I'm going to find out who it was, and I'll send you over to the Lutherans and let them deal with you. Because people who laugh in church deserve...well, they deserve to have gas masks sewed to their butts." Cleopatra sensed a butt theme developing.

"Now, as I was saying, loyalty. The only way to get along in this damn world is to make friends and be loyal to them. That's why I hate people who laugh in church. They're not loyal. Not loyal to the priest. Not loyal to the rest of the congregation. And I say to you, if someone's not loyal, tell 'em to hit the road. You have enough problems just being alive without some disloyal mammyjammer causing you more problems for no good reason."

"Mammyjammer?" a hushed voice in the back echoed, puzzled.

Father O'Grotten rolled on. "Yes, people who aren't loyal are more disgusting than a gallon jug full of snake snot. I think disloyal people should be given wood putty enemas." Another butt reference...and was a wood putty enema *possible*? Well, it would be another thing to look up on the Internet. (When Cleopatra finally remembered to look it up seven years later, she was *shocked* at what she found.)

An old woman got up and walked toward the door.

"Hey, woman!" Father O'Grotten shouted. "Where do you think you're going?"

She turned, frightened. "Your language..." she ventured.

"This," Father O'Grotten announced with a great deal of satisfaction, "is exactly what I'm talking about. This woman has no loyalty whatsoever. And do you know how we deal with people like her?" He leaned forward and pointed at the door. "Get out. *Get out of here and don't come back*. Ever. Unless you're going to donate a whole lot of money. Good God, I'd rather swallow a mouthful of bees than be in the same room with someone who's not loyal."

Sobbing, the woman ran much faster than she appeared to be able to run. In a second, the door was shut behind her.

"Let that be a lesson to the rest of you." Father O'Grotten's voice boomed throughout the church with just a little more reverb than it had previously had.

Cleopatra gazed upon this man in wonder. Yes, he was a priest. Father Willis O'Grotten was a priest in the truest sense of the word.

***

At the county jail, Mr. Sigmoid sat in a cell considering his situation. Things looked bad for him, very bad, and he was worried. The police had lots of evidence and witnesses. What if I confess, he wondered, and throw myself on the mercy of the court? Will they go easy on me? He would have to ask his lawyer.

But it didn't come to that. The police had to release Mr. Sigmoid. See, here's the thing: Diuretic paint thinner, especially the illegal German stuff, evaporates extremely quickly after you open the container, and all the containers at the party had been opened. By the time Monday morning came around, it was gone. All the police had was a bunch of empty cans. And the cans didn't even have "German Diuretic Paint Thinner" labels because it would have been foolish for the dealers to label an illegal, highly controlled substance. So the evidence was gone because the police officers didn't document it quickly enough.

But the school board didn't waste any time. As soon as Mr. Sigmoid was out of police custody, they had him come to headquarters so he could listen to them rake him over the coals for getting arrested with diuretic paint thinner, the illegal German stuff. They didn't need evidence or proof. The news reports, the rumors, the "appearance of impropriety" were enough to get him in trouble with the school board.

Mr. Sigmoid listened to them, feeling as if he were naked, out on the ice in a huge hockey rink that was crowded with people making fun of him. That had happened to him one time (purely by accident, you understand), and this felt exactly the same.

"Mr. Sigmoid, public servants aren't supposed to do such things."

"Mr. Sigmoid, you've involved the school system in a terrible scandal."

"Mr. Sigmoid, look at this headline." SCUMBAG SCHOOL SUPERINTENDENT ARRESTED FOR PERVERTED BEHAVIOR. LOCAL PARENTS SHOCKED.

Well, Mr. Sigmoid took issue with "perverted." The newspaper was clearly making stuff up.

"And this one." "SIGMOID SHOULD BE DROWNED IN A VAT OF WATERMELON JUICE," ANGRY PARENT SAYS.

He took issue with "watermelon juice," too. The worst he deserved was to be drowned in a vat of grape juice.

"Mr. Sigmoid, you're a dork."

"And when was the last time you brushed your teeth?"

"I've always thought his handwriting was awfully childish looking."

"And he drives too close to the car in front of him."

"Who thinks he should be fired?"

Everyone shouted "I do!" enthusiastically, and then one guy in the back, caught up in the excitement, shouted, "I'm Spartacus!"

The head of the committee said, "Get out of here, Sigmoid. You're yesterday's leftovers. You're ancient history. It's out on the street with you, boy. We'll see to it you never work in this town again."

So Mr. Sigmoid, after all that unfair treatment, all that harsh and unfair treatment, slunk (slank?) out of the room much in the same way Billy-Bob had slinked away from the front porch after the commotion. But this was worse. Mr. Sigmoid stood on the sidewalk and shivered. It was cold, and the wind was blowing, and the ground was covered with lots of snow and ice. (Actually it was warm and pleasant, being early in the summer, but I'm saying it was all wintry because it had become a hard, hard winter in his soul.) So Mr. Sigmoid gathered his coat up under his chin and trudged off, alone and cold and miserable and hungry and wet. And his rheumatism was starting to act up again. Two little boys hit him in the back of the head with snowballs. He slipped and fell on the ice. Tears were freezing on his face. A dog barked at him.

Then he looked up, Mr. Sigmoid did, and saw one of Mr. Schurk's notices on a telephone pole. Charcoal Vendor Wanted. He could do that. It wasn't as good a job as being the school superintendent, but he wasn't the school superintendent anymore. He could sell charcoal, maybe, until he could find another job, a good job that would be exciting and challenging, that would be more in keeping with his talents and interests, that would pay loads of money and confer a tremendous amount of prestige. A job that would be important, creative, productive, and interesting. A job that would help him develop himself intellectually, emotionally, and spiritually. A job that would give him plenty of opportunities to help people and make positive contributions to society, to improve the world. A job that would allow him to do things that would make people remember him for years and years. A job that would qualify him for his own Wikipedia entry. And gosh darn it, was that too much to ask for?

And no more diuretic paint thinner. Boy, had Mr. Sigmoid ever learned his lesson about *that*!

He tore the paper off the pole and went to the nearest phone booth. It took his last tenth of a handful of money coin, the last money he had in the world—actually, he had six hundred and five handfuls of money in the bank, but it's a better story if the coin was the last money he had—and called Mr. Schurk. "I'd like to be a vendor," he said. Of course, as we already said, he wouldn't *really* like it, but it was more desirable than starving to death and freezing in the gutter. Actually, his house was all paid for, and it had a powerful and well-maintained furnace, but for this part of the story we'll say it wasn't and it didn't.

"Yes," Mr. Schurk said. "I have an opening in the rich people's neighborhood. I need to find someone as soon as possible. The vendors I have there now, I'm promoting them to bigger and better things."

Ah, Mr. Sigmoid thought. There's room for upward mobility in this company. This is starting to sound better.

So he went to talk to Mr. Schurk. And by a strange coincidence of the sort you see only in unbelievably silly novels (if you were ever to read such a thing), it just so happened that Mr. Sigmoid and Mr. Schurk looked exactly alike. Exactly.

So when Mr. Sigmoid walked into Schurk Enterprises World Headquarters, Mr. Schurk's secretary, Miss Spikenhammer, thought her boss was walking in.

"Mr. Schurk," she said, "aren't you...already in your office?"

Mr. Sigmoid stopped, puzzled. He rolled his eyes
around to help him think, but it didn't work. "I came in
to talk to Mr. Schurk," he said.

Then Miss Spikenhammer decided Mr. Schurk was
joking with her. And when the boss, or a person you
believe to be the boss, does something that's supposed
to be funny, you play along, whether the joke is funny
or not. "Okay. Well, go on in," she said.

This "playing along" sounded kind of odd to Mr.
Sigmoid, but he went into Mr. Schurk's office. Mr.
Schurk, reading some paperwork, heard the door open
and looked up to see...himself.

"Mr. Schurk?" himself—er, Mr. Sigmoid—said. "I'm
Mr. Sigmoid."

Ordinarily, Mr. Schurk would have been outraged
at someone barging into his office unannounced. But
ordinarily, the barging-in person wouldn't have been
a dead ringer. "Gosh," Mr. Schurk said. "We could be
twins." It made him think about stuff. He thought that
in his line of work, not as a charcoal magnate but as
something closer to what you might think of as a mob
boss, it could come in handy to have a lookalike. Sometimes people got mad and went out looking for him.

And he was righter than he could have imagined
about being twins because they were really authentic,
true-blue, official twins. Yes! They had been separated
at birth, and Mr. Sigmoid was raised by their real parents. But the night they were born, Mr. Schurk left the
hospital. How could a six-hour-old baby do something
like that? Good question. Well, six-hour-old babies are
short, and it just so happened that no one looked down.

So Mr. Schurk wandered out, unnoticed, and somehow ended up in a swamp, where he was found and raised by wolves. He hadn't intended to run away. It just worked out like that.

And now, not knowing they were real twins or related in any way, the two were reunited.

"So you're Mr. Sigmoid, the guy in all the papers," Mr. Schurk said.

"Yes, that's me. But I'm innocent."

"You didn't really do all that stuff?"

Mr. Sigmoid didn't think a party with diuretic paint thinner that evaporated before the police could log it as evidence could be described as "all that stuff," but he didn't want to argue with a potential employer. So he said, "No, of course not." After all, you don't want the aforementioned potential employer to think you're a criminal. He might have a beautiful daughter and not want to have to worry about the hired help.

"Listen," Mr. Schurk said. "The kind of organization I have here, it helps to be guilty of a few things. You fit in better, if you catch my drift."

"Oh?"

"Yeah. We, uh, sometimes conduct operations that we'd rather people didn't find out about. Shady, you might say."

Well, if that was the type of people Mr. Sigmoid was dealing with, he might be able make a lot of money. Shady dealings always involve a lot of money. He might be able to take home a suitcase full of handfuls of money every day. That would be a gas!

"Yeah, I did it," Mr. Sigmoid said, trying to sound tough. "I'm also the one who blew up Cortlandt Homes, I'm the one who shot Joe Gillis at Norma Desmond's house, and I burned Rosebud. What do you think of that?"

"Interesting."

"Yes, and I led the charge up San Juan Hill. Teddy Roosevelt paid me to let him take the credit for it." It wasn't illegal, but it would show that he had his tough-guy credentials in order.

"Is that right?" Actually, it wasn't, because the Neuralgia sister had told him the truth.

"Absolutely."

"Don't overdo it, Mr. Sigmoid."

"Oh. Okay."

"But I think you would fit right in. Sometimes we have, uh, shall we say, special assignments for some of our people. Such as, f'rinstance, these vendors you're replacing. For security reasons I can't tell you what their special project is, but I can tell you it's big. I mean, like as big as a hippopotamus. No, make that a hippopotamus and a giraffe together. Yeah, *that* big. The reason I mention it is to show you that this is a company with plenty of opportunity. If you can prove yourself, I might promote you and let you handle some, uh, special assignments."

"I'd like that. I'm a special guy, so special assignments would be just right for me."

Mr. Schurk stood up and shook Mr. Sigmoid's hand. "I think we can work together," Mr. Schurk said. "Mr. Sigmoid, you're my kind of man."

Mr. Sigmoid wasn't sure what Mr. Schurk meant by that. The idea nagged at him, a tiny little bit, that it might be a romantic overture. He decided to pretend he didn't think so. "Thank you," Mr. Sigmoid said. "I promise you'll be pleased. With my job performance, that is. On the job, I mean."

So he had a job. And if this Mr. Schurk guy, his new employer, was into some shady dealings, well, what had Mr. Sigmoid to do with that? He didn't have to join in with any of that bad-guy-type stuff. Heck no. And if Mr. Schurk tried to make him do something mean to somebody, he could always refuse. After all, there was a law that said employers couldn't make people who work for them do illegal things. There was that law, so Mr. Schurk couldn't fire him for refusing to blow up somebody's house or whatever. Of course, it was a shame that that kind of thing had to go on at all, but it was really none of his concern. He was just an average guy trying to eke out a living, although he was certainly far above average and deserved to get rich. That is, he couldn't be said to be guilty himself, not if he tried his best to stay away from underhanded behavior.

7. The Special Project

Much in the same way as the school board didn't waste any time getting rid of Mr. Sigmoid, the Neuralgia Sisters didn't waste any time—they wasted no time at all—getting to work on their special project. After all, the quicker they got rid of Mr. Antwerp's people, the quicker Mr. Schurk could expand out of town and leave them in complete charge. (And complete is the best kind of charge, as Nancy pointed out to Norma.)

The first victim, the one they started with, was the one in the redneck neighborhood. He was a little, skinny guy named Johnny Abacus. They kidnapped him one afternoon after he had finished selling his charcoal. They forced him into their car at gunpoint, the way you see spies do it in those movies on TV that you can never remember having been out in the theaters, and they took him to an abandoned warehouse, also like in the movies. They tied him to a chair.

"What are you going to do to me?" Johnny Abacus asked. He wasn't sure about anything. He didn't know who they were or why they had kidnapped him, and he was obviously in a bad position because he couldn't stop them from doing anything they wanted. (Well, they couldn't force him to say an unpronounceable word, but why would they want to?) And they looked mean. These girls, they would probably lead soldiers in a fierce charge against enemy forces. (Well, they might want to make him say an unpronounceable word just for fun. They were like that, you know.)

"We've got plans for you, skinny boy. Big plans," Nancy said. She spoke threateningly because she wanted him to be scared. It wasn't strictly necessary, since he had already decided they looked really mean, and he could only think of two things that they would be likely to do to him, one of which was to kill him, a scary thing, and the other was to do wild and woolly things to his body, things like what people do with no clothes on, and judging by the way these girls looked, that would probably kill him too, so either way he was dead, but between the two he would rather have the wild and woolly way out if given the choice; actually, it would be pretty good to try out that stuff with these women anyway, what with him being a real red-blooded American male, but if they thought he wanted it, they'd probably chain him to something heavy like an air compressor and throw him off a pier, or something equally boring, so the key was to play it cool.

"We could cut his knees off," Nancy said.

"That wouldn't bother me," Johnny Abacus said. "And I don't care whether you have sex with me or not."

"We could cut his gizzard out," Norma said.

"Go ahead. See if I care. And I'm not concerned about sex, either."

"Let's force-feed him a bag of rusty washers," Nancy said.

"I had that for breakfast this morning. I had sex this morning, too, so it's no big deal whether I have sex now or not."

"How about sewing a gas mask to his butt?" Norma suggested.

Well, that bothered Johnny Abacus. When he was a little kid in school, about Goliath's age, and the photographer came to take pictures of his class, Johnny's pictures got mixed up with those from another job the photographer was doing. Little Johnny was given pictures of a fireman in a gas mask. For four weeks, he was convinced that his face looked like a gas mask, until he finally looked in a mirror. Even though the truth was clear to him now, the damage was done. Johnny Abacus was whacked out, for life, over gas masks.

But he was safe from Norma and Nancy's dreaded threat. They couldn't find a gas mask. They decided next to force-feed him a bag of rusty washers, thinking he had only been playing it cool when he said he had had some for breakfast. Yes, they believed it would really be an awful, terribly awful thing to do, and besides that, if he had really had rusty washers for breakfast, he certainly wouldn't want more again so soon. But alas, all they could find was a bag of new, shiny ones. So they did something else. Here's what happened:

Norma and Nancy got Johnny, poor Johnny Abacus, into their car and drove around downtown looking for something. And after a while, Norma pointed. "Look, Nancy," she said. "There's what we're looking for."

"Yeah, that's it," Nancy said. She pulled over to the curb and parked.

"See that guy over there, up on that ladder?" Norma said. Down the street a little way, in the middle of the block, a guy had a tall, tall ladder propped up against a building. He was up there, standing on the ladder, working on something. Norma and Nancy couldn't tell what he was doing on account of the angle they were watching from, but it didn't matter. All they were interested in was the ladder. (Actually, what the guy was doing—and Norma and Nancy wouldn't have known what he was doing even if they could have gotten a good view of it because it's a highly specialized task—was cleaning evil spirit vomit off the building. Don't ask how it got there. The story is far too involved to explain in parentheses.)

Norma handed Johnny Abacus a little hand mirror. "Okay," Norma said. "Here's what we want you to do. We want you to walk under that ladder, and while you're under it, drop this mirror and make sure it breaks."

Now, understand that on the one hand, Johnny Abacus didn't believe in any of that superstitious nonsense. Walk under a ladder? Bad luck? Pffft. Break a mirror? Bad luck? Pffft. Who cares? Who the heck cares?

On the other hand, he couldn't help but feel a little uneasy over the prospect of tempting fate. "I'm not so sure about that," he said.

"We dare you," Nancy said.

"We *double-dog* dare you," Norma said.

On the third hand, if these women were double-dog daring him, what choice did he have?

With a little cloud of dread forming above him, Johnny Abacus got out of the car, mirror in hand. He looked at the guy on the ladder, scoped out the distance he had to walk, and blinked his eyes a couple times. While he was doing all this, Nancy (Nancy Neuralgia) ran ahead and made some additional preparations.

"Get going," Norma said to Johnny. "We don't have all day. We want to get this over with so we can go home and giggle like little girls about it."

Johnny frowned. "Do you think I'm wearing the right shoes for this?"

"Quit stalling. Walk."

Johnny took a deep breath and started toward the ladder. When he was about halfway there, Nancy, from a doorway, shoved a black cat out in front of him—ack! another bad luck vector! She had placed an open can of tuna on the sidewalk across the street, and exactly according to plan, the cat made straight for the can— right across Johnny's path. Johnny stopped and looked back at Norma. She gave him a hard, hard look and mouthed "double-dog dare" at him.

He gulped apprehensively. This was all too much. But he was into it now, and there was no way out except to hope for the best.

So Johnny Abacus continued. He walked across the path the cat had taken and went under the ladder. "Hey, buddy," the worker shouted from above him. "Watch out! You're walking under my ladder!" The worker was horrified. He had never seen such blatant and reckless disregard for bad luck safety. (Of course, he had never run afoul of the Neuralgia Sisters, either.) Bystanders turned and looked. They were shocked. Some pulled their cell phones out and started shooting video.

Johnny pretended not to hear the worker. He paused under the ladder long enough to drop the mirror. It shattered into dozens of little pieces the size of toenail clippings.

Then Johnny stepped out from under the ladder on

the other side. He had done it.

His cell phone rang. Surprised, he answered. "Mr. Abacus, this is Helen Consternation from Greater Tibia Savings and Loan. I'm sorry, but it would appear that someone hacked into your account, withdrew all your money, and used the entire amount to buy artificial cheese-flavored food product. Mr. Abacus, you don't have any money left."

"Oh, no."

And no sooner was Johnny Abacus off the phone with Helen Consternation than another call came in. This time it was Harold Elstree calling, his neighbor across the street. "Hey, Johnny, something weird happened. Your house suddenly shot up into the air for no apparent reason."

"Huh?"

"Yeah. It went up about two hundred feet and came down and landed in Herb Smooble's backyard about ten minutes ago."

"Oh, no. If it's in Smooble's yard, he won't give it back."

"Sorry, man."

Then a long-dormant genetic condition became active due to the stress of losing his money and his house, and Johnny's hair fell out. Yeah, all at once. A soft breeze blew it away slowly.

Then a text message came: "Johnny, I want a divorce. Love, your wife." Oh, gosh, it didn't let up. His money, his house, and his hair had all vanished...and now, the lady vanishes.

The bad luck was already piling high, but the worst was yet to come. A UFO from the planet Akamaxas appeared over the horizon and drifted around over the tops of the buildings. It stopped directly above Johnny Abacus, and a bright beam of bluish light came down and covered him. When the beam turned off, Johnny was gone. Aliens had transported him into their UFO, and they zipped away as quick as you please. They were taking him back to Akamaxas to make him write pop songs.

TV reporters came and interviewed witnesses. Everyone had a completely different description of the UFO, including one guy who said it looked like a giant statue of a goat. Now, of course, I wasn't there myself, but if I had been, it would have looked like Santa's sleigh to me. They do that, UFOs do. They generate a confusion field so that people never see them the way they really look. What did this one really look like? A hockey stick.

So anyway, Johnny Abacus was gone. What really burns me up about the whole thing is that he was supporting his bedridden mother, his brother who had been stricken with the mystery brain disease, and his uncle who had a heart condition and couldn't work. That is, Johnny had been supporting them, but now that he was on another planet he couldn't sell charcoal in the redneck neighborhood anymore. Akamaxas was way too far away to commute.

Johnny had also been the chairman of a committee that was trying to raise money to feed starving children. He coached a little league baseball team, too, and not only taught his players the fundamentals of the game, but teamwork and sportsmanship, too. He taught them how to be good winners and gracious losers, and that those things were more important than winning games, although you should always give it all you've got and try to win. All the boys liked him, and so did their parents. And now, all that was over.

After the TV people left, the Neuralgia Sisters called Mr. Antwerp at home. Norma made the call. Or was it Nancy? It's nearly impossible to tell them apart, even for me. We'll say it was Norma. "Hey, An-*twerp*," she said. "The thing that happened to your guy in the redneck neighborhood...we did that to him. And something bad will happen to anybody else you hire to work there."

But Mr. Antwerp hadn't heard about the whole mess. Not at all, because he had spent the whole evening brushing his teeth and hadn't seen the news. "What are you talking about?" he asked.

Norma—or Nancy, or somebody—told him about Johnny's bad luck story.

"Yeah, well, you can't scare me that easily," he said, although being on the phone with her was giving him an uneasy feeling.

***

Mr. Antwerp believed the Neuralgia Sisters' phone call was a prank until he heard about it on the news the next morning. He heard about Johnny Abacus's spectacular run of bad luck on the news, that is, not about the phone call. The news people didn't know about the phone call.

"Oh, my goodness," he thought. "It really happened." It looked as if someone was trying to put him out of business. Gosh, but that wasn't nice.

He called his other people right away. He called Ellen Compote, the woman who sold charcoal in the suburban neighborhood, and warned her about walking under ladders and dropping mirrors. Then he called Goliath. He was particularly worried about Goliath, since he was a little kid and would be an easy target.

"I saw all about it on the news last night," Goliath told him.

"Please be careful," Mr. Antwerp said. "You're my best person. I think you have a brilliant career in charcoal ahead of you. Maybe you could get that big kid next door to you, that Billy-Bob kid, to be a bodyguard."

"I think he's mad at me," Goliath said. It did seem that way. After all, Billy-Bob *did* hit him and try to choke his wrist. When you do stuff like that it usually means you're mad at somebody. Probably the person you're doing it to, who in this case was Goliath, and if Billy-Bob was the best person Goliath could get to watch out for him, he might as well give up right away and save everyone a lot of trouble.

"Well, whatever you do, please be careful," Mr. Antwerp said. "I think someone's trying to put me out of business, and if I'm right, you're probably in for it."

Goliath said he would be careful, and then he hung up. Of course, you have to be careful these days, what with people like Billy-Bob running around wanting to do Heaven-knows-what to nice women and punching people in the knee. And Billy-Bob wasn't trying to run anybody out of business, as far as Goliath knew.

It worried him, all this threatening stuff did, and he thought about it a lot at school that day. Miss Cranberry noticed he wasn't paying attention to the lesson on fermentation, which was puzzling because Goliath had always been interested in fermentation.

"Goliath, you're not paying attention to my lesson

on fermentation," she said.

But he didn't hear that, either, because he wasn't paying attention. Miss Cranberry walked over and nudged his shoulder, much in the same way Emma Lou Josephine Vernacular Hortense Hortense P. Barnacle had nudged Roger Glass Door Knob. But of course, Goliath didn't fall over because he was still alive. What he did was look up at Miss Cranberry. "What's wrong?" she asked him.

"I'm worried," Goliath said.

This sounded serious. Miss Cranberry waited for him to say more, but Goliath looked around and didn't say anything. So to keep the kids busy, Miss Cranberry told them to diagram the chemical stuff that goes on when wine ferments, and then she took Goliath, little Goliath, out into the hall. No, she didn't beat him up. She had caught on that he didn't want to talk about his problems in front of the other kids. "What are you worried about?" she asked.

"Mr. Antwerp thinks somebody's trying to run him out of business. He says some bad guys are responsible for what happened to Johnny Abacus, and they might try to get me."

Well, Miss Cranberry had heard about Johnny Abacus. She heard it on the radio that morning, and it was awful. She also knew how important Goliath's job was to him. It was very important.

"Oh, that's scary," she said.

But Goliath didn't have anything else to say about it. What else is there to say after you've told somebody you're afraid of getting abducted by aliens because a bad guy is trying to run your boss out of business?

So Miss Cranberry gave him, Goliath, that is, a

strip of bacon to munch on and sent him home.

Eunice Mae, in her seat, began biting her nails. She didn't know what was going on, but it was obviously awful even if it wasn't awfully obvious. Were some bad guys trying to do something evil to Goliath? Or could it be that the bank was going to take his house away? She'd heard about banks doing that to folks, although she wasn't clear as to why. Or maybe—worst of all— somebody may have stolen his TV set.

***

And in the redneck neighborhood, a new charcoal ven- dor appeared. It was Leo Kegg. You know, Harley's boy. He wanted to sell some charcoal and make a little extra spending money.

***

Later on that same night, Miss Cranberry was at Dex- ter Kroger's house, and Dexter Kroger was there, too, and they were watching *Bowling for Penicillin*. Goli- ath, that cute little boy, the one who had so much trou- ble with arithmetic, and who had been involved in that commotion on Mr. Sigmoid's front porch, had big prob- lems, she told him. And the rest of it, too—Miss Cran- berry told Dexter Kroger all about the rest of it, about Johnny Abacus and Mr. Antwerp and everything.

"Do you think that big, goofy kid on the front porch was working for Mr. Schurk? Is that why he was trying to beat Goliath up?" Dexter asked. It wasn't, of course, but they never did get the real story behind the infa- mous Front Porch Commotion.

"You know, I bet it was," Miss Cranberry said.

The news was on now. "A survey conducted by the Department of Defense found that the general public considers bricklayers, of all those who do not cook professionally, to make the best homemade pizzas. They were followed, in order, by cartoonists, surfers, truck drivers, and geologists. However, double-blind taste tests conducted with pizzas made by people of various occupations revealed that the best ones are actually made by teachers' assistants, telephone operators, and face painters."

"What can we do about it?" Miss Cranberry asked.

"Try new recipes," Dexter Kroger said.

"I mean, about Goliath."

"I don't know."

A commercial was on. "Face it," the man said. "You're inept, especially in the kitchen. You can't even fill a pan with water unless you have an instruction book, which you couldn't read anyway. And whatever the heck you think you try to do in the morning for breakfast would be amusing if it weren't so pathetic. But with the new Baconmatic, there is a glimmer of hope, slight though it is. Merely warm the Baconmatic up for an hour and a half before operating it, and then feed in a slice of bacon between the two rollers on top. In only forty-five minutes it comes out the opening in the side, cooked to delicious perfection. No more messy grease spattering all over the kitchen. No more burning yourself on a hot stove. No more trichinosis because you don't know how to tell when it's done. Available in seven different gaudy-looking suburban-type linoleum patterns to fit any kitchen decor. Great gift for dad, mom, or sis! Not so good for grandpa, but get him one anyway. Only thirty-nine ninety-five for one, or eighty-nine ninety-nine for two. Call 1-800-555-2345. That's 1-800-555-2345. 1-800-555-3245. Remember, 1-800-555-2345. Dial it now, if you can. Operators are standing by now. That's 1-800-555-2345. 1-800-555-2435. And be sure to dial the one."

Miss Cranberry thought about that strip of bacon she had given Goliath. She hadn't used a Baconmatic. She hoped she had cooked it adequately. Gosh, one more thing to worry about.

"That goofy kid is obviously working for someone," Dexter Kroger said. "We could find him and make him tell us who. Get to the bottom of all this."

"Dexter, you're so masterful," Miss Cranberry said. She liked a real take-charge kind of guy, and Dexter Kroger was one of those. A real take-charge kind of guy.

"And you how to bake a good potato," Dexter said. Miss Cranberry had baked him a potato for supper earlier, and she put toothpaste on it so he wouldn't have to brush his teeth afterward. She might fall short on the bacon front, but she was aces with potatoes, for sure. "I feel as if I'm eating at a fast-food restaurant," he had told her. "All we need now are some deep-fried chicken scraps."

But that had happened much earlier in the day, and now Dexter had forgotten all about chicken and scraps therefrom. "I know what I can do," Dexter Kroger said. "I was thinking: I've seen him on my dust route. I can talk to him tomorrow."

8. Showdown in the Basement

In the suburban neighborhood—right around the corner from Ellen Compote's charcoal-vending spot, actually—Dexter Kroger came to that daggone ol' Billy-Bob's house. It was late afternoon, just the right time to catch the kid after school but before his parents came home from work. He, Dexter, rang the doorbell and whistled a quiet little tune to himself while he waited.

(And how do dust collectors get into the house if no one's home? They don't, obviously. The homeowner leaves the dust in a big trash bag out on the front porch. I mean, it's not like the collectors have a skeleton key that can get them in. That would be silly.)

After a minute, Billy-Bob answered the door. He didn't recognize Dexter Kroger because he had been looking down at Dexter's shoes during The Big Front Porch Commotion, and Dexter was wearing his work boots now.

"I've come for your dust," Dexter Kroger said. (And how many times have we all said that?)

Billy-Bob let him in. Dexter went down into the basement and took the filter out of the dryer. He put the lint in his collection bag and replaced the filter. He noticed a cardboard box with a whole bunch of dust and lint in it, off in the corner, so he emptied that into his bag, too.

Billy-Bob watched him carefully, as if he didn't trust Dexter out of his sight. Well, Dexter wouldn't steal anything because he was an A-One all right guy. When the Midwest Stagnant Air Company hired him, they gave him a lie detector test and asked him all kinds of questions like did he ever steal from any place he'd worked before, or did he drink or take drugs, or had he ever bought an unregistered computer mouse or gotten away without paying for a haircut, and they were satisfied that he was an A-One all right guy. (And you're wondering how he passed a lie detector test if he had to tell them he hadn't sniffed any diuretic paint thinner. Well, at the time, he hadn't. Things change over the years, don't they?)

In Billy-Bob's basement, Dexter was ready to leave. He went to the bottom of the stairs, with Billy-Bob right behind him. Dexter went up a couple of steps, so as to be a little higher for psychological effect, and turned around.

"Who are you working for, kid?" he asked. He had an idea that a dull-witted dumbo like this Billy-Bob kid could be taken off-guard easily with a sudden question. The element of surprise, and all that stuff.

"Huh?" Billy-Bob said. He didn't work for anybody. He didn't have a job. He went to school.

Oh, ho, Dexter thought. The kid's being cagey. Didn't think he was that smart. But Dexter was clever-erer—more clever—than any dorky kid. "Don't pretend you don't know what I'm talking about. I can stand here all day and wait for an answer. You might as well make it easy on yourself and tell me now."

"I don't know what you're talking about," Billy-Bob said, pouting. He was pouting because he had to pee, and it didn't look as though this guy was going to let him go up to the bathroom. He, Billy-Bob, didn't think he could fight his way past him. The guy was big and had a really intimidating attitude. Although Billy-Bob didn't know those big words, that was the general idea. And *Gilligan's Island* was about ready to start. Billy-Bob liked *Gilligan's Island*, even if he couldn't follow the story. That Gilligan sure was funny. And Ginger was beautiful. He knew on account of they said so all the time. If he ever got a shot at Ginger...oh, boy! But she was stuck on that island.

The show was going to start pretty soon, and he was going to miss it and probably end up peeing in his pants, too, right in front of this strange guy who was going to stay right there, blocking his way, until Billy-Bob told him whatever it was he wanted to know. But he couldn't figure it out. He didn't know what it was the guy wanted, didn't have an inkling. Even if he did, he might not be able to talk about it because it was really hard to concentrate, having to pee so bad. The problem would be gone if he ended up peeing in his pants, but it would be awfully embarrassing. Yeah, that would be a whole new problem! Why hadn't his mom ever told him to always go to the bathroom before answering the door?

Billy-Bob fingered the spool of typewriter ribbon around his neck. He already had a whole bunch of ink on his shirt, and some on his pants, and now he was getting it on his hands. Dexter thought it was pretty stupid, especially since it was a black-and-red ribbon, so Billy-Bob was messing in two colors, not just one.

"Look, kid," Dexter said. "I know why you were beating up little Goliath on the porch at the party. Remember that?"

Well, sure, Billy-Bob remembered. "Yeah," he spat at Dexter. "If you know why, then what am I supposed to tell you?"

"Who put you up to it? Who was behind the whole thing?"

Put him up to it? What in the name of Thurston Howell the Third was that supposed to mean, Billy-Bob wondered. The fight was because of Miss Cranberry. Well, maybe that was what this guy wanted to know. Anyway, Billy-Bob didn't care whether he got the truth or not, whatever it might be. All he cared about was getting this guy to leave, and he, Billy-Bob, was going to have to tell him something. "Miss Cranberry," Billy-Bob said.

"Come on, now. You don't really expect me to believe that."

Billy-Bob was at a loss. Miss Cranberry was the only answer he could think of. "It's true," he pleaded. "I did it to get Miss Cranberry to like me."

Dexter started to snicker, and then he remembered something. He remembered that during The Big Front Porch Commotion, Goliath had been babbling about Billy-Bob wanting to do "that baby-making thing" to Miss Cranberry. Hmmmm...Could it be true? Well, it all seemed to fit. There was evidence of someone trying to run Mr. Antwerp out of the charcoal business: Johnny Abacus had been abducted in broad daylight in front of dozens of witnesses, and Mr. Antwerp received a threatening phone call. Another vendor—Goliath, that is—had been attacked by this kid here, possibly with intent to kill. Yes, it could all be related. It probably was; it would be the simplest explanation for everything.

And let's consider Miss Cranberry. She probably wouldn't be the Master Bad Guy, the one who wanted to run Mr. Antwerp out of business. Dexter couldn't see that she would have any interest in it from that angle. But, hypothetically, if you were the Master Bad Guy, who would you hire to get rid of Goliath, if you wanted to get rid of him? Someone like Miss Cranberry, obviously. She knew him fairly well, and she was a trusted authority figure to him. She would know exactly what to do. And she might be open to the possibility of making a few extra handfuls of money on the side. That electronic sundial she had given him, Dexter Kroger, for his birthday looked pretty expensive, he had to admit. Perfect! What about the concern she had shown when she was telling him about Goliath's problems? All an act, a great big act!

Of course, having planned how to get rid of Goliath, she wouldn't do the dirty work herself. Oh, no, that was what Billy-Bob was for. Why should Miss Cranberry, being intelligent and sensible, risk getting caught committing such a crime when she could get a stupid kid to do it for her? AND—what better payment to offer Billy-Bob than to let him...uh...do stuff...with her? He was probably terribly frustrated when it came to girls. Eek! It was icky to think of her with this kid. Dexter hoped she had only *promised* to do stuff with him and had no intention of actually coming across. At any rate, everything fit together perfectly, and it was disgusting. No, not disgusting. It was sordid. It was disgusting and sordid. And vile. And not nice.

But—why would she have encouraged him to come over here and question this kid, who was squirming around as if he had to pee, if that were the case? She must have known that he, Billy-Bob, would let the beans out of the bag and blow the whole scheme. Or at least that he would be likely to. It didn't make a bit of sense that she would tell Dexter to come over here and do this...unless, of course, she expected that he, Dexter, wouldn't believe the kid. After all, (a) Billy-Bob had no credibility, (b) the scheme *did* sound pretty far-fetched and would sound farfetched even if a credible person told him about it, and (c) Miss Cranberry would of course deny it all, and she could naturally expect him to believe her rather than this mess of a kid here. Yes, Miss Cranberry would think she was perfectly safe letting Dexter question Billy-Bob. Actually, it would have looked suspicious for her to tell him *not* to do it!

But what Miss Cranberry didn't know was that he, Dexter, had seen every *Columbo* episode, so he knew how to piece together intricate plots from one little clue. And although it never worked out this way for Columbo, he also knew that in real life, the person you'd least suspect was almost always the one who was actually guilty.

It was fiendishly clever! And who would think such a thing of Miss Cranberry, who looked so fresh and wholesome, like the girl on those snack cake boxes except all grown up? Right off the ol' farm. Who would ever suspect?

The whole thing was disturbing, quite disturbing. Miss Cranberry was so nice, and Dexter liked her quite a bit. In fact, he thought she was pretty swell. He had kinda pictured what it might be like if they were to get married, living in a big house with seven bathrooms and a tennis court in the closet. She was—well, he had *believed* she was—that kind of woman. It would be hard to give up the idea that they might have a future together, and maybe he would want a little bit more conclusive proof that she was an evil evildoer before he took any action. But he was going to have to follow up on all this in some way.

Dexter gathered up his dust bag. "Okay, kid, I don't think you're to blame for any of it. They were using you because you were convenient and unbelievably stupid. But don't you *ever* let me catch you anywhere near Goliath again, you hear?"

"Yes, sir," Billy-Bob said. He didn't care. He just wanted to go to the bathroom. "Can I go pee now?"

"Sure. Knock yourself out." Dexter left, and Billy-Bob wondered why Dexter wanted him to knock himself out. But he'd show that ol' guy. He wouldn't do it!

***

Later, Dexter mused over the Miss Cranberry situation. Not the real Miss Cranberry situation, which was perfectly innocent, but his own evil version of it. He mulled it around in his head, trying to decide what do to. It wouldn't be easy. He couldn't push her around the way he did Billy-Bob. No, from now on, he would need much more ingenuity and cleverness. You have to be subtle with a woman—that is to say, with an *adversary*—like Miss Cranberry.

But Dexter was a clever and resourceful guy. He

was up to the task.

Dexter, she's innocent! Really, she is! She's whole-some and pure of heart!

Oh, it's no use. He's not listening.

***

Speaking of wholesomeness and purity of heart, Cato (ha!) and his friend George Baklava were getting ready to go out for the evening. They were going to go to a few bars and drink some drinks, listen to bands play Du-ran Duran songs, find a couple of beautiful women, and take them home and play bouncy-bouncy with them.

George and Cato, they had been best friends since high school (along with Roger Glass Door Knob, the poor devil). They belonged to the Pornography Club, the Siesta Club, and the Young Extortionists' Society.

George got into a lot of trouble back then, but it was never his fault. One time he was sitting in a classroom, and a bunch of people in the back were whispering and passing notes around while the teacher was writing a bunch of junk on the chalkboard. She heard the noise, turned around, and, thinking George was involved, said, "George, what's afoot?"

George said, "It's that thing at the end of your leg."

He wasn't trying to be a smarty-pants, but it sure sounded that way to the teacher. He got suspended from the Pornography Club for a whole month. Talk about harsh!

That was the kind of stuff that happened to George Baklava, the poor misunderstood boy.

Anyway, Cato dropped by George's place to pick him up. George came out munching on a big, huge, red apple.

"If you get apple juice all over the interior of my car, you're going to be sorry," Cato said.

"Relax. I want to have a snack before drinking, and I'm not going to get any kind of juice all over the interior of your car." What George didn't realize was that his pores were oozing some kind of ectoplasmic juice, and he left a trail of it wherever he went. But it didn't matter because it couldn't be perceived in this plane of reality.

They went to the Slipknot Inn first. It wasn't a great place to meet women, but it was one of their favorite places to sit and have a beer. A fine punk band called Guys Who Are Kind Of Confused was playing. Their repertoire of original songs ranged from "I'm Kind of Confused" and "This is Confusing" all the way to "The Confusion in this Room Is So Thick That It's Hard to Walk Around."

Then George and Cato cruised out to the hot pickup spot in town, the Meatmarket. "This is the hottest pickup spot in town," Cato observed as they turned into the parking lot. Of course, they didn't really turn into the parking lot, in the sense of morphing into a flat surface of asphalt. Cato merely turned his steering wheel so that the car would go on top of the parking lot.

Inside, The Insteps were playing a Duran Duran tune—I don't know which one, but one of them—and they had a guy in front of them juggling potatoes. The Insteps liked to be theatrical. Their lead singer sometimes made gestures as he sang. Occasionally, the gestures were appropriate.

"Lots of women are here," George said. It was true. Lots of women were in the place, attractive women, and George was excited.

Cato went to the bar and ordered a Siberian Blow-torch, an exotic drink that, although totally rancid-tasting, was considered trendy. If a woman saw a cute guy like Cato drinking a Siberian Blowtorch, well, he was already halfway in. Even Billy-Bob might have had some luck at the Meatmarket if he were to be seen with a Siberian Blowtorch in his hand. On second thought, probably not. But anyone else would.

Cato ordered one for George, too.

"I don't want that thing," George said. "They taste like something you would feed your plants."

"What kind of plant food are we talking about? And how do you know what plant food tastes like, anyway?"

"I would prefer not to talk about that part of my life. Let's just say I don't like these drinks and leave it at that."

"George, it doesn't matter what you don't like. Don't you want to meet women?"

"Men were meeting women for thousands of years before there was ever any such thing as a Siberian Blowtorch."

Cato, not wanting to argue about it any more, wandered off toward a tall redhead dressed in leather. This redhead was, of course, a woman, or Cato wouldn't have walked over to her.

"Hello," he said. "You know, I can rub my stomach and pat my head at the same time." It was a line he always had a great deal of success with. He smiled at her, knowing that he had oodles of boyish charm. He had so much he couldn't take it all with him when he went out.

"With the same hand?" she asked.

"Hey, you're on your toes. I like a woman who's on her toes. Why don't we head on back to my place and do some nutmeg and read Plato?"

"All right," the woman said. "But I would rather go back to my place instead."

"No problem."

"I just have to let my sister know I'm leaving. She's in the ladies' room."

"I happen to have a friend with me. Let me go get him. You stay here." He walked away, looking for George and glancing back every six seconds to make sure the woman wasn't going off with someone else.

He spotted George at the bar, playing with a miniature ashtray and sipping a less fashionable drink called a Monkey's Nose. "Oh, you don't want to be seen with that," Cato said. "But it doesn't matter. I found a hot one, and she has a sister. Come on."

"But I don't have a Siberian Blowtorch," George said sarcastically.

"Come on."

"But they're going to have a trivia contest in a few minutes."

Cato grabbed George's arm and dragged him over to the redhead. "This is my friend George," he said. "My name's Cato."

"I'm Nancy Neuralgia," the redhead said. "My sister Norma should be out any minute now."

"Oh, good."

"By the way, we're twins. We're out on the town tonight to celebrate our first big career move."

Oh, boy, Cato thought. Things are going great.

9. The Sort-Of Vacant Lot

The next morning, Dexter Kroger stopped sleeping and woke up. He woke up, and he knew exactly what he had to do about Miss Cranberry. He had pondered the situation carefully and had slept on it. He had considered calling the police and reporting her car stolen, so that when she went out driving, a cop would stop her and she'd have to spend a bunch of time proving she was herself. He had considered calling her on the phone, disguising his voice, and calling her a fart. He had considered renting a devil suit and breaking into her house while she was home and squishing a bowl of mayonnaise pudding into her face.

But none of that would solve the problem. I mean, how many times have all of us done all those things, right? And how many problems does it solve? None. What Dexter had to do, then, was find some evidence against her, something that would prove she was involved in trying to run Mr. Antwerp out of business, something that would persuade the police to arrest her and put her in jail for a really long time. Or at least long enough for the novelty of being locked up to wear off.

He reported for work, Dexter did, and got his dust

collection truck. But before he went on his regular route, he took himself a little detour and wheeled over toward her house. Yes, it was going to be a good day. The sun was shining, the birds were tweetering, and Miss Cranberry was at school with, Dexter knew, all kinds of incriminating evidence lying around all over her house. Gee, he would probably trip over a big pile of it going in the door. Yeah, he was going to get her.

At a stop sign, he glanced over at a vacant lot and noticed something that looked like a great big guy all beat up, lying on the ground out in the middle of the empty space. Well, it wasn't really empty because the whole thing was covered by a layer of mud, and clumps of grass had sprouted up here and there, and a few tree stumps were poking up, but we can still think of it as empty space because mud and clumps of grass and tree stumps don't actually serve any useful purpose. Not to people, anyway. Not usually.

Dexter looked at the guy. Maybe he should stop to see what was going on. The great big guy might need help, and Dexter could...well, do something. Maybe. Or the guy might not need help. At any rate, it didn't look right.

So Dexter pulled over and parked by the side of the road. As he walked closer, he could see the person, the great big guy, was in bad shape. His clothes were ripped to smithereens, and every inch of his skin was cut and bruised, and broken bones were poking out, and blood and other alien substances were smeared all over him and splattered around in the mud. Gee, a guy in that kind of shape must be dead.

But no, Dexter could see him breathing, so he carefully moved closer, and holy smoke, it wasn't a big guy.

It was two average-size guys!

"What happened?" Dexter asked. He picked the one guy's head up and gave him a little slap on the cheek. Not to beat him up or anything; just to bring him around, to get his attention.

"Huh? Where am I?" the guy said. His voice was croaky sounding. He could barely talk.

"You're in a vacant lot. What happened?"

"Oh, uh...Oh, those women, were they ever wild! Gee whiz, that was the most fun I've ever had in my life!" It was Cato, of course, with his friend George under him.

Dexter was appalled. Appalled and shocked. But who was he to judge? "I'll call an ambulance," he said. Dexter stood up and whipped out his cell phone. Being the stylish and trendy kind of guy that he was, he had, of course, the stylish and trendy Mompel Mobile Phone Model XR3-71000-SRB11-7768-LMNOP in the stylish color of...well, it was so cutting-edge that it didn't have a color, and it had the optional tertiary keypad that existed in subreality, the Heorot four-dimensional display, and access to the fabled Stilte Network, which many people didn't believe to actually exist. Indeed, it didn't! And if it did, it wouldn't carry any signals. That was how *exclusive* it was, and that was why the access fee was a hundred handfuls of money a month! Although both phones could cut your hair (his favorite feature), he chose the Model XR3-71000-SRB11-7768-LMNOP over the Model XR3-71000-SRB11-7768-LM-NO because for only an extra five hundred and seventy handfuls of money, it gave you the ability to perform a tonsillectomy on yourself. You never know when something like that might come in handy, do you?

So, holding the phone in such a way as to be sure that Cato could see what kind of stylish, trendy device he had, Dexter called an ambulance. "Two guys are in a vacant lot all beat up," he said. "I mean the guys are all beat up, not the lot. Send an ambulance to twenty-three Skidoo Lane."

And then Dexter realized he had to get moving, like, right away. He still had to search Miss Cranberry's house and then get back to his dust collection route and finish up on time. Feeling sure that these poor guys would be taken care of, Dexter figured he could be on his way.

At that moment, the old codger who lived next door stepped out to get his morning newspaper. He watched as Dexter ran swiftly and gracefully, watched as Dexter ran like the wind through the vacant lot, dodging tree stumps and leaping over puddles with great dexterity, the way an all-pro college football player might make a big play out there on the ol' gridiron. The old codger watched as Dexter capped off the run with a spectacular jump across the ditch that ran alongside the road and landed next to the door of his truck. In an instant, Dexter was gone.

The old codger was curious, so he went to see what was going on. He walked out across his front yard and into the vacant lot, even though he hadn't shaved yet. And do you know what he saw? He saw the same thing Dexter Kroger had seen, except from a different angle. He went over to Cato and George. "Are you all right?" he asked.

Well, the strain of trying to talk to Dexter had pooped poor Cato out, so all he could do was kind of creak or groan, or maybe gurgle or gargle, but not talk.

It had been one heck of a wild night, the night before had. He and George had gone to the Neuralgia Sisters' house for a little party, a glass of lemonade and some TV, and a nice sedate game of Show Me Yours and I'll Show You Mine. That was what the boys had in mind, but it sure didn't turn out that way. Not at all! The Neuralgia Sisters had a big ol' huge collection of stuff they liked to use when they entertained guys. They had handcuffs, leather whips, rubber gloves, mirrors, video cameras, sound effects records, blow-up dolls, gymnastics equipment, a pair of sphygmomanometers, a half-dozen gas masks, a jackhammer, a life-sized poster of Herman Melville, an ice hockey goal, a torque wrench, a watermelon patch, a suitcase full of laxatives, an ant farm, a carton of correction fluid, a revolving door, a fire hydrant, a metronome (amplified), a blender, two anchors, a riding lawn mower, a dozen rolls of wallpaper, a Geiger counter, and an abacus (to keep count).

They used, the Neuralgia Sisters, all their equipment to entertain themselves and George and Cato, but George and Cato ended up a lot more entertained than they had expected. They were men of the world, and they had seen a lot. They were used to the strange and exotic, but this! Holy smoke! These women were intense with that stuff—Johnny Abacus had been right about that—and the guys eventually ended up in no condition to continue. And they were of no use if they were going to tire out that easily, so Norma and Nancy drove them out to the next subdivision and left them for dead in this vacant (except for mud and clumps of grass and tree stumps) lot. And then, because it was a big night of celebration on account of their shiny new promotion, the Neuralgia Sisters went back to the Meatmarket and found themselves a pair of sturdier fellows. Real Men. Men like Dexter Kroger, but not him specifically, because right then he had been home sleeping.

Anyway, that was what happened to Cato and George, and that was why they couldn't talk anymore. The old codger thought about all kinds of stuff for a while, stuff like steel and silver and red paint and paper and fermentation, and then he thought about these two guys a little bit and decided he should call an ambulance.

Right then, one arrived. Wow! The old codger was impressed—they were dispatching them by telepathy now! The ambulance guys loaded Cato and George onto stretchers, put them in the ambulance, and drove away. The old codger supervised the whole thing with the utmost approval.

Then the police came and asked the old codger what he knew about it. "What do you know about it?" they asked.

"Well, I was stepping out to get the paper, and I saw this guy go running out of the vacant lot. You know, the way he ran was really something. A guy like that could probably run a pretty far distance. An unbelievably far distance, maybe. Anyway, he jumped into a truck and drove off real fast. It was like he was trying to make a quick getaway. I think he done it. I think he beat these guys up." Of course, Cato and George hadn't actually been beaten, but it sure looked that way.

"Can you describe the guy?"

"Sure I can. He was a ne'er-do-well. I could feel it all the way across the yard. I can tell these things.

I was in the fifth grade with John Dillinger, did you know that? And I knew John would turn out bad. We sat together at lunch every day and talked about girls, but I knew he would turn out bad." The old codger had indeed picked up ne'er-do-well vibes from Dexter, but only because Dexter had recently talked to his ne'er-do-well brother Earl on the phone, and some of the ne'er-do-well vibes came through the phone connection and got on Dexter. Few people could detect them; the old codger was extra-sensitive.

"What did he look like?"

"He was a big guy. He looked all muscular and athletic, like maybe he used to be an all-pro football player in college. And he had dark hair."

"I mean the guy you saw running away, not John Dillinger."

"Yeah, I know. That's who I'm talking about, dillweed."

"What kind of truck was it?"

"It was a Midwest Stagnant Air Company dust collection truck. It said so in big letters on the side. The license number was 517-86." The old codger was also extra-observant.

***

Meanwhile, Cato and George were arriving at the hospital. A family in the neighborhood, the Ganglia family, ran a small hospital right in their house—what a marvel of the modern entrepreneurial spirit!—and the ambulance people had taken them there because it was the closest medical facility.

The Ganglias had a great big dog in the backyard,

and he barked and woke Cato up as the ambulance was pulling into the driveway. Cato didn't open his eyes, though, because they were swollen shut. It was just as well. He'd never heard of people operating hospitals in their houses, and it would have upset him greatly to find out where he'd been taken. So he lay on the stretcher and listened.

"Hey, lady, we got a couple emergency cases here," Cato heard a guy say.

"I'm Dottie. I just clean up around here."

"Well, where do we take them?"

"What do you mean, where do you take them? Take them inside! You don't want to leave them out here, do you? It's summer. There are lots of mosquitoes."

Cato felt his stretcher being taken out of the ambulance and rolled into the hospital.

"Hey, kid, where do we take these guys?"

Hey, kid? Cato wondered. What was going on here? Wouldn't the ambulance guys know where to take new patients? And if not, wouldn't the hospital have the emergency room entrance clearly marked, like with big ol' signs, so you could find it easily? Wouldn't someone be on duty at the entrance, someone who wasn't a kid?

A *kid*, fer Pete's sake?

"Leave them here. No, wait. They'll bleed on the carpet, and mom'll get mad. Better put 'em in the kitchen."

Carpet?

Mom?

Kitchen?

Holy smoke! What was going on here? Had he been taken to—gasp!—someone's house? It had a carpet (that wasn't to be bled on), a mom (who would get mad), and a kitchen. Hospitals had kitchens, but not carpets, at least not in the places where they might put people who were bleeding, and they had moms, but just because some of the employees and/or patients happened to be moms, and some women *became* moms in hospitals, but getting mad didn't have anything to do with any of that, and...

Why would they put him in the kitchen? Was a guy with a leather mask and a chainsaw lurking around back there, waiting for fresh victims? Was he, Cato the Ladies' Man, about to become sausage? If so, he hoped it would at least be spicy, but he somehow doubted that hospital food was likely to be spicy.

In his helpless condition, he couldn't keep them from doing anything they wanted to him. Even that little Goliath boy, if he hypothetically happened for some reason to be there, could do anything he might want— do anything to Cato, that is, and do it with impunity. Goliath could punch him in the knee, or poke him in the eye, or pour motor oil in his belly button, and Cato wouldn't be able to do anything but lie there being helpless. On the other hand, Goliath wouldn't want to do anything icky to anybody. But what did that matter, since Goliath wasn't around?

Why was Cato thinking about Goliath, anyway?

And then, from the other room, Cato heard heavy breathing and moaning and groaning, like the sounds married people make when they do married people things, or like the sounds unmarried people make when they do married people things. A man moaned, "Oh, Helen, I love you."

And a woman moaned, "Oh, Freeman, I love you, too."

Then more breathing and stuff. After a minute, the woman, sounding weary, said, "Freeman, it isn't working."

"What?"

"It's not the least bit exciting having a torrid doctor-nurse love affair when we're married to each other. Big deal."

"But Helen, we *have* to have a torrid affair. That's the way it's done at all the real hospitals. Don't you ever watch TV?"

At the *real* hospitals? So this, apparently, was a *fake* hospital? Was it any kind of hospital at all? Cato wanted to start trembling in fear, but as we've seen, he couldn't move. Not even enough to tremble. That made him more fearful.

This was turning out to be a real bad time to be helpless.

"It's too distracting trying to pretend it's illicit. Besides, we have to get ready for Mr. Bunn's bypass operation."

"Oh, all right."

Cato heard the rustle of clothing and the zipping of zippers, and then footsteps. Okay, a bypass operation. So he was indeed in a hospital. That was a little more comforting. But only a little.

A minute later, footfalls suddenly pounded through the hallway. "HELEN! The heart-lung machine's gone!"

"What?"

"The heart-lung machine's gone. What happened to it?"

"Now, Freeman, it's not my job to keep track of your stuff. You're always losing things. Your watch, your car keys—"

"Helen, the heart-lung machine's a huge piece of equipment. It never leaves the room!"

"Maybe Dottie moved it when she swept up last night."

The kid's voice joined in. "Hey, dad, they brought in two guys a few minutes ago. They're all banged up and bloody."

"In a minute, Johnny. The heart-lung machine's missing."

"The heart-lung machine?"

"Yes, it's missing, and we need it. Mr. Bunn needs his bypass operation as soon as possible. It's urgent."

"Oh, uh, well..." Johnny sounded sheepish. Cato could almost hear the baa-aa.

"What is it, Johnny?" Freeman asked.

"I traded it to Leo Kegg. For a frog."

"MY GOD! HELEN, DID YOU HEAR...HELEN! MY GOD!" And then heavy breathing. But this time it wasn't like people doing married people things. It was rapid, extremely rapid, gasping, panic-stricken, like someone trying to inhale a bag of cotton candy.

"Johnny, that machine was daddy's. You can't go around trading other people's things off. Now go over to Leo's house and get the machine back." Helen sounded soothingly mother-like when she said that. Her voice was comforting to Cato—so much that his pain eased considerably. His own mother's voice sounded like someone tearing a garbage can lid in half.

"I don't think he'll trade back," Johnny said.

"Why not?"

"The frog died last night." And, of course, Leo couldn't trade back, regardless. He had sold the machine to Irving the pawnshop guy. That Leo, what a little operator!

"Oh, I'll have to go over there," Freeman said, disgusted. Cato could smell the disgust. It came oozing down the hallway and into the kitchen. It nudged his stretcher up against the refrigerator.

Cato fell asleep. He was happier that way.

***

Later, Cato woke up again. He heard the clanging and banging of equipment being moved around.

"Okay," Freeman said. "Let's see what's going on with these two guys."

Cato heard the sounds of plugs being plugged in and switches being switched and buttons being butted, etc. "Let's get this guy first," Freeman said. "He's in much worse shape." Cato heard a thud. "Oh, no, I can't get near him. He must have had an apple within the last twenty-four hours."

He had to be talking about George. Cato hadn't eaten an apple. Ever.

"What can we do?" Helen asked.

"I'll have to talk you through it. First, we have to sew his head back on."

Then Cato died. He floated up out of his body, looked down, and saw Freeman and Helen, doctor and nurse, trying to sew George's head back on in what looked to be a bedroom that had been equipped as an operating room. Then Cato started floating through a tunnel toward a bright light. He came out in a sunny pasture full of sunflowers and butterflies. And George was waiting for him. Wow, this was neat.

"We must be dead," Cato said.

"We are. My grandfather welcomed me a few minutes ago. I'm supposed to follow him that way," George said, pointing. "That's the way they do it, you know. A dead relative greets you and shows you around. I wanted to stick around here for a minute and say hi to you first."

From off in the distance, Cato could see a person coming. He wondered who it could be. God? St. Peter? The angel Gabriel? A dead relative?

The person got closer because he kept on coming toward them. And the person turned out to be Cato's Uncle Fudd.

"Hello, Cato," Uncle Fudd said.

"Hello, Uncle Fudd," Cato said.

"How do you like it here in Wherever It Is That People Go When They Die?"

"It's nice, so far. Is there any place around here to get a drink?"

Uncle Fudd kind of grimaced in embarrassment. "Well, see, Cato, it's like this. You only get to stay here a few minutes. Your friend George, he's honest-to-gosh dead, and he gets to stay permanently, but you have to return to Earth. I had you brought here so you could take a message back to your mother."

Jeepers, Cato thought. A message from beyond the grave. What message could be so important that Uncle Fudd would have his beloved nephew killed—although just temporarily—so he bring it back to the world of the living? Maybe his mother was in danger of ending up in that hot, eternally loathsome location. Maybe Earth was about to be invaded by a band of roving pirates from the eighteenth dimension.

"I owe your mother a tenth of a handful of money,"

Uncle Fudd said. "I've owed it to her for twenty-seven years, and it's really bothering me. Tell her that if she looks in the piano bench I left her, under the music books, she'll find a whole handful." Uncle Fudd looked at Cato with, for some reason, what seemed to be a hopeful expression on his face.

Cato didn't say anything. George was snickering.

"She can keep it all," Uncle Fudd added, as if he were making some sort of concession.

"In the piano bench," Cato said, stunned. George was snickering louder.

"That's right."

"She can keep it all."

"Yeah. I mean, I don't have any use for it here."

Cato rolled all this stuff around in his head for a few moments, the way a diuretic paint thinner connoisseur might roll a diuretic paint thinner-soaked rag around in his hands before sniffing. George was still snickering. Uncle Fudd didn't say anything.

"Well?" Cato finally asked.

"Well what?"

"What's the important message?"

Uncle Fudd looked surprised. "That's it," he said, as if Cato were defective for thinking there might be something else.

Cato put his hands on his hips, and then he let them hang. He wanted desperately to do something really dramatic with them, but he didn't know what. Would it be awful to slap a dead relative in Wherever It Is That People Go When They Die? They might blackball him if he did. "We don't want no rowdies in here," they'd tell him when he died for real. "You're scheduled to go south, boy."

George was snickering more.

"Stop snickering," Cato snapped. "You're really dead."

"Yes. I like it here, and I get to stay."

Cato turned back to Uncle Fudd. "Let me get this straight. You had it fixed up for me to die of those injuries so you could get that dinky little message back to mom?"

"Well, it's not quite like that."

Cato was getting cross. "What is it like?" he demanded. He really wanted to know. He wanted to know what kind of scatterbrain he had for an uncle.

"Well, I mean, it took a lot of work to get you here. I had to arrange for you to meet the Neuralgia Sisters. In order to do that, I had to see to it that they could get a job so they could afford to go out drinking. Otherwise, they wouldn't have been at that bar, and you'd never have met them. So I had to figure out what kind of job would be good for them. It had to be one where they could use their best talents and it wouldn't matter that they hadn't paid attention in school. Charcoal vending, for example, because they wouldn't have to do anything but stand around and intimidate people into buying. But before they could get the job, I had to create an opening at Schurk Enterprises. So I made Roger Glass Door Knob forget his wallet so that he would die at the hair stylist's. I'm sorry to do that to your friend, but he's happy here.

"So the Neuralgia Sisters were all set up to meet you. But you weren't set up to meet them yet; you had started dating Emma Lou Josephine Vernacular Hortense Hortense P. Barnacle, and if you had kept on dating her, you wouldn't have gone to the bar. So I had to break you two up. What would do that? Jealousy.

"I knew Miss Cranberry and Miss Fluorine were regular customers at the hair salon where Emma Lou Josephine Vernacular Hortense Hortense P. Barnacle worked, so all I needed was some event that would get them in there. I wanted them to go together, so they could sit and talk while Emma Lou Josephine Vernacular Hortense Hortense P. Barnacle overheard them. A party given by their boss, the school superintendent, would be the perfect thing. Not only would they go to the party, but they would want to look nice for it.

"So I gave Mr. Sigmoid the idea to have the diuretic paint thinner party. Actually, it was supposed to be some kind of generic party, nothing special. I didn't know he was going to have diuretic paint thinner there. But it was all right because it provided another incentive for the women to go.

"But since the party was illegal, and I hadn't counted on your showing up at it, I had to make sure you left with Miss Fluorine before the police came. I didn't know they would come, but I thought it was likely. That made it a lucky coincidence that I...uh, brought Roger Glass Door Knob here—it left Miss Fluorine available to leave with you. It was all incredibly difficult. But it worked out all right for you, because you ended up getting a little bouncy-bouncy in the deal."

Cato started to call Uncle Fudd a pee-pee head, but decided not to because Uncle Fudd was right. This big plan, after all, had gotten him in close with Miss Fluorine.

10. Investigations

The policemen, the ones who were investigating the case of Cato and George, they drove to the Midwest Stagnant Air Company to find out who the culprit was. Gosh, but their job sure was getting interesting. First, they got to raid a diuretic paint thinner party—at the school superintendent's house, no less—and don't think they'd forgotten about those human sacrifices just because they never found any evidence. And now they had a couple of brutal beatings, with the victims left for dead in a sort-of vacant lot and everything. Wow, neat!

They got right in to see Mr. Midwest, even though they didn't have an appointment, because they were policemen investigating a serious crime. As they walked into the office, Mr. Midwest was blasting one of his employees in half with a shotgun. He buzzed the intercom. "Miss Satyricon, could you get Mr. Purvis in here to clean up this mess? I blasted Harry from here to Kingdom Come and back."

"Yes, sir. That's a shame, sir. He was a good checkers player."

"Well, I had to." Mr. Midwest clicked the intercom off and turned his attention to the policemen. "He asked for a raise. It's in the contract that we have a legal right to gun down any employee who asks for a raise. You start with one guy, and before you know it, they all want one. That's the trouble. With Harry it's a tragedy because he was with me from the beginning, when I was operating out of a broom closet on an aircraft carrier. But that's how it goes sometimes."

The police officers shook their heads sadly.

Mr. Midwest gestured toward two chairs in front of his desk. "Won't you sit down? What can I do for you fellows?"

The policemen stepped around the mess and sat down. "We're here to investigate a beating that took place this morning. Two guys were left for dead in a vacant lot. One guy died, and the other's unconscious. We have reason to think one of your employees was involved in it."

"It was probably Harry here. As you can see, he was a real troublemaker."

"Our witness said it was one of your truck drivers. He got the license plate number." And he gave Mr. Midwest a piece of paper with the number written on it.

Mr. Midwest buzzed his intercom again. "Miss Satyricon, can you tell me who drives the truck with plate number 517-86?"

"Yes, sir. I'll look it up right away."

"We only have six drivers," Mr. Midwest said, "and I can't imagine any of them doing something like this. They're all a bunch of great guys and gals. We give 'em lie detector tests to make sure they're A-One all right guys and gals before we hire them. You know that charcoal vendor who got abducted by aliens? One of my drivers, Elmer Cunkus, took over coaching the guy's

Little League team. And another of my drivers, Ellie McPooble, took over as the chairman of the committee to raise money to feed starving children."

"That's admirable," one of the police officers said. What else could he say?

Mr. Midwest's intercom beeped. "Yes?" he said.

"Sir, Dexter Kroger drives that truck."

"Thank you." He clicked the intercom off and turned to the police officers. "Well, guys, there you have it. Dexter Kroger is your man."

"What kind of noble thing does he do to help people?"

"Gosh, I don't know. Maybe nothing."

"Then he must be the one."

"Yeah," Mr. Midwest said. "But he took that lie detector test I was talking about, and he passed. Doesn't that prove he wouldn't hurt people?"

The officers paused and looked at each other. "Well," one of them said, "maybe it proves he wouldn't have hurt anyone at the time he took the test. Who knows what he would do now?"

It was an uncomfortable thought for Mr. Midwest, but he didn't have an answer.

"What's his address?" the other police officer asked.

"Miss Satyricon can give it to you."

***

After the officers left, Miss Satyricon sat at her desk being worried about Dexter. She didn't know why the police were interested in his truck, but she figured no good could come of it.

She went into Mr. Midwest's office. "Mr. Midwest,

why were those policemen asking about Dexter Kro-ger?"

He looked up, his mouth gaping open. For some rea-son, she had an urge to throw a ping-pong ball in. It was a good thing she didn't have one. "I don't think I'm supposed to talk about it," he said.

"But it's okay. I'm your secretary. I'm supposed to know everything that goes on around here. I think it's, like, the law."

"Is that right?"

"Sure."

He looked doubtful. She smiled at him.

***

Meanwhile, Dexter was in the middle of paying Miss Cranberry a visit. Or he would have been if she were home, but since she was at school teaching little kids, including Goliath, Dexter was paying her uninhabited house a visit, which was just the way he wanted it.

He had parked his dust collection truck around the corner—he didn't want the neighbors to see it in the driveway. Then Dexter snuck up through Miss Cran-berry's backyard and got in through a broken window. The glass part wasn't broken, but the frame was loosely sitting in place, held there by a few strips of duct tape. So Dexter eased the window out, put it on the ground leaning against the house, and climbed in through the open window hole. He was pleased with himself. He would have pretended he was a secret agent, but he was too grown-up for that.

Dexter liked Miss Cranberry's house. In the center of her living room, she had a big, huge display case containing her trophy from winning the Miss Wholesome contest at the state fair. The walls were papered with thousands of copies of the cover of Robert Anton Wilson's book *Cosmic Trigger*. And at one end of the room was a life-size sculpture of a popular rock group called the Exploding Sperm Whales. The dining room sported an exquisitely beautiful chandelier made of the solidified tears of a panda. In the kitchen she had two Baconmatics because she liked to have two slices of bacon for breakfast.

Giving the place a quick once-over, he didn't see anything that looked amiss. But really, as much as he had hoped differently, she wouldn't leave incriminating evidence lying out where anyone could see it. A schoolteacher, of all people, should know better than that; knowledge was her livelihood. He would have to dig around.

It was then that Dexter noticed that he had tracked mud into the house. He took off his work boots and left them sitting on top of the last footprints so that he wouldn't make any more of a mess. He was mad at himself for being so careless. Miss Cranberry probably never tracked mud into anyone's house when she was up to no good, and here he was doing it right in her house. Daggone it. He was going to have to be smarter than this.

The next place to check was either the bathroom or the bedroom. He chose the bedroom because there's something, uh, sacred about a bathroom. He wouldn't go in there unless he couldn't find anything in the bedroom. Besides, the bedroom would probably be more interesting, anyway, on general principles.

So in he went, into the bedroom, and he spotted the

old cigar box she kept in the corner. Aha! He opened the
box and saw a whole lot of stuff packed inside. There
was a checkers game, and an electric typewriter, and
a goldfish bowl, and a print of the third reel of Andy
Warhol's *Trash*. And there was a Monumental Pursuit
game, and a Timesink CRM-114 51-inch television,
eight copies of Philip K. Dick's novel *Ubik*, a petrified
zebra, and two fake beards. Plus, a plastic replica of the
Rosetta Stone, a broken xylophone (which she kept for
its sentimental value—her favorite pet parakeet, Ker-
mit, had played it until he was killed when his electric
perch short-circuited), a globe of Jupiter, a Gibson SG
electric guitar, three original and unknown works of M.
C. Escher, a player piano, and a small piece of dirty fur.
There was also an invisible Hamburger Sty coffee mug,
but, of course, he couldn't see it. And way down at the
bottom of it all, under everything, a folded-up sheet of
paper.

Dexter picked up the paper. He knew it was a crime
to read other people's mail, but this wasn't mail anymore. For that matter, it might never have been mail.
Whatever it was, as far as he was concerned, it was
nothing more than a piece of paper he had found in a
box. He unfolded it and read:

Dear Miss Cranberry,

*This little note is just to let you know how much
our night together meant to me. Your warmth, sen-
sitivity, and understanding made my first time free
from the embarrassment and anxiety that I had
feared would characterize it. Our encounter has
raised my self-confidence immeasurably and has im-
proved my sense of masculinity. Although I know we*

can never have a relationship, I will always remember you with much fondness and appreciation.

Affectionately,
Billy-Bob

Billy-Bob?

BILLY-BOB!

But that was a halfway decently written note. Well, at least it wasn't illiterate, anyway. Sort of dumb, but nice. And certainly hokey, but it seemed sincere. A much better note than that Billy-Bob kid he had talked to in the basement could ever hope to write. Well, he might have gotten someone to write it for him, maybe, but anyway, Billy-Bob's name was on it. There was no denying that, because Billy-Bob's name was Billy-Bob, and what the letter said...well, that proved, unfortunately, Dexter's theory.

The conclusion was obvious. Miss Cranberry and Billy-Bob had...oh, no.

Oh, how sordid!

Dexter was disillusioned. He was disappointed. He was distraught. He didn't want to believe such things about Miss Cranberry, that she would be involved in such an evil conspiracy or that she would do that kind of thing with Billy-Bob. But he didn't know what else to think. The evidence seemed crystal clear. Dexter didn't see room for the slightest shadow of a doubt that Miss Cranberry was a bad guy.

Now, I'll admit it looked incriminating. It looked bad, but it really wasn't. The letter had been written four years earlier by Billy-Bob Wazoo, who was a different Billy-Bob from Dexter and Goliath's Billy-Bob, who was Billy-Bob Kierkegaard, not that Billy-Bob Kierkegaard was really Dexter and Goliath's, but he was the one causing trouble for them at the moment, although Dexter's college football team had a seventh-string halfback named Billy-Bob Runamok who became an accountant for a radiator manufacturer in Denver and died four years later in a nasty accounts payable accident.

But here's the poop on Billy-Bob Wazoo: Miss Cranberry met him at the St. Louis Historical Belt Loop Museum. He impressed her by being cute and shy and sensitive and all that crud. She was young (not that she was old when our story took place—far from it) and free-spirited and eager to explore the wonders of the world. She took him home and consummated him up one wall and across the ceiling and almost out the window, believing all the while that she was initiating this young man into the Eternal Mysteries of Ecstasy or some such nonsense. But the young and innocent, naive bit was merely an act that he had carefully worked up and cultivated for the benefit of women like Miss Cranberry. She was his six hundred and fifteenth "first time."

And if you're wondering why he bothered to write a note like that after getting what he wanted, he did it to make sure none of the women would become suspicious of his little ploy. Think about this: Would you want six hundred and fifteen women mad at you for tricking them into bed under false pretenses?

To be fair to Dexter, he couldn't have known about Billy-Bob Wazoo. On the other hand, I have to say he should have trusted Miss Cranberry enough not to go jumping off to half-baked conclusions on the basis of a note like that. And I also have to say it serves him right that he started getting queasy at the idea of Miss Cranberry and Billy-Bob together.

Dexter had to retain his composure, though, so he could finish up being nosy...er, finish his investigation at Miss Cranberry's house and get on with his route. He took a deep breath, did a few push-ups, went to the kitchen, and poured himself a glass of crabgrass tea— Miss Cranberry wouldn't notice as long as he remembered to wash the glass.

Dexter went back to the bedroom and opened the closet. Nothing was there but a roll of duct tape. Ah, more evidence! Goliath had been spouting off about duct tape during the Great Front Porch Commotion. Of course, it never occurred to him that she might have used it to hold the loose window in place. He grabbed the tape and the letter and prepared for his escape.

Then his stylish (etc.) cell phone rang. He whipped it out and answered.

"Dexter," Miss Satyricon said, "don't come back to the plant. And don't go home."

"Okay." Dexter didn't ask why; he was a sucker for a pretty face. And even though he couldn't see her over the phone, he knew she had a pretty face because he had seen her before. Besides, he was in a hurry to leave.

"Don't you want to know why?" she asked.

"Uh, sure."

"The police are looking for you. They think you killed a guy."

"I didn't."

"I know. I don't doubt you for an instant." And she

meant it. "But they think you did."

Dexter thanked Miss Satyricon for the warning and hung up. Wanted for murder? What on earth was going on? It was bizarre. But he didn't have time to waste being surprised. He had to keep his wits about him, and he was going to have to be extremely careful. The police take murder seriously. But then again, when he turned in this evidence against Miss Cranberry, he would become a hero. The police would probably drop the charges against him. He would have helped bust up the gang of desperate criminals who were trying to run Mr. Antwerp out of business. Those scummy people had already caused an alien abduction, and they were probably planning worse stuff for the rest of Mr. Antwerp's people. Further, they might be the ones who had killed whoever it was the police thought Dexter killed!

Yeah...Who was it they thought he had killed, anyway? He tried to remember. Had he ever killed anyone? He didn't think so. Had he done anything that might appear to be murder? Uh...well, he wasn't sure, but he wasn't going to figure it out standing in Miss Cranberry's house, where he didn't belong. Right now, he had to get this evidence to the police as quickly as possible. Dexter cleaned up the muddy footprints, put on his boots, and washed his tea glass. The only thing left now was to make his escape.

Climbing out the window, he lost his balance. He grabbed at the curtain, ripping it and pulling it out with him, along with the curtain rod. His foot whammed through the window pane that was leaning against the house, making a loud, sparkling, CRASH. He landed with a thump that was sort of like the thump of the delivery person dropping a canvas bag of charcoal on the sidewalk for a vendor.

Dexter was dazed. He thought about charcoal, and then about fermentation, and then he remembered why he was there. He stood up and surveyed the scene: the broken glass on the ground, the torn curtain in his hand. Fortunately, his heavy work boots had protected him from the broken glass, but this looked bad, bad. He could fix it not to look bad, bad, though.

He laid the window frame flat on the ground and carefully, oh-so-carefully, arranged the shards of glass to make it look as if the window had fallen there, sort of like as if the wind had blown it out. As he continued trying to make it look more like an accident, it looked less and less like one. Eventually, he ended up with something that looked like a mosaic of a snowy mountain with two goats on top. No matter; Miss Cranberry wouldn't believe the wind had blown out from a closed-up house, anyway. Dexter momentarily wished he had a camera, and then he convinced himself that Miss Cranberry wouldn't suspect that he was the one responsible for this, uneasy though he was about it. And then, after all that, he realized (once again) that he shouldn't linger.

He sighed, tossed the curtain down, and started toward his truck. No, he couldn't take the truck—the police would be watching for it! But he was headed to the police station anyway, right? But it would be better if he could walk into the police station, on his own and with the evidence, rather than let them pick him up out on the street before he could get to the police station.

Ah, but then again, the police station was a pretty far distance to walk.

But then *again*, if he was careful, if he were to sneak around and skulk about behind buildings and such, he could make it there without being seen.

***

And Goliath, after school he went to the shopping mall. It was his sister Othello's birthday, and they were going to have a party that night. He had to get her a present. He didn't know what he was going to buy, even though he had been thinking about it for weeks. But he was sure it would be all right. Goliath knew sales people were always helpful about these things. Like, for example, that Irving guy at the pawnshop had been oh so helpful when he sold Goliath that eight-track tape player to give his mother for Christmas. "This technology is the *future*," the man had predicted. And he had been right. It was so futuristic they couldn't find any tapes to play in it!

But this time Goliath didn't go to the pawnshop. Every time he went there, that Irving guy, nice and helpful though he was, talked him into spending more money than he should. So here he was, Goliath, that is, at the mall.

He went into Stinky's Department Store and looked around.

"Can I help you?" a salesperson asked. She was a nice lady with a name tag that said "Ann Onimous." Goliath thought he recognized her, and of course he did. She was the lady who had answered the door at the diuretic paint thinner party. She didn't seem to recognize him, though. But she was pretty, and she smelled nice. Goliath, in his little-boy way, was developing a crush on her.

"I'm looking for a birthday sister for my present," he said. He was addled.

"How about an air compressor? We're having a clearance sale this week."

"No, she already has one," he said, Goliath.

"Would she like a wok?"

"No, our mom won't let us have a pet."

Ann Onimous giggled. "You cook with it," she said.

"Oh, no. That wouldn't do at all." Goliath wasn't *that* addled.

"Well, how about a nice picture for her room?"

"Yeah, that would be the perfect thing." Goliath *was* that addled.

Ann Onimous took Goliath over to the picture department, and he looked at all the nifty pictures. He looked at pictures of translucent waves rolling over the ocean. He looked at pictures of babbling brooks wending their way through forests. He looked at pictures of big-eyed children and dogs. He looked at a picture of a vacant lot with a truck parked in front of it. Finally, Goliath found one he liked. It was a picture of Jean-Paul Sartre bench-pressing three hundred pounds. Yeah, it was a good picture, and Goliath liked it, so he bought it. As he left, Ann Onimous said to one of her coworkers, "What a cute little boy."

And also as Goliath left, Billy-Bob was standing around out in the concourse, or whatever they call the big open area in a shopping mall where there aren't any stores, like the sidewalk, except that it's not really a sidewalk because it's not at the side of anything but in the middle. Anyway, that daggone ol' Billy-Bob was out there, being a dork, and dorkiness is always dorkier in public, so there he was with a little toy mugwump hanging on a string around his neck. He went up to Goliath.

"Hey, Goliath, whatcha got?"

"A picture of Jean-Paul Sartre bench pressing three hundred pounds."

"Let me see."

Goliath took the picture out of the bag and showed it to Billy-Bob. Billy-Bob looked at it. "That Jean-Paul Sartre, he looks like a real smart guy. I bet he does a lot of thinking."

"Yeah," Goliath said. "Only I think he's dead now."

"Why'd you buy the picture?"

"It's for Othello," Goliath said. "Today's her birthday, and this is my present for her. We're having a party tonight."

When Billy-Bob heard that, he hauled off and started feeling bad. He deserved to be invited because he had gone out on a date with Othello, whose birthday it was, and he had taken her to a movie with Laurence I'll Live in Hay (or whatever his name was) in it. And she wouldn't let him do naked things with her, so he at least deserved to be invited to her party. She owed it to him, gosh darn it. "How come I didn't get invited?" he asked.

"She's mad at you," Goliath said. Surely Billy-Bob should know that. When a boy wants to do naked things with a girl and the girl doesn't want to, the girl often gets mad at the boy.

"But it was all Cato's fault," Billy-Bob said.

"Gee, Billy-Bob, I'm sorry, but I can't do anything about it, no matter whose fault it is."

Well, Billy-Bob figured that if he had gotten Othello

to like him before by giving her a present, why wouldn't it work again? It would, that was why. It would work, and here was Goliath right in front of him with a present for Othello, a cool picture of John Paul Salt bench-pressing three hundred pounds. Heck, he (Billy-Bob) could give it to Othello, and then they could go see *Wuthering Heights* again, and this time she'd probably do naked things with him. This was a much better present than that ol' tongue depressor Cato had told him to give her. His dad had given his mom one just like it, this picture, and she was so overwhelmed that she fainted. On Valentine's Day, no less. Not only that, but Goliath was her brother, Othello's brother, that is, not Billy-Bob's mother's brother, so he, Goliath, knew her better and would be able to pick out the perfect present. So this picture must be perfect! Billy-Bob didn't think Othello liked the tongue depressor because it was still sitting out there on her porch. She hadn't even taken it inside!

"Can I give her that picture?" Billy-Bob asked.

"But I bought it myself. It took a long time to pick it out, and I don't know whether I could find something else to give her."

"You have to. You got everything all messed up when I wanted to dance for Miss Cranberry."

Goliath didn't see what that had to do with Othello's birthday, but he didn't want to ask. He wanted to end the conversation so he could go home. "I did not. I was going to warn her, in case she didn't want to do baby-making things."

"I didn't want to do baby-making things. I wanted to dance."

"Just dance?"

"Yeah, dance. She said I was a big, clumsy kid."

"Well, aren't you?"

And that made Billy-Bob mad. It was bad enough for Miss Cranberry to say something like that, but at least she was a grownup and probably knew what she was talking about. But this miserable little puke Goliath, what did *he* know about anything at all? He was only in the third grade, and Billy-Bob had heard that he flunked the lesson on fermentation. Billy-Bob had never had a lesson on fermentation, at least not that he could remember, but he was sure that if he ever did, he would learn it and pass. He had to be better than Goliath at *something*. It stood to reason because he was older. "No, I'm not," he said.

"Well, okay, but I have to go now," Goliath said. "If I'm late they'll think it's because I didn't want to eat Othello's cooking, and I'll get in trouble."

"Give me the picture first."

"Can't you buy something yourself?"

"I don't know what to get her. Besides, I spent all my money on that tongue depressor. So hand it over."

"I don't have it," Goliath said, thinking Billy-Bob had meant for him to hand over the tongue...er, air compressor.

Billy-Bob, that clunky ol' Billy-Bob, reached out, and he grabbed it. The picture, that is. He grabbed it, and Goliath kept on holding onto it, so they tugged and pulled, and the frame cracked, and since Billy-Bob was bigger and stronger, he was able to get it. "See?" he said. "That wasn't so hard, was it?"

"Give me that picture back!" Goliath said.

"Why would I take it if I was going to give it right back? Gee, Goliath, you ain't as bright as everybody says." And then Billy-Bob kicked Goliath in the knee.

Goliath fell down. Then he sat up and watched Billy-Bob walk away with the picture. After Billy-Bob was gone Goliath stayed right where he was, sitting on the floor in the middle of the mall, all alone and by himself, waiting for his knee to quit hurting. It was the same knee Billy-Bob had punched during the Front Porch Commotion. People walked around Goliath, mumbling and murmuring about how this little kid needed to get up before someone stepped on him. Finally, his knee felt better. He got up and started walking home. He didn't have enough money to get Othello another present, so he had to go empty handed.

11. Othello's Red-Letter Day

It was a Red-Letter Day for Othello. Not only was it her birthday, but she had written an opera. Yes indeed, an entire opera. After school, while Goliath was at the mall and Cleopatra was at the corner store buying some synchronicity for the birthday party (you don't want to get it too far in advance because it gets stale quickly), Othello was left all alone for a while.

And when Cleopatra came home, Othello was sitting at the kitchen table with a huge, thick manuscript in front of her. "Guess what I just did," Othello said.

"What?"

"I wrote an opera? I mean, I wrote an opera."

"An opera? In an hour? How'd you do that?"

"By accident. The phone rang, and I was trying to write down a message for you."

"Let me see it."

The title of the opera was *Three Chipmunks and a Fox*. It was about a soldier who went off to war, and he married a beautiful young lady in the country where he was fighting. Then he went back to the fighting and got lost. He ended up in a small town in Idaho and found work as a stop sign proofreader. Meanwhile, his lovely bride searched the world, high and low, for him. She thought she found him in New York City, but it was really the soldier's twin brother. And the twin brother, having a more than healthy appreciation for beautiful women, pretended he was her husband so he could... well, you know what.

Then a band of roving pirates from the eighteenth dimension invaded the small town in Idaho and took our hero captive. They wrapped him up in duct tape so he couldn't move and carried him back to the eighteenth dimension, where they put him on display in a museum.

The twin brother, the opportunistic twin brother, talked in his sleep. One night he started babbling about pretending to be his brother, and he was so loud that our lovely young lady woke up. She heard him babble the whole thing in his sleep and got so mad that her brainwaves ripped open a portal to the eighteenth dimension (loudly and violently, I might add). She fell through and was reunited with her real husband in the museum. The pirates, seeing how much in love these young people were, decided they couldn't keep them as a museum exhibit anymore. So they let them return home.

The couple went to live in Idaho, where he continued his career as a stop sign proofreader and she embarked on a career as a goldfish inspector. They lived happily ever after.

"It looks like a real winner," Cleopatra said. "I love stories that have pirate museum curators from the eighteenth dimension. What are you going to do with it?"

"I want to let it sit in the closet and collect dust for the rest of my life," Othello said. "And then, after I die, they can find it among my stuff and produce it, and I'll become famous."

Cleopatra was so charmed with the opera and Othello's plans for it that she forgot to ask what the phone message was.

Later, Goliath came home. And when Cleopatra saw that he had no present, she got mad. She had told him, Goliath, SHE HAD TOLD HIM, to make sure he bought Othello a birthday present. "Make sure you buy Othello a birthday present," she had said.

"Okay," Goliath had said.

And now, here he was without one.

"Where's Othello's birthday present?" Cleopatra asked.

"Billy-Bob took it away from me."

"Why would he do that? It's not his present."

"He wanted to give it to Othello himself."

"He wouldn't do that. He's such a good boy. He sent Othello that nice tongue depressor and took her to the movies and everything." She didn't know about Billy-Bob wanting to do nasty things with Othello. To her, he was still a good boy.

"He didn't have enough money to buy her something himself."

"Quit lying, Goliath. A nice boy like Billy-Bob, he could get some money some way if he didn't have any."

"But mom—"

"The party's going to start in a few minutes, and Othello's friends will be here, and they'll see that her own brother didn't think enough of her to get her a present for her birthday. That's a pretty shoddy way to treat your family, especially someone who's blind and deserves extra nice treatment, and who cooks your

meals for you. And especially after I told you, and reminded you, and told you again to make sure you get
her a present."

"But it wasn't my fault!"

"And then to blame the whole thing on that nice
boy, Billy-Bob. Goliath, I thought I'd raised you up
better than that." Although, of course, she couldn't remember a whole bunch of raising up Goliath because of
the mysterious brain disease. Further, she had never
actually told Goliath to get Othello a birthday present.
She just thought she had.

Othello came out of the bathroom with a towel
wrapped around her. I'm tempted to make joke to the
effect that she hadn't been taking a shower, but she
had been, and I won't. "Othello, Goliath didn't buy you
a birthday present," Cleopatra told her.

Othello stopped walking and stood still. She was
hurt. "I bought you a present for your birthday," she
said. "I bought you that electron microscope, remember?"

"Yes," Cleopatra said. "We got it at the flea mar-
ket."

"I bought you a present," Goliath pleaded, "but Billy-Bob took it away from me. He's going to give it to
you himself." He started to tell her what it was, but he
didn't want to spoil the surprise.

Well, Othello didn't hardly believe that, not for half
a millimeter of a second. Billy-Bob couldn't possibly
know it was her birthday, and if he did, he was too
creepy to get her a present. If he did get her a present, he probably would do it by taking one that Goliath
had bought, but he wouldn't have had the chance because Goliath hadn't bought her one in the first place,

so that was that. "I don't hardly believe you," she said. Then she turned around and went into her room to get dressed.

"You see how disappointed your sister is?" Cleopatra said.

"It's all Billy-Bob's fault," Goliath said. He was starting to cry. And he was getting hungry, too. "Growl," his stomach said. "Growl."

Then somebody rang the doorbell. Cleopatra opened the door and said, "You're a disgrace to the family."

Well, Billy-Bob was standing out there, out on the front porch, holding The Picture. "No I'm not," he said.

"I'm sorry," Cleopatra said. "I meant Goliath. Come on in, Billy-Bob. You're a nice boy."

Billy-Bob came in. "I bought a birthday present for Othello," he said. "Har har. Goliath tried to take it away from me at the shopping mall, har har. That's how come the frame's cracked."

Cleopatra looked at the frame, and sure enough, it was cracked. What an outrage! Not only did Goliath not buy his loving, devoted sister a present for her birthday, but he went so far as to mess up one that somebody else had bought her. Now that was going too far, as if merely not buying a present weren't. Oh, where did it all end? Where had she gone wrong? Goliath had been such a good boy, or had seemed so. Gosh, but it was heartbreaking. "Billy-Bob, could you excuse Goliath and me for a minute so we can have a little talk?" she said, and then she stuck an ashtray in Billy-Bob's hands so he would have something to keep himself occupied. Then she took Goliath into the kitchen.

"Goliath," she said, "you're a big disappointment to me. You...you..." And then she remembered Father

O'Grotten and his sermon. "You have no loyalty."

"Sure I do, mom."

"You clearly don't, young man. And Father O'Grotten, that blessed man, told us Sunday how we should deal with people of your ilk, people who have no loyalty." She stopped and hyperventilated for a few breaths, hoping to make her face turn all red so she would look like Father O'Grotten. Then she pointed to the door. "Go."

"What?" little Goliath said. He didn't understand. He didn't even know what "ilk" meant.

"I'm kicking you out of the house. It's hard enough getting along in this stinking world without disloyal people making it more difficult for no good reason."

"What?" little Goliath said again.

"Well, that's what Father O'Grotten said, anyway. And he's wiser than any of us. So go."

"But mom—"

"And don't forget to send us money every week."

Goliath could see that his mother was serious. He sighed. His chin quivered. He looked up at Cleopatra's face and saw nothing but a rock-hard expression. He sighed again and slunk out the front door.

Cleopatra, in the house, sat down to compose a letter to Father O'Grotten. She wanted to tell him how his sermon had helped her home life.

Across the street, Eunice Mae was visiting her friend Alma, who lived over there—across the street from Goliath, that is. They were in the front yard jumping rope. Since no one had taught them the right way to do it, they were laying the rope out on the ground and jumping over it.

"Look, Eunice Mae," Alma said, pointing. "There's

Goliath. He looks sad."

Eunice Mae looked. She saw Goliath slinking down the front walk. Yes, indeed, he looked sad. "Hey, Goliath," Eunice Mae shouted. "What's wrong?"

Goliath stopped. "My mother kicked me out of the house."

Eunice Mae was flabbergasted. Goliath, the Man She Loved, was in a pickle! She had to do something. "My goodness! Well, why don't you come over to my house for supper tonight?"

Goliath cheered up a little. "Okay. But first, I want to go somewhere and be alone for a while."

"Come over at six o'clock," Eunice Mae said.

"Sure thing, Eunice Mae."

Goliath walked away, walked away slowly. Eunice Mae watched him disappear into the distance, not realizing that he didn't have a watch—or that he didn't know where she lived.

"Alma," she said, "I have a date with Goliath."

***

Meanwhile, Miss Cranberry was standing in her backyard looking at the window on the ground. She was frustrated. This was the third time—*the third time*—the air conditioner had kicked on with enough force to blast this window out into the backyard. And this time it had taken the curtain out too! Why can't those guys get it fixed properly?

She would have to make some phone calls to get this repaired as soon as possible. Someone might see the empty window hole and climb in and go through all her stuff. It would be embarrassing if they found that note from Billy-Bob Wazoo.

It was interesting, though. This time the shards of glass had somehow ended up looking like a mosaic of a snowy mountain with two goats on top. What were the chances of that? She went inside to get her camera.

***

The Neuralgia Sisters were plotting again. They were getting ready to take out their next target—Mr. Antwerp's vendor in the suburban neighborhood, Ellen Compote.

Ellen had gone to work for Mr. Antwerp when she was a mere fifteen years old. He hired her because she was fresh looking and wholesome, almost as wholesome as Miss Cranberry, and she had an oh-so-bright smile. At first, he didn't want to put her out on the street selling charcoal because he was afraid she would be robbed. So he had her work around the office, doing things like installing a kitchen and ripping the asbestos out of the ceiling. But then he hired Goliath, who at the time was only seven. Mr. Antwerp decided that since he had a seven-year-old boy out on the street vending, a fifteen-year-old girl could do just as well. And she did.

Ellen did so well that her sisters, Tina and Mary Catherine Probang—Ellen thought the name Probang was silly, so she changed her own name to Compote—could go off on their search—or more accurately, quest—for the Holy Grail, secure in the knowledge that someone was home drudging away, keeping the dust off the television set, paying the gravity bill, and, most important, sending them money. Tina and Mary Catherine had been on their quest for seven years when all this stuff happened that you're reading about here. (You *are* reading this, aren't you?)

Norma and Nancy had been watching Ellen Compote for quite some time. In fact, they had been watching her since before they started their job as charcoal vendors because they were nosy and it was fun. They followed her to work and to lunch at Hamburger Sty every day. (Ellen got the Atomic Burger, the biggest burger in town—three six-pound hamburger patties, cheese, lettuce, tomato slices, pickles, onions, an ounce of black caviar, a handful of beer nuts, a magazine centerfold, two skeleton keys, an Osmond Brothers 45 single, a sixty-watt light bulb, a small chunk of uranium 235, six tenpenny nails, a Civil War sword, a small television antenna, an original Dennis the Menace cartoon drawing, a roll of electrician's tape, a snare drum, a ceramic cookie jar, a four-inch cube of transparent oak, a gas mask, a revolving door, and a small piece of dirty fur, all served up between two oyster crackers. You could also get bacon on it, but Ellen thought that was excessive.) They followed her home at night. They knew when she watched television, and they knew when she talked on the phone. They knew when she fed the cement geese in her front yard. They knew all about her. The only problem was that she didn't do anything illegal or scandalous. She didn't do anything interesting at all. Well, that is to say, she volunteered to help inner city children learn to read, and she was the chairperson of a committee to help find loving homes for stray kittens, and she organized numerous fundraising events to benefit that strange brain disease I can't be bothered to think of a name for.

But the Neuralgia Sisters didn't think any of that

stuff was interesting. They didn't even understand it. They were just having fun being spies. Dexter might have been too mature to pretend he was a secret agent when he was sneaking around, but Norma and Nancy weren't.

For their special project, the Neuralgia Sisters didn't need any of information they gathered. They already knew what they were going to do, and to do it, all they needed to know was where her charcoal-vending corner was.

And when it came time to lower the boom, they drove there. "Would you like to buy some charcoal?" Ellen asked.

"Get in the car," Nancy said.

Ellen sniffed. She was puzzled.

"Get in the car," Norma said.

Well, the consensus was that she should get into the car; she was outvoted two to one, so she got in. They drove to a warehouse—it was the same warehouse the Neuralgia Sisters had taken poor Johnny Abacus to. They went there, and in a matter of minutes Ellen found herself tied to a chair. It wasn't voluntary, though, nor was she distracted by thoughts of adult activities.

Norma and Nancy said sinister things to scare her.

"This is going to be bad," Norma said.

"Real bad," Nancy said.

"*Really* bad," Ellen said, correcting her.

"Are you sure it's not real bad?"

"Well, now that you mention it, I'm not all that sure."

"We might do something like, say, stick bubble gum in your hair," Norma said.

"Or we might run over you with a steamroller and use you as a bookmark."

But they knew what they were going to do, and what they were going to do wasn't any of that. Nancy stayed at the warehouse to keep an eye on Ellen, and Norma went out to the hardware store. She gave the clerk a list of stuff she wanted. Heavy-duty wire, screws, things like that. The clerk was scared of her, so he gathered everything up as quickly as he could. His arms were a blur. Then he wanted to give her the stuff for free. But Norma paid him for it because she wanted to look normal. "We're not going to use this to commit a crime," she said.

And then she didn't go back to the warehouse.

No, Norma went to the local neighborhood Consu-Mart and looked at the television sets. She found a nice, big Farnsworth model 1927 with a great picture and a cool-looking remote control. Yes, it would do just fine.

***

Meanwhile, it was getting dark, and Goliath was wandering around looking for a place to spend the night. He was hungry, and as he got hungrier, he regretted not asking Eunice Mae where she lived. It wasn't that he hadn't wanted to go to her house. Being upset, he just hadn't thought to ask.

As he walked along the sidewalk, a man and a woman sitting in a front yard noticed him. "Hey, little boy," the woman said.

He stopped. "Who, me?"

"Yes. Why do you look so sad?"

Goliath hesitated. He didn't want to tell complete strangers that he had gotten kicked out of the house. But then again, he couldn't think of anything else to tell them. "My mom...kicked me out of the house," he mumbled.

"Oh, that's awful," the woman said. "Do you have a place to stay?"

Again, he hesitated. Then, "No."

The woman looked heartbroken. She glanced over at the man, and he nodded. "Do you want to stay with us?" she asked.

"Well, you sure do have a nice-looking place."

"Oh, no, the house isn't ours. We live here." She pointed at a hollowed-out dictionary under a tree in the middle of the yard. "It's small, but our daughters have moved out. So we have room for another child."

Once upon a time, Goliath would have scoffed at it. Now, it looked pretty good.

12. Bus Stop Blues

Norma took all the stuff she bought back to the warehouse. She and Nancy fixed up Ellen, poor Ellen, like Alex in *A Clockwork Orange*. First they put her in a room that used to be the boss' office, back when a real business was operating there. (The warehouse had been a storage facility for a diuretic paint thinner company, the legal domestic stuff.) They strapped her to a chair and put a clamp on her head to hold it firmly in place. They put little clips on her eyelids to keep them open and rigged up a squirt gun on a timer to spray eye drops, so her eyes wouldn't dry out. Then they set up the television set in front of her and hooked it up to the cable (which they had spliced in from a house around the corner—will their crimes never end?).

Nancy turned the TV on and flipped through the channels. She stopped briefly at Belt Loop Channel. Ellen, being the fashion maven that she was, perked up. Nancy waited a few moments to let Ellen get into the show and then punched buttons on the remote.

"Hey, I was watching that," Ellen said.

Nancy didn't reply. She punched more buttons and landed on the Earthworm Channel. Ellen, being the nature lover that she was, perked up. Nancy waited a few moments to let Ellen get into the show and then punched buttons on the remote.

"Hey, I was watching that," Ellen said.

Nancy didn't reply. She punched more buttons and landed on See-Spin, the channel that showed footage of legislative bodies sitting around before sessions waiting for the rest of the members to show up. Ellen shuddered.

Nancy put the remote down and got all up in Ellen's face. "Yes, my dear. We're going to *bore* you to death. Bye-*bye!*" And then the Neuralgia Sisters left the room so they wouldn't be weakened by the boredom vibrations from the TV.

"What shall we do while we wait?" Norma said.

"Let's play Big Business Tycoon," Nancy said.

They played two games. Norma won the first. She ended up with all the most expensive property, plus Carburetor State University, National Motors, the US Army, Delaware, and a small tattoo shop in Carbondale. Nancy won the second game, having accumulated all the major television networks, the National Goalball League, the planet Saturn, and a Mothers of Invention record.

After the second game, they went out to eat and then caught a baseball game that went into extra innings. They went to see *Goodfellas*. Then it was back to the warehouse with them.

Norma cracked the office door open and looked in. Ellen was all bound up immobile, just as they had left her, so Norma couldn't tell anything by the way she acted. But Ellen was making little "Gughgugh" sounds and drooling on herself.

Norma closed the door. "Well," she said, "if we stop

now, she'll probably never focus her eyes again, be able to operate a machine more complex than a wheelbarrow, use words with more that one syllable, remember her address or phone number, or understand what the lines on a hockey rink are for. And she'll certainly never sell charcoal again."

"What do you think, then? Do we stop now or go for the kill?"

"Let's pin a note on her shirt and let her wander loose," Norma said.

Nancy liked that idea. "I like that idea," she said.

They sat down and wrote a note:

Dear whoever finds this girl:
Please take her to Mr. Antwerp's office. He'll know what happened and why.

"Let's test her," Nancy said. They went back into the room where Ellen, poor Ellen Compote, was, and Norma snapped her fingers in front of Ellen's face. Ellen didn't reack—I mean react, but she didn't reack either. Norma poked her arm with a hatpin. Again, no reaction. Not that Norma expected one; she just wanted to poke somebody with a hatpin.

"She's wasted," Nancy said. "This girl's brain has gone belly-up."

"Chw," Ellen said, and drooled on herself.

"Let's take her out and turn her loose," Norma said.

They put Ellen in the car and drove out near Mr. Antwerp's office. "We should be careful where we leave her," Nancy said. "She might wander out in front of a bus or something."

"I know what to do," Norma said. She got out of

the car and opened Ellen's door. Norma led Ellen by the arm to a nearby bus stop and sat her down. "Stay," Norma said.

"Ttq," Ellen said. Her arm twitched.

Norma and Nancy Neuralgia grinned with satisfaction and went back home. They drank hot chocolate, congratulated each other, and giggled like little girls.

Ellen Compote sat at the bus stop all night. Her only movement was that she sneezed when a mosquito flew up her nose.

The next morning, the city came to life. People were hustling and bustling about, on their way to the dentist to get their teeth cleaned, or to offices to interview for jobs as paperweights, or to the county courthouse to register for being too smart.

No one noticed poor Ellen in her state of affliction until a passerby saw that a dog was peeing on her foot and she wasn't doing anything about it.

At the same time, in the suburban neighborhood, a new charcoal vendor was setting up shop. Pandy O'Smidlington had finished her job interview with Mr. Schurk only minutes ago, and she was ready to start selling charcoal and lots of it. Yes, Pandy was excited about this new opportunity.

***

At the hollowed-out dictionary, Goliath was waking up. Mr. and Mrs. Neuralgia waited until the people who lived in the house left for work, and then they went in and scavenged for breakfast. They found some All-American Powerhouse Synthetic Pre-Processed Breakfast Food Product Bars, which provide 0.05

percent of your daily nutritional needs, and besides that, almost make your stomach feel as if you've eaten something. Goliath was uncomfortable. He sensed that what they were doing was wrong, even if Mr. and Mrs. Neuralgia insisted that it was all right.

All through breakfast, they regaled him with stories about how awful their daughters were, how they got some kind of job, the girls did, and they were successful at it, whatever it was (the girls hadn't told their parents what the job was) and made big wads of money. And they bought a big house, the girls did, but left their poor parents to continue living in that hollowed-out dictionary out there in the front yard. Mr. and Mrs. Neuralgia had never seen Norma and Nancy's house. They didn't know where it was, but they knew all about it because the girls came back one day to gloat. And they were sure—they just *knew*—this new house had bedrooms, lots and lots of bedrooms, and most of them were undoubtedly being left unused. And they probably had a tennis court in the closet.

Mr. and Mrs. Neuralgia said they were thinking about changing their names to distance themselves from their ungrateful offspring. They were going to become Mr. and Mrs. Smith.

Goliath agreed that Norma and Nancy were bad.

***

Eunice Mae saw Goliath at school that day, but she didn't have a chance to talk to him, to find out whether he was all right and why he hadn't come over for supper. She noticed that he was in the same clothes he had worn the day before, and he looked somewhat the worse for wear. Not seriously, but sorta like as if he had spent the night in some tiny, uncomfortable, cramped-up place.

Poor Goliath, she thought.

That night, Eunice Mae was watching the news, and she saw a story about Ellen Compote.

"Ellen Compote," the anchor said, "a vendor for the Antwerp Charcoal Company, was found at a bus stop this morning in a state of catatonia. Compote, experts believe, can understand simple sentences, but cannot speak, and apparently cannot focus her eyes or understand what the lines on a hockey rink are for. Police suspect foul play because of a note found pinned to her shirt. They also believe this case is related to the alien abduction of poor Johnny Abacus, another Antwerp vendor."

Supper was ready. Eunice Mae sat down at the table and worried about Goliath. Maybe the reason he had looked so much the worse for wear at school was because those bad charcoal vending villains had been chasing him around all night! That must be why he hadn't shown up to have supper at her house.

"Eunice Mae, you're not eating your supper," Eunice Mae's Mom said.

"Is something wrong?" Eunice Mae's Dad asked.

"Oh, I'm not hungry," Eunice Mae said.

"You look worried to me," Eunice Mae's Mom said. "Eunice Mae's Dad, don't you think she looks worried?" (The reason they named their daughter Eunice Mae was because their names were Eunice Mae's Mom and Eunice Mae's Dad. It would have been embarrassing for the whole family if their child had been a boy. You think I'm kidding, but it's true.)

"Yes, I do, Eunice Mae's Mom. But I reckon she'll talk about it when she's ready. Eunice Mae, you may be excused."

"Thank you," Eunice Mae said. She got up and went to her room. She did her homework because that was what Goliath would want her to do.

***

And over at Miss Cranberry's house, Miss Cranberry saw the Ellen Compote story on the TV news. It was dreadful, absolutely dreadful. Miss Cranberry used to babysit Ellen, years ago. Ellen had always been such a nice girl. And she fried bacon so well, too. What a loss.

And then there was the Antwerp thing. Another vendor bites the dust. And that could only mean Goliath's turn was probably going to come pretty soon.

Gosh!

She had to do something, and quick. She had to... she had to...well...

She had to keep an eye on Goliath. Yeah! She could follow him around and watch him, and if something was about to happen, she would swoop down and help him.

She could get Dexter Kroger, too, because things might get rough. Yeah! It would be great! Goliath would be at school during the early part of the day, right there where she worked because she was a teacher, and Goliath's teacher at that. She could keep an eye on him during school hours and no one would suspect a thing because she was supposed to be there anyway, in the same room with him.

And then after school she could follow him. Goliath

would be at his corner, perched on his stool selling charcoal, and it's easy to follow someone who's sitting still. She'd have to stay out of sight, of course, because Goliath shouldn't know about this. And Dexter Kroger could join her after work in case any rough stuff happened. Out there, at Goliath's charcoal corner, was probably where the rough stuff would happen, if it was going to happen.

It was an elegant plan!

And romantic, too. It was something she and Dexter could do together, side by side.

***

Meanwhile, Dexter Kroger was lurking behind Mifford's Wood Screw Shop (which truthfully advertised the world's largest assortment of exotic wood screws from all over the world, making the establishment a favorite of collectors). He was coming to the conclusion that he shouldn't barge into the police station with this evidence he had found. The more he thought about it, the more he became afraid the police would lock him up, regardless of any evidence he might have in regard to the Miss Cranberry Case. He should take some time to figure out exactly the right way to go about this.

He needed an apartment. Any old, dumpy place would do, just a place to hide for a few days until he could get his plans worked out. He would have to find it pretty quickly because he wanted to see the ball game tonight. Beer and baseball. Yeah. And it looked to be a pretty good game, with the East Patella Pencil-Neck Geeks against the Grubsville Ignorant Twerps. Last summer the two teams had battled it out neck-and-neck for fourth place, through the whole season, and the Ignorant Twerps finally pulled it out in the last game when one of their fans shot the Pencil-Neck Geek center fielder, allowing the winning run to score in the bottom of the ninth.

It was an iffy situation at best. Dexter's general, overall situation, that is, not the baseball situation. Dexter hoped he wouldn't end up living in a closet in a radiator factory in Denver. It had happened to a close friend of his, and he didn't relish the prospect.

He force-grew a mustache, which took about ten minutes. Thus disguised, Dexter went to the bank and got all his money out, even though the lady didn't approve because he should save his money for a rainy day. He told her that if this wasn't a rainy day, he didn't know what was (although he couldn't tell her why). She was doubtful, but she had to let him take it. It was his money.

Then he went and got himself a newspaper. He read all the ads for apartments, ones that were available to be rented, while he ate a chili dog with cream cheese and acetate. One ad looked good—the place had steel wool carpeting inside and pretzel trees in the backyard.

He called the number, and the landlord told him the pretzel trees grew those great big thick ones, not the little, tiny, skinny ones that most trees have. It sounded good to Dexter, so he went to look at the place.

The building was a big ol' Victorian mansion type of place, divided into small apartments. The landlord met Dexter inside the front door, in the entrance hall.

"The apartment's on the top floor," the landlord said. "Come on up."

They went upstairs and into the apartment. Dexter

looked at everything. He looked at the kitchen, the bathroom, the spinning wheel, the rocket launcher, the scale model of Vancouver. The apartment had all the necessities, but it didn't have any extras. Still, what more did Dexter need at the moment? Yes, this place would do nicely. It was a place where he could lay low for a while and figure out what to do next.

"The other tenants are kind of flaky, but mostly they're likeable folks," the landlord said. "Just watch out for Mr. Tate, the lodger downstairs. Sometimes he can be a troublemaker."

"Do I have to pay the utilities?" Dexter asked.

"Yes."

"How much do they usually run?"

"About two handfuls of money for the water bill, five for the electricity, and one for the gravity bill. The gravity lines are brand new, so the bill should be low for a long time."

"I like it. How much do you want for it?"

"Six handfuls of money per month and a six-handful deposit," the landlord said.

"I'll take it."

"Great. I'm sure you'll like it here. Let's go ahead and sign the paperwork, and you can move in anytime." The landlord opened a folder he had been carrying. He took out a copy of his standard lease agreement, put it on the kitchen table, and made a few notations. Then he slid the lease over in front of Dexter. "If everything looks good, sign at the bottom and you'll be all set," the landlord said.

Dexter looked at the lease, a month-to-month agreement with various details filled in. At the bottom was a blank line for his signature next to another line where

the landlord had already signed his name: Mr. Schurk.
Yes, everything seemed to be in order.

Dexter signed the lease as Hector Rogers and paid
Mr. Schurk.

***

After finishing his charcoal-vending day, Goliath wandered around, looking for a place to spend the night.
The Neuralgias were expecting him back at the hollowed-out dictionary, but he didn't want to go there.
They were nice people, no bout adoubt it, but it was
depressing being around them. Besides, that hollowed-out dictionary was awfully cramped-up. He had
never been able to get comfortable in there, and he still
had a crick in his neck.

He came to the Elmo Lincoln Memorial River and
noticed a generous amount of space on the bank where
the bridge went over. Yeah, that looked like a good
place to spend the night, a good, out-of-the-way place.
He shuffled down the hill and went under the bridge.
He could see a big, indistinct lump of something, but in
the dim light, he couldn't tell what it was. It might be a
big rock. It might be a huge blop of really, really, thick
applesauce. It might be anything.

Goliath sat on the ground.

The lump moved. Goliath gasped. The lump moved
some more, and in a few seconds had oriented itself
into a big, sort of humanoid creature. "Hey, dinner...
uh, I mean, hey, kid. Where did you come from?" Its
voice was deep and raspy and scary.

Goliath didn't know what to say. The creature
stared at him. Goliath pointed. "From over there," he

said.

"Come over here," the creature said.

"Who...who are you?"

"My name is Hrobigothr. I'm a troll."

"You're not going to eat me, are you?"

"Huh? What gave you that idea? I'm just lonesome. I want someone to talk to."

"Then why did you call me dinner?"

"I mistook you for someone else. I...uh...have a friend. His name is Dinner. Yeah, that's it. My friend's name is Dinner."

That sounded odd to Goliath, but he felt he'd better not argue the point. "I was looking for a place to spend the night," he said. "If this is where you live, I'll leave."

Hrobigothr looked Goliath over carefully. "Don't you have a home?"

"No," Goliath said. And then, without any further prompting, the whole, sorry story poured out of him, the story of Billy-Bob and Othello's birthday present, of getting kicked out of the house, of some mysterious bad guy disposing of his coworkers, of spending the previous night all cramped up in a hollowed-out dictionary. The whole story.

"Gosh, kid, that's tough," Hrobigothr said. "Look, you can stay here tonight. You can stay here as long as you want. I'll make sure nothing happens to you."

Goliath could tell that Hrobigothr was sincere.

13. Complaints and Stuff

Dexter sat down to watch the game. He was just in time to hear "The Star-Spangled Banner." It was a good, rousing version, and as the singer was finishing up, his (Dexter's) phone rang. The caller ID said it was Miss Cranberry.

Dexter wondered whether he should answer. Well, you and I know why she was calling. She wanted to ask him to help her watch over Goliath. And I can tell you that if Dexter answered, and she asked him, it would become clear to him that she had Goliath's best interests at heart. Dexter would realize that she was a good guy after all.

But Dexter, suspicious Dexter, was afraid she knew he was to blame for her window. Maybe a neighbor had seen him lurking around her house that day and said something to her. Maybe he hadn't cleaned up his muddy footprints well enough. Maybe something else. No matter how she had figured it out, he was sure—he just *knew*—she was calling to accuse him of breaking into her house.

It's best if I don't answer, he thought. The crowd at the game cheered for the singer, and the ringing stopped.

Miss Cranberry, disappointed, flipped her phone shut and turned on the Belt Loop Channel. *In the Loop* was on, a reality show in which contestants competed to see who could sell the greatest number of belt loops door-to-door. She was rooting for Pimmy, the shy contestant who had trouble talking to people. No one expected her to win, but lots of people on the Internet message boards loved her because she had heart. You can go far in this world if you have heart. That is to say, if you have heart and you're as cute as Pimmy, who was as cute as a box of six kittens and seven puppies. She also had a large number of male fans simply because she had boobs the size of basketballs. And because she wore clothing so tight that some thought it must be painful. Actually, now that I think about it, it probably didn't matter that she had heart.

On Dexter's TV, the baseball game started and went on for a while. In the top of the seventh inning, the score was tied. One of the Pencil-Neck Geeks was on first base, and he tried to steal second as the Ignorant Twerp pitcher threw to his first baseman. The Geek was caught between bases, and two Twerps were running him down. The Geek stopped suddenly and pulled a cell phone out of his pocket. "Wait a minute, guys," he said. "I have to take this call." He talked for a couple minutes on the phone, ambling about aimlessly, while the Twerps stood around watching. Then, seeing an opening, the Geek made a break for it. Caught unaware, the Twerp with the ball threw to second, but the Geek slid in, safe. Then, when he got up to brush the dirt off his uniform, he stepped off the base and a Twerp player tagged him out. Dexter was excited. "Oh, boy," he said. That was how excited he was.

"That's the third out," the announcer said. "Time for the seventh-inning stretch." Then a commercial. It was for the brand new BioSource Energy Device, a gizmo you could plug your TV set into. The BioSource Energy Device, or BED, sucked energy from the bodies of living creatures in the house to power the TV, thus saving scads of money on the electric bill. It was almost completely painless. Some backward-thinking individuals criticized it, though. They said after a couple hours it made people too weak to get up and turn the set off, so you were stuck there watching the daggone TV until someone came to rescue you. Or until the device sucked all the life out of you, whichever might come first.

On the upside, you could use it to exterminate the bugs in the house. All you had to do was leave your TV on while the family was out, and the BED would suck enough energy from the bugs to kill them. Actually, it sounded pretty good.

Dexter got another beer, and an old man knocked on the door and popped his head in.

"Hello," the old man said. "I'm Mr. Tate. Isn't anyone else here yet?"

"Huh?" Dexter said.

"Clever boy, you are. Where's the ham sandwiches and deviled eggs? You got a beer?"

"What are you talking about?" Dexter asked. He was confused. Even though he was a lot smarter than Billy-Bob, some things still confused him. Such as this.

"Oh, then you must have barbecue and potato salad. That's just as good."

"No, I don't," Dexter said. "I don't know what you're talking about."

"For the tenants' meeting, you fool. We're having a

tenants' meeting here tonight."

"Nobody told me."

Mr. Tate walked over to the TV and turned it off. "We can't have any of that foolishness going on. We have serious business to discuss. If you want, I'll help you whip up the ham sandwiches before the others get here." He gave Dexter a conspiratorial grin. "No one else has to know you weren't ready."

"I think you're being a bit presumptuous," Dexter said.

"If you wanted barbecue, you should have started it earlier. I don't think we have enough time now."

"I mean about the meeting."

"The announcement's been up on the bulletin board in the laundry room for a whole week. 'As soon as somebody moves into the empty apartment, we're having a meeting.' That's what it says, and it's been there long enough for everyone to see it."

"But I just moved in a couple hours ago."

"That's plenty of time. It should only take a few seconds to read the notice."

"Besides, I do my laundry at my parents' house."

"Don't they have a bulletin board?"

"Mr. Tate, you're being ridiculous."

Mr. Tate started toward the kitchen. "Do you have any rye bread?"

"No. I'd like to watch the game, if you don't mind."

"Hi! We're not late, are we?" A middle-aged couple stood inside the door. They were Ann and Ed Socrates, although Dexter didn't know their names.

"Hey, everybody, this is getting—" he said, but couldn't say "ridiculous" because Mr. Tate interrupted him.

"He says he didn't know anything about the meeting."

"He does now, doesn't he?" Ed Socrates said. Dexter couldn't decide whether the man was offensively jocular or feebleminded, or both.

"Where are the ham and cheese sandwiches?" Ann Socrates asked.

"What's all this about sandwiches?" Dexter asked.

"It's customary. You've got a lot to learn, son," Mr. Tate said with an air of wisdom. It was this kind of behavior that made people notice that his hair was a dignified gray. Well, that and the fact that it was gray.

"By the way, Mrs. Warren said she couldn't make it to the meeting tonight," Ed said.

"I guess we'll have to run her out of the building," Mr. Tate proclaimed.

"Yeah, she's divorced anyway," Ann said. "Ed, go into the kitchen and make some ham sandwiches."

"Yes, dear." Ed promptly disappeared into the kitchen and started making noise.

"Young man," Ann said to Dexter, "you're going to have to learn to be a better host."

"We've been through all that," Mr. Tate said. "He'll do better next time."

"Is there any rye bread?" Ed called out from the kitchen.

"No, there's not," Dexter said.

"Do you have any white bread?" Ann asked Dexter.

"Sure."

"Honey, use white."

"Okay." Ed sounded doubtful, as if it was bizarre to think you could eat ham on white bread. Dexter decided he was feebleminded. He was right, and he didn't even know that Ed had been fired from being a movie cameraman in Russia because he didn't have a long enough attention span. Sergei Eisenstein, in frustration, had literally kicked him in the butt when he left.

"What's this meeting all about?" Dexter asked.

"We have complaints," Ann explained. "Big complaints, and we have to decide what to do."

"Reasonable enough, don't you think?" Mr. Tate said.

"Uh, sure."

"Do you have motor oil?" Ed asked from the kitchen.

"On the refrigerator door," Ann shouted at him.

A tall, gangly kid walked in and proudly announced, "I like a good forty-weight motor oil." He was Bert Mc-Ccc, and he was young, younger than Dexter Kroger, but older than Goliath. He was even older than Billy-Bob.

"Shall we start the meeting?" Mr. Tate said.

"Hello? Hello? Where are you guys?" A woman's voice drifted in from the hallway.

"We're in here," Ann said.

"I seem to be lost. Can you help me?" the woman pleaded. She sounded lost.

"I'll talk you in," Ann said. "Can you tell where my voice is coming from?"

"It sounds like it's directly below me."

"Can't be," Mr. Tate said. "We're on the top floor. I told you we need the ceilings raised around here."

"That's the first complaint," Ann said. "Someone write it down."

"Ceilings raised?" Dexter said.

"Yes. From their present height of twelve feet to

eighteen feet."

"But they would have to completely tear down the house and rebuild it. This is a three-story building."

"That's the problem with America these days. Everybody's lazy. Everything's too hard."

"That's Trudy out there, isn't it?" Ann said.

"Then how can she be lost?" Mr. Tate said. "She lives next door to this apartment."

"Good," Ann said. "That could be important. Trudy!"

"Yes?"

"You live next door to here!"

"Wow! Ain't that a hoot! Say, it's getting foggy out here."

"It's just your imagination."

"That's impossible," Mr. Tate said. "She has no imagination. She sold it to a pawnshop, along with the air compressor she got from that secret admirer." He snorted in contempt. "The air compressor didn't even work. Imagine that!"

Footsteps approached in the hallway, and Trudy peeked around the doorframe. "Oh, I'm sorry to interrupt," she said. "I was looking for the tenants' meeting."

"That's all right," Bert said. "I think it's next door."

"No, he's an idiot, dear," Ann said. "The meeting's here."

Trudy came in and sat down. "Oh, good. I'll wait here until the other tenants start showing up," she said.

Ed appeared with the sandwiches. He carried a plate that had two sick-looking things on it. "Who's she?" he asked, noticing Trudy. "Does she live here?"

"That's Trudy," Ann explained. "She lives next door."

"Then what's she doing here?"

"I got lost," Trudy said.

"Let's get on with the meeting," Mr. Tate said. "I hope everyone has a lot of complaints."

"I don't have a girlfriend," Bert said.

"Well, that goes without saying," Mr. Tate said. "But it's a good complaint, so I'll write it down."

"Wait a minute," Dexter said. "That's not a legitimate complaint against a landlord."

"I think he should provide Bert with a girlfriend, if Bert wants one. It would be a big improvement," Ann said.

"Yeah," Mr. Tate said. "He'll never get one on his own."

"Maybe if he cut his hair differently," Trudy suggested.

"Tighter pants," Ann said. "He should wear tighter pants."

"Naw, he'd still look like a dork," Mr. Tate said.

"That's another complaint," Bert said. "Everyone makes fun of me."

Mr. Tate scribbled it down on his list. "Come on, people," he said. "We need a bunch more. You were supposed to have a bunch of complaints ready for this meeting."

"Why are you so concerned about getting a lot of things to complain about?" Dexter asked.

"We want to make sure we have enough," Mr. Tate explained.

"Are you going to take him to court?"

"No, of course not."

"Then what?"

"Hang him," Mr. Tate said. "What else?"

"Hang him?"

"Sure."

"Oh, come on."

"That's what we always do when things get bad around here," Mr. Tate said. "We hang the landlord. String the sucker up."

"You've hung landlords before?" Oh, what a day of surprises for Dexter Kroger.

"Yeah, three so far."

"But one turned out not to really be the landlord," Trudy said.

"Oh, that's right," Ed remembered. "We had to do it all over again."

"We've only hung two landlords," Ann said. "And one bonus guy."

"I still think that one guy really was the landlord," Bert said.

"He said he wasn't," Ed said.

"Of course he did," Mr. Tate said. "We were, like, all up in his face looking angry and waving a noose around and saying things like, 'We're looking for our landlord so we can hang him.' If you were the landlord, what would you say?"

"I still don't think he was," Bert said.

"How do you get away with hanging these people?" Dexter asked.

"We blame it on John Wilkes Booth," Ann told him.

"That's ridiculous!"

"No it's not. It's plausible. He's a known killer."

"But he's been dead well over a hundred years."

"That's the whole point," Ed said. "He can't defend

himself."

"But how can he hang anybody if he's dead?"

"You mean he's still alive?" Trudy sounded scared.

"If he is, we're in big trouble," Ed said.

"He's dead," Mr. Tate said. "It's in every history book."

"You don't believe everything you read, do you?" Ann demanded.

"We seem to have a real problem here," Ed said. "We need to find out about John Wilkes Booth."

"Didn't he invent the phone booth?" Bert asked.

"Yeah, right," Trudy said. "So that means..."

"He was dead before the phone was invented," Dexter said.

"What do you know?" Ann spat out. "You don't want to hang the landlord."

"Maybe if we could find out when the phone was invented, it would solve the problem," Bert suggested.

So Dexter did the only thing he could do at that point. He zoned out and wished he could watch the ball game while the rest of them alternated between wondering how they could find out whether John Wilkes Booth was still alive and writing down a whole bunch of complaints. It took a long time. Finally, Dexter realized the meeting had wound down when Mr. Tate nudged his arm and asked, "Don't you have any complaints, Hector?"

"Ah, no. I guess I haven't been here long enough. Maybe next time."

"All right," Mr. Tate said. "Everybody go get a good night's sleep, and tomorrow, at eight in the morning, we'll meet in the entrance hall and go hang the landlord. All right?"

"All right!" everybody jumped up and cheered—that is, everybody except Dexter, who was kind of dazed by the whole thing. The others rushed out and went to their rooms to do some sleeping so they would be rested up in the morning. Mr. Tate was the last one out, and at the door he turned and said something to Dexter.

"See you tomorrow morning," Mr. Tate said.

Dexter didn't say anything. What could he say? He watched Mr. Tate close the door, and then, left alone, he turned the TV back on.

"Starting off the bottom of the ninth," the announcer said, "the first Ignorant Twerp batter will be Jack Salmon. He broke his leg in the fifth inning, so he may be a bit slower now."

***

The next morning the tenants, without Dexter Kroger, met in the entrance hall. They all had weapons, things like claw hammers and tennis rackets and sticks with nails through the end. Things like TV wrestlers use— rolls of coins and sacks full of earwax. Trudy had some empty bottles, but not quite getting the idea, she had gotten plastic ones because they're safer than the glass ones. Bert had read *Invisibility Secrets of the Ninjas*. He really did think he was invisible, but that was only because people ignored him most of the time.

Mr. Tate was late. The others stood around and waited for him because he was their leader, and they couldn't do anything without him. There were plenty of chairs and couches in the room, but all the furniture was old and dilapidated and moldy and might collapse if somebody sat on it, or if not, it might give them a disease. No one likes diseases.

"Where's Hector Rogers?" Trudy asked.

"Do you have a crush on him?" Ed Socrates said. A spider ran up his leg.

"Maybe I do, and maybe I don't." Trudy would never tell Ed if she did. A hunk of plaster fell from the ceiling and bonked her on the shoulder.

"Where's Mr. Tate?" Ann Socrates said. "He's more important."

"Do you have a crush on Mr. Tate?" Bert asked.

"I have a new knock-knock joke," Ann said. "Bert, you start."

"Okay. Knock, knock."

"Who's there?"

Bert's mouth fell open. A light bulb burned out.

Mr. Tate came in. "Okay, gang, let's go," he said.

"Hector Rogers isn't here," Trudy said.

"Well, he's going to have to miss out on this one," Mr. Tate said. "I don't want to wait around. He didn't have any complaints, anyway."

They gathered their weapons and went out to the bus stop. Two buses went by, ones that were going places they didn't want to go—"they" being the tenants, that is, not the buses—places like the Randy Smedley Memorial Underwater Ping-Pong Arena, and Onpersoonlijk Inc.'s big DNA factory down by the river, which was always a big tourist attraction.

Finally, the right bus came. The sign on the front said, "SCHURK ENTERPRISES AT THE INTOLERANCE BUILDING."

"This is the one," Mr. Tate said.

They got on the bus. As they sat down, Mr. Tate said, "Okay, everybody. Hold your weapons up high, and look as mean and angry as you can." Other passengers glanced at them apprehensively and tried to ignore them, but Mr. Tate, standing up at the front of the bus, was putting on too good a show. "Bare your teeth, Bert," he said. Bert wasn't paying attention. He was still confused by the knock-knock joke.

"Trudy, growl a little louder," Mr. Tate said. "I wish we had brought some torches. We could look like a mob of angry villagers." The other passengers shifted around nervously. They were afraid of Mr. Tate. They didn't need to be, of course, because they weren't landlords, but they were anyway.

At the next stop, the other passengers got off the bus. One guy turned around at the door and shook his fist at Mr. Tate.

"Gosh," Ed Socrates said. "Maybe we'd better not do this." He was worried. A guy had shaken his fist at one of them.

"We might as well go ahead with it this time," Ann Socrates said, "since we've already gotten started."

The bus driver turned around. "You people aren't going to commit a crime, are you?"

"We're going to hang our landlord," Mr. Tate said.

"Oh." The bus driver went back to his driving.

At the Intolerance Building, Mr. Tate inspected his army before they got off the bus. "Everybody, bare your teeth and bug your eyes out." Bert bugged his eyes out so hard that, well, gosh, they popped right out of their sockets. They hung down his face, dangling on their muscles, swinging to and fro and smacking against his nose, sort of but not quite like bolas.

"Help," Bert said.

"Bert, daggone it, put your eyes back in," Ann

Socrates said.

Trudy reached over and popped Bert's eyes back in place. "There you go, Bert," she said, wiping her hands on his sleeve.

"Gosh, I don't mean to be ungrateful, but I think you got them in the wrong sockets."

"It's probably an improvement," Mr. Tate said. "Now, on the count of three, everybody rush into the building and up to the thirteenth floor. That's where his office is. Use the stairs, because you can't charge fiercely on an elevator. Any questions?"

"Yeah," Bert said. "Who's there?"

14. Teddy Roosevelt

Mr. Tate's nostrils flared. "One, two, three, *CHARGE!*" he shouted.

The tenants gushed out of the bus. "Scream and shout," Mr. Tate exhorted. (Because in situations like this, the leader never "orders" or "commands." He, or she, always "exhorts." Keep that in mind the next time you're leading an unruly mob.)

"Geronimo!" Ann Socrates shouted.

"Sitting Bull!" Ed Socrates shouted.

"Chicken intestines!" Bert shouted.

Trudy didn't shout because it wasn't ladylike. She also had trouble running because she was wearing a tight skirt.

Inside the stairwell, a guy in a cruddy suit was leaning against the wall smoking a cigarette. He was seedy-looking and needed a shave. He had a tattoo of a ball of cotton on the back of his hand. That is to say, it wasn't really clear what the tattoo was supposed to be, but most people who saw it preferred to think it was a ball of cotton. Maybe kind of a dirty ball of cotton, but still... "What floor?" the guy asked.

"Thirteenth," Ed said.

"Who are you?" Ann asked.

"I'm the stair operator. It's customary to tip me five handfuls of money per floor."

"What? All we have to do is walk up."

"Well, yeah. But you'd be surprised how many gullible people come in here. I make out pretty good, really."

Ed was looking through his wallet. "Let's see," he mused. "Thirteen floors at five handfuls per... That's sixty-five handfuls of money, plus five percent sales tax..."

Ann slapped him, just hard enough to get his attention. "You idiot. Everyone knows the sales tax on tips in this state is six and a half percent."

The guy flashed a dirty look at Ed but then accepted the tip with a big smile.

The other tenants were already on their way up. Mr. Tate was pretending he was Teddy Roosevelt leading the charge up San Juan Hill.

It was a long way up, and since no one was in very good condition, they had to stop and rest after every floor. They hadn't brought lunch, but Bert had packed some games in his backpack. He had a pin the tail on the snail set, an electric jai-alai game, and some other stuff I can't think of, but it doesn't matter.

They played pin the tail on the snail the first few stops. After that they switched over to twenty questions, but by the ninth floor they were too out of breath. "Things aren't going so well," Mr. Tate said. He looked up at the thirty-nine steps remaining and sighed.

At the landing on the thirteenth floor, everybody was pooped out.

"Can we spend the night here and hang him in the morning?" Bert gasped.

"It's only two thirty in the afternoon," Mr. Tate said. He was more frustrated than Miss Cranberry when she tried to teach Goliath arithmetic.

After some bickering and squabbling and threatening to go home, the others finally got Mr. Tate to let them take a short nap before going to get Mr. Schurk. Mr. Tate was annoyed because he wanted it to be a fierce charge, fast and noisy and violent. He wanted them to be like storm troopers, like guerilla fighters, like…well, like people who were competent. This was disillusioning. "This is disillusioning," he mumbled. He decided to quit pretending he was Teddy Roosevelt, mostly because he was afraid an angry ghost of Teddy Roosevelt would appear before him and severely berate him.

Bert dreamed he was a squirrel. Ann dreamed she was a robot. Trudy dreamed she was cupcake that was being eaten by a robotic squirrel.

Later, everyone woke up, everyone except Mr. Tate, who couldn't wake up because he had never gone to sleep—that is, never that afternoon, not never at all; he'd stayed awake to act as a lookout. So anyway, they woke up, and Mr. Tate gave them a final pep talk. "Let's get him" was what he said.

They opened the door and charged into the hallway. "This way," Mr. Tate exhorted. Up ahead was a door with "SCHURK ENTERPRISES" painted on it. Mr. Tate flung the door open, and they rushed in.

Mr. Schurk's secretary, Miss Spikenhammer, was sitting at her desk reading a Flippo McTurgid novel called *Spider Flambé*. It was very thick. "Do you have an appointment?" she asked.

"No," Ed Socrates said. "How soon can we get one?"

Miss Spikenhammer started to look at her appointment book, and Mr. Tate spoke up. "We don't need an appointment. We're angry tenants, and we're here to hang Mr. Schurk."

"He's on the phone right now, long distance. If you'd care to wait, he could see you in a few minutes."

"You don't understand, young lady," Mr. Tate said. "We're not supposed to care about what he's doing. We're supposed to barge right in and hang him."

"Well, all right, but I'll warn you. He's not going to like this." Miss Spikenhammer rang her intercom.

"Yes?" Mr. Schurk said.

"Sir, some of your tenants from the slum...er, I mean, the apartment building, are here to hang you."

"Have them wait."

"They say they're not supposed to."

Silence. The tenants looked at one another, and then Mr. Tate carefully tiptoed over to Mr. Schurk's office door and opened it. He stepped in and saw a bookcase sliding shut over a secret passage. "Come on!" he shouted, and ran to catch the bookcase before it finished shutting. He jammed his baseball bat into the opening and, with great effort and no help, pushed it back open.

Bert started to run into Mr. Schurk's office, and then he turned around. "Do you know this knock-knock joke?" he asked. "Knock knock."

"You're a dork," Miss Spikenhammer said.

"You're a dork who?"

Ann reached around the doorway and grabbed Bert.

***

Behind the bookcase, Mr. Schurk had a secret sliding board, specially installed in case he had to make a
quick escape. He dove in headfirst, with the tenants in
hot pursuit. A grate that appeared to cover a heating
duct on the twelfth floor automatically flipped open.
He whooshed out, did a highly impressive roll on the
floor, and came up running. He ran to the elevators and
pushed the down button. As the tenants rushed up to
him, he held his hand out to stop them. "You can't grab
me here," he said. "You have to chase me down, fair
and square."

"Aw, geez," Ed Socrates said. "This is lousy."

"Yes, but if we got him here and now, while he's
waiting for the elevator, it wouldn't be an accomplish-
ment to be proud of," Mr. Tate pointed out. Trudy nodded thoughtfully, digesting the wisdom.

Everyone stood around awkwardly until the elevator came. Mr. Schurk stepped in. The tenants started
to follow, but he stopped them. "You have to take a different one," he said. The door closed, and he was gone.

The next elevator came a few seconds later. Riding down, the tenants practiced their angry shouting.
"Bert, you're starting to get the hang of it," Mr. Tate
said.

They reached the lobby in time to see Mr. Schurk
heading out the front door. "Charge!" Mr. Tate shouted. A couple of folks in the lobby got caught up in the
enthusiasm and joined the mob.

Outside, Billy-Bob was standing around on the
sidewalk with a copy of a certain well-known dental
floss collectors' magazine hanging on a string around
his neck. He was sort of not doing anything, which was
what he usually did. He watched as everybody ran by.

Gosh, it sure looked exciting, and maybe it would be fun to run along with them, but Billy-Bob didn't feel like running. He picked his nose a time or two, trying to see whether he could duplicate the stylistic flourish he had seen Goliath use. The kid might be a miserable little puke, but that flourish sure was cool.

Meanwhile, the mob chasing Mr. Schurk was growing. People on the sidewalk, people who didn't know what was going on but who needed the exercise, joined in. "Why are we running?" they asked.

"We're chasing a guy," others answered.

"Why?"

"To hang him."

"Oh, boy!" None of the join-in-ers asked why the mob wanted to hang a guy. And why would they? If the reason turned out to be something they disagreed with, it would spoil the fun. So they worked themselves up into an unthinking frenzy.

Mr. Schurk could see the mob was growing, and he was getting more and more scared. He ran as fast as he could. He climbed fences, but the mob could climb fences, too. In fact, it was easier for them because they had more arms and legs.

Mr. Schurk came to the Elmo Lincoln Memorial River. He started to run to the bridge, but decided not to. He swam across, hoping the mob wouldn't notice the bridge or be able to swim. Most of them noticed the bridge. The ones who didn't knew how to swim. (This was, incidentally, the bridge Hrobigothr lived under. But he was at the movies. If he had been home, he would have grabbed Mr. Schurk, as well as a whole bunch of the people chasing him, and eaten them.)

He went into a Hamburger Sty restaurant, hoping

the mob would be a bunch of gourmets who would never go into such a place.

But they had all been raised on Hamburger Sty. They went in and were more welcome than Mr. Schurk because he was all wet and dripping and was making muddy footprints on the floor. Some of the mob stopped for lunch. All that running was making them hungry.

Mr. Schurk ran out the side door, and by a fantastic coincidence, he found himself on the street where Dexter's dust collection truck was parked. An idea came to him: he could get in it and drive, and that would be a lot faster than running. Why did he zero in on Dexter's truck after running past hundreds of other parked vehicles? It was his favorite color.

So Mr. Schurk got into the truck. He began fooling around with the wires under the dash, trying to hot-wire it. But he didn't know how. He did what would have been a wrong thing in a normal truck, a thing that would have caused the atoms in his body to become anticharged with subneutral quarkons, which in turn would have weakened the pull of gravity on him, which in turn would have caused him spend the rest of his life floating two hundred feet up in the air, drifting around at the mercy of the wind and the birds and the clouds and airplanes. But the wires in this truck were messed up already, so the thing that Mr. Schurk did, the thing that would have been wrong in a normal truck, caused the engine in this one to start right up. Mr. Schurk drove away, careful to observe all traffic laws because he didn't want to get pulled over by a cop.

The mob began flagging down passing motorists. Reluctant but seeing no other choice, Mr. Schurk picked up speed. His pursuers picked up speed. Soon a whole bunch—a cluster, a flock, a bundle—of cars could be seen chasing Mr. Schurk, recklessly tearing through the streets. "Could be seen?" Yes, not only in person by people who were standing on the sidewalk being innocent bystanders, but also on television by people who happened to be watching a well-known cable channel that always interrupted whatever it was showing to cover a car chase.

Mr. Schurk ran some red lights and drove between huge semi trucks that were close together. He knocked over apple carts and narrowly avoided a couple of guys carrying a huge plate glass window.

Mr. Schurk drove past a police car. Two cops were in the car, and they thought something was wrong. Dust collection trucks weren't supposed to drive that fast, not even if they were behind schedule. Not only was it against the law, but it was bad for the dust. It could get bruised if you transported it at high speeds.

The cops fell in between Mr. Schurk and The Mob. One cop called the license number of the truck into the police station.

"That's Dexter Kroger's truck," the people at the police station said. "Get him. He's wanted for murder."

Mr. Schurk almost hit a young mother with her baby in a stroller.

Meanwhile, Dexter Kroger was wandering around the neighborhood. He was looking for something that would help him make sense of this whole mess, something that would clear up all the mysteries of life and his relationship to the world. He was looking for a mysterious stranger to give him advice, or for a sultry, seductive woman to take him home and feed him and explore the heights of ecstasy. But mostly, he was looking for dental floss. He had something stuck between his teeth, and it sure was bothersome.

So Dexter was wandering around in a daze, thinking about stuff and not paying attention. He crossed the street just as Mr. Schurk came barreling through, and POW! Dexter got knocked down and hit his head on a manhole cover. And do you know what? It knocked some sense into his head. He suddenly saw how foolish he had been. Miss Cranberry was innocent! Innocent of everything! How could she have done any of that horrible stuff that he had thought she did? How? She couldn't have, that was how! His unreasonably suspicious mind had concocted all those foul, icky, evil ideas because...well, for no good reason, actually.

Dexter felt great! He was enlightened! He suddenly felt the way you feel when you can't think of a word, and worry about it for days and days, and then you finally think of it. He felt the way you feel when you manage to cook macaroni without any of it sticking to the pot. He felt the way you feel when you finally get through to your cable company on the phone.

And as he was basking in all this good feeling, he looked up and saw the cars of the angry mob bearing down on him, the police car way out in front. Gosh, but it was scary! Try it yourself sometime. You'll be scared, too. Your hair might not stand up on end, but Dexter's did. It looked funny.

The police car was mere inches away when he jumped. Dexter was still quite athletic from having been an all-pro football player in college, so he was able to jump high enough to let it drive under him. He came down in front of the angry mob, but he didn't notice them because he was distracted by a kitten standing in front of a nearby building.

And as another wave of "Miss Cranberry Is Innocent" exhilaration washed over Dexter, the cars driven by the angry mob clobbered him and knocked the sense back out of his head. He wandered over to the sidewalk and immediately realized what he had to do. Or, that is to say, he realized what he *thought* he had to do. What he *really* had to do was go to the emergency room and get X-rays of his head taken. What he *thought* he had to do was follow Miss Cranberry. He had to keep an eye on her. He had to watch her, and it wouldn't be too bad, either, because she was nice to look at.

She would be teaching children right now, so he went toward the school building. He would wait across the street and then follow her when she got off work.

***

In the teachers' lounge, Miss Cranberry was taking a break. She tried to call Dexter again but couldn't get through. His phone had been damaged when he got clobbered by the cars. She sat next to the window, gazing at the very spot under a tree where Dexter would show up five minutes later to wait for her. She got up and went back to her classroom.

***

Back at the chase, the police had called in more units, and they set up roadblocks. Mr. Schurk, speeding through the commercial district, saw a line of police cars across the road up ahead. Trying to drive around them, he crashed into Annette's Caulk Boutique.

The police cars that were chasing him screeched to a stop, and cops came running at Mr. Schurk from all directions, guns out. "Dexter Kroger, you're under arrest," they said. "You have the right to a haircut at the state's expense. You have the right to use any of the vending machines at the jail. If you give up these rights, the judge may ridicule you at your trial."

All Mr. Schurk could think was, who's Dexter Kroger?

15. Hung Out to Dry

The Neuralgia Sisters were home, practicing looking
mean. Nancy would scowl at Norma and say, "Take
this!" and growl, and then Norma would scowl back and
say, "Take *this*!" and growl louder. They were trying to
frighten each other, but it didn't work because each one
was too busy trying to look scary to pay attention to the
other. The neighbors felt uneasy, though.

The phone rang. "Answer the phone," Norma said.

"No, you answer it," Nancy said.

The phone kept ringing. The Neuralgia Sisters
didn't normally bicker, but they were caught up in
practicing meanness.

"Well, *somebody'd* better get it," Norma said.

A neighbor, thoroughly frightened, came in and answered the phone. His hand was shaking so much the
wires in the receiver started coming loose.

The neighbor listened to the caller. The sound was
full of static because of the loose wires, but he could
still understand. "It's somebody named Mr. Schurk,"
he told the sisters. "He's been arrested. The police
think he's some guy named Dexter Kroger, and this
Kroger guy's wanted for murder. So Mr. Schurk needs
somebody to go down to the police station and identify

him so they'll let him go."

"Tell him we'll be there later on," Norma said. "After we finish practicing."

The neighbor told Mr. Schurk the sisters would be down there later, hung up, and left. He was so scared that he ran out of the house the same way Cato had run out of the hair salon, except the neighbor didn't leave a trail of blood. He was pretty sure he didn't, anyway.

After a few minutes, Nancy had an idea. "Why should we go down there and tell the police he's not the guy they want?"

"Yeah! We could let him get convicted of murder..."

"And then take over the business!"

The Neuralgia Sisters were pleased with themselves. They gave each other a high-five, giggled like little girls, and went back to practicing meanness.

After a few more minutes, Norma had another idea. "You know," she said, "we could go down there and tell them he's Dexter Kroger."

Nancy was ecstatic. Or at least sort of happy. "Yeah. That would *really* fry his bun!"

They went outside, knocked a couple of kids off their bicycles, and pedaled down to the police station.

"Hi," Nancy said to the desk sergeant. "We're the Neuralgia Sisters. We got a phone call from somebody who said he was our boss. He said you thought he was Dexter Kroger."

"Oh, yeah," the sergeant said. "Henderson, bring the Kroger guy out here."

"We know Dexter Kroger, too," Norma said. "So we can identify the man you arrested, no matter who he is."

"It's impressive, sergeant, the way your shirt accentuates your muscles," Nancy said. She figured it might be good to have friends on the police force.

"Well, gosh." The sergeant blushed. "Thank you. I'm a pretty good cook, too. Would you like me to cook dinner for you?"

"I'm on a diet," Nancy said. She didn't want him to be *that* friendly.

Henderson came back with Mr. Schurk. "Norma! Nancy! Thank God you're here! Oh, what an awful place this is! Oh, what awful people they had me locked up with! You wouldn't believe what those hardened criminals wanted to do to me! Can a raccoon fit in—"

"Dexter, we're disappointed in you," Nancy said.

Mr. Schurk's face went all white.

"I knew you'd come to this," Norma said, "*Dexter*."

His jaw dropped so far that he could have licked his own belly button.

"Officer, this man is Dexter Kroger," Nancy said.

"Yes, he is," Norma said.

"Norma! Nancy! What are you doing to me?" Mr. Schurk pleaded. "Don't tell him that!"

"Yes, officer," Norma said. "We knew this would eventually happen. The guy was raised in a swamp by wolves. It was inevitable."

Mr. Schurk was speechless with astonishment. He didn't say anything. He tried to figure out how Norma and Nancy knew he'd been raised in a swamp by wolves. They didn't, really. They were making stuff up. That it happened to be true was a coincidence—the only coincidence in this whole story.

"You could say he was a victim of his upbringing," Nancy said. "But he still can't be allowed to run free."

"Yes," Norma said. "He should be locked up for the rest of his life."

The sergeant was still beaming inside from Nancy's compliment. "Well, thank you, ladies," he said. "You have helped bring a desperate criminal to justice."

Mr. Schurk looked at the Neuralgia Sisters as if he wanted to sew them together by their elbows and use them as a garden rake. (What kind of look would that be? you may ask. Sorry, but I can't describe it any better.)

"Don't be like that, Dexter," Norma said.

"Yes," Nancy said. "You made your bed, now lie in it."

Then Mr. Schurk started looking as if he wished he could become a stick of margarine and be melted over a bag of popcorn, and then be spilled by a four-year-old kid on the floor of a movie theater and get walked on by everybody. That was what he looked like, but actually, he just wished he had some dental floss. He had something stuck between his teeth, and it sure was bothersome.

Norma and Nancy—that is, Norma and Nancy Neuralgia—were happy with themselves. "Let's go to our new office," Norma said.

"Yes, let's do."

At the Intolerance building, Billy-Bob was still standing around out front. He didn't have anything better to do. After all, he was Billy-Bob.

And upstairs, at the office that had formerly been the headquarters of Schurk Enterprises, Miss Spikenhammer was still at her desk when the Neuralgia Sisters came in. "Do you have an appointment?" she asked.

"Get lost," Norma said. As the Neuralgia Sisters went into Mr. Schurk's office, Miss Spikenhammer began gathering her things up. "Can I let my boyfriend know where I am?" she asked.

Norma and Nancy ignored her. They were busy looking around. The first thing they did was check out the safe because that was undoubtedly where the good stuff would be.

"Do you know the combination?" Nancy asked.

"No, but I can intimidate it open," Norma said. She glared at the safe with her meanest, most evil look. "Open up," she snarled. The door swung open immediately.

They looked in and saw a briefcase. Norma pulled it out of the safe and laid it on Mr. Schurk's desk. A label on the front read "TO BE USED ONLY IN CASE OF EMERGENCY." The sisters looked at each other, curious. But their curiosity wasn't going to be satisfied by looking at each other.

Nancy opened the briefcase. Inside were four large Seal-O-Matic food storage bags with brown, ooey-gooey-looking stuff in them. The bags had yellow labels that said, "Extra Smarts."

"Extra Smarts?" Nancy said. She smirked, thinking highly of herself. "Heck, we don't need this."

"No, we don't," Norma agreed. "We're real hot shots. We're plenty smart. We could take over the world using one-tenth of the smarts we have." She slammed the briefcase shut, picked it up, and threw it out the window. It broke through with a spectacular crash.

Down below, it landed in front of Billy-Bob in a shower of glass particles. He looked at the briefcase for ten minutes or so and then bent down and opened it. He didn't know what was in the bags because he couldn't read the labels, but the stuff in them looked good. It looked like pudding. He opened a bag, scooped his finger into the goo, and dabbed a bit onto his tongue. Big surprise—this wasn't like any pudding he had ever eaten. It tasted like a sopping wet, stuffed Andrew Jackson doll spiced with nutmeg. We're talking about *stale* nutmeg, but nutmeg nonetheless. Billy-Bob had eaten stuff that tasted worse, though. Lots of stuff. Lots worse.

Then he started feeling all swirly in his head, as if he had vertigo, and his vision went out of focus, and then into real hyper-sharp focus. The swirly feeling went away. He looked around and blinked. He was different.

"Wow," he said. "I think I'm smarter." He looked at the bag. "Extra Smarts," he read. "Yes, if I can read the label, I *am* smarter!" The pudding-type stuff...had made him, like, intelligent!

Well, Billy-Bob could see only one thing to do. He ate the rest of the goo in the bag. He felt more swirly feelings in his head, and his vision did that focus thing again.

"My goodness," he said, "I feel quite intelligent. Further, I believe that it is imperative to stimulate the ubiquitous, incessant, meretricious unctuousness into a state of omnipresent, perdurable, specious ostentatiousness."

Then Billy-Bob started wondering what this goo was made of. He opened another bag and, as before, got a sample on his fingertip for a taste. But this time he knew what he was tasting. "I would say it's roughly five parts obliquity, one part sodium cogitate, one part esemplastic, and seven parts tedium." It was a good formula, Billy-Bob thought in big words, bigger words than I could ever hope—or want—to use, but it was merely a good formula for *temporary* smarts. It might last an hour or so, depending on a variety of factors including the day's humidity. That was why Mr. Schurk had labeled the briefcase for emergency use only. He had a limited supply—sodium cogitate was fabulously rare. It could be obtained only from one single plant that grew far inside the depths of a cave whose entrance was at the top of a high mountain in Siberia (guarded, as legend has it, by an ill-tempered troll), and it had to be harvested at exactly noon on leap day by a fair-haired maiden on her thirteenth birthday after she had been fasting for five days.

But Billy-Bob, with his newfound smarts, knew how to make it permanent. All he had to do was add mustard.

Now, you'll be wondering why Mr. Schurk hadn't added mustard himself. Billy-Bob, now smarter than either you or I, understood that the way the formula worked, the dumber you are before eating this stuff, the smarter you end up after.

So Mr. Schurk, being a pretty bright guy to begin with, would have gotten only a little bit smarter, certainly not smart enough to figure out the mustard thing. And then Billy-Bob thought, I like the sound of that. I might put a rock and roll band together so I can call it The Mustard Thing. (Author's note to self: Remember to do this if Billy-Bob doesn't.)

On the other hand, a person who starts out astonishingly dumb, a person like Billy-Bob, would end up astonishingly intelligent. Yes, now Billy-Bob was probably the smartest person in the whole city. And he could make it permanent if he could find some mustard. But he had to do it quickly. If the smarts he had eaten wore off first, he wouldn't remember to add mustard to the remaining bags. So it would have to be his first order of business as a newly minted genius.

He, Billy-Bob, walked a few steps down the street and saw a pretty girl. "You have a pulchritudinous countenance, miss." She got wide-eyed and ran away. Oh, well. On to Hamburger Sty. They'd give him some packets of mustard.

***

Meanwhile, the Neuralgia Sisters were looking through Mr. Schurk's desk. His daily things-to-do calendar had stuff like "Sell drugs to children," "Kick a puppy," and "Egg cars" written on it.

They looked through the file cabinet. It had folders labeled "Underhanded Doings," "Nasty Business," "Dirty Deeds Done Daggone Expensively," etc. In the bottom drawer, in the back, the sisters found a file titled "Plans for World Domination." Norma picked it up. "Hey, Nancy," she said. "This looks interesting."

They opened the file. It had lots of charts and diagrams and calculations. It had lots of doodling in the margins. The doodling was stuff like awful things happening to police officers. It didn't have anything to do with the plans. But the plans were to extort sixty-four pavillion handfuls of money and the title of "Head Guy in Charge of Everything, and I Do Mean Everything" from the UN. Mr. Schurk was going to do this by threatening to extinguish the sun. He was going to get a heavy-duty water pump and put it on top of the highest mountain he could find near the equator, so that he would be as close as possible to the sun, and run a special heavy-duty steel-belted radial hose down to the ocean as a water supply.

"A short, ten-minute squirt will make the sun flicker, thus convincing them I can actually do it," he wrote in the notes. "A good, heavy, forty-five minute gush will certainly put it out completely, but only if I absolutely have to. Under no circumstances should I put out the sun just for fun. Not even to impress a woman."

"Hey," Nancy said. "We could do this."

Norma considered the idea. "We could, couldn't we?"

***

Dr. Ganglia had sent Cato home from the hospital—not because Cato was getting better (even though he was), but because he, Dr. Ganglia, was jealous. He was convinced that Cato was trying to get Nurse Helen interested in doing naked things with him. And he was right, of course. Cato had indeed been trying to do that very thing. It was going to be a long, long time before he would be able to actually *do* naked things with a woman again, but even laid up in the hospital, he was operating. It was a reflex.

Now Cato was propped up in bed, and Miss Fluorine was feeding him some kind of squashed food because he couldn't chew very well. She had finished massaging his nose a few minutes earlier. A nose massage isn't all that great, but the rest of Cato, except for his mouth and eyes and a couple other necessary places, was covered by a cast. And Miss Fluorine wanted to give Cato a massage. Why couldn't she have given him a massage on one of the other necessary places not covered by the cast? It was much too sore. It was the sorest part of him.

Anyway, Miss Fluorine was feeding Cato, and they were making goo-goo eyes at each other. The mailman stuck his head in through the window. "Here's some mail for you, Cato," the mailman said.

Miss Fluorine reached for the envelope. The mailman snatched it away. "It's addressed to Cato," he said.

"It's all right," Cato said.

Miss Fluorine took the envelope and opened it. "It's a get well card," she said.

"Oh, yeah? Who's it from?"

She opened it. "It's from your mother. She says she found a tenth of a handful of money in that old piano bench your Uncle Fudd left her. She spent it on the card."

Cato didn't want to think about it. He sniffed, and then he looked up at her. "Miss Fluorine, I've been thinking."

"Yes?"

"I've been…well, I've had a lot of girlfriends. I was having a pretty good time, but lately, lying here with every bone in my body broken in at least one place has given me time to think. That is, during the times when I *can* think, when the pain's not too bad and I'm not all doped up with drugs, which isn't often.

"But I've been thinking a little bit, and I realize I'm lucky to be alive."

"We're *all* lucky to be alive, Cato. We have birds and trees and sunshine and butterflies to show us how beautiful the world is, and cute little boys like Goliath to give us hope for the future, and cell phones with built-in calculators so we can figure out the best bargains at the supermarket..."

"Miss Fluorine, what I'm trying to say is that I was lucky to survive that night with the Neuralgia Sisters. I can't go on like that anymore. I'm ready to settle down. Miss Fluorine, will you marry me?"

Talking about other women you've played with isn't the best way to frame a marriage proposal, but Cato didn't have a clear idea of real romance. Nonetheless, Miss Fluorine could tell he was sincere. And she was convinced that under all that shallowness was true marriage material, a man who could appreciate her for the woman she was, a man she could live with in a big house with seven bathrooms and a tennis court in the closet. A man she could raise a family with, maybe a little boy like Goliath or a girl like Eunice Mae. Or both. It would be quite the picture of domesticity to look at their bright, shining faces across the supper table. And, of course, it didn't hurt that Cato was cute.

"Cato," she said, "I would love to marry you." And then she leaned over and kissed him.

"Ouch," Cato said. His lips were sore, but he didn't mind the kiss.

The mailman, inspired by this display of young love, walked away whistling a bright, happy tune.

16. Water Pump

The Neuralgia Sisters went shopping for a water pump. First, they went to the five-and-dime (although they weren't quite clear on what a "dime" was). "Do you have water pumps?" Norma asked the clerk.

"No."

"Well, get some." The Neuralgia Sisters turned and walked out. The clerk went to the store manager and told him to order some water pumps. The manager didn't know that Norma and Nancy had been there, but the clerk was scared enough for both of them. The manager called some distributors and found one who had water pumps. He ordered a half-dozen, and they sat in the back corner of the store until it went out of business thirty-three years later.

Then—"then" being after Norma and Nancy left the five-and-dime, not thirty-three years later—the Neuralgia Sisters walked into the pawnshop where Billy-Bob had gone shopping earlier.

Irving the pawnshop guy showed them Trudy's imagination in the Paradine case, but since it wasn't a water pump, and since they figured they had all the imagination anyone could ever hope to need and then some, they weren't going for it.

Then he showed them the Ganglias' heart-lung machine. Under different circumstances the sisters could have been convinced that it was a water pump, but unfortunately for Irving, he had already impressed them as a con artist. They weren't going to believe him.

The Neuralgia Sisters wandered around downtown some more and ran across a shop called Just Water Pumps. They went in, and it was a nice, cozy place, with little round tables in the back corner where you could sit with your friends and sip tea and gossip, or maybe sit all by yourself with your laptop computer and work on your screenplay. "We're looking for a water pump," they told the salesman.

"Well, you came to the right place," the salesman said. "Exactly what features are you looking for?"

"Power. Raw power and lots of it," Norma said. "Gimme danger. We want a water pump that, if it were a golfer, could drive a ball through an anvil at five hundred yards. We want a water pump that could put out a fire ninety-three million miles away."

"Not that we have plans to do anything like that," Nancy hastened to add.

"I have exactly what you need." The salesman was smiling. "Right over here. It's the Goliath Super XR-5000." Of course, it was just a coincidence that the pump was named Goliath. The pump people named it after the Goliath in the Bible, not our Goliath. If they were going to name a water pump after our Goliath, it would be a small, cute, bright one with a big smile. But this was a huge pump, taller than any of them, and wider than a hippopotamus. And we're talking about a fat hippopotamus. It was massive. The Neuralgia Sisters were impressed.

"And it's funny you should mention anvils," the salesman continued. "This baby'll knock a hole in an anvil from a thousand yards away. The water pressure can kill a man at a distance of six miles. And we're talking about a big, strong, healthy man, not just a little, sickly, fragile guy. They found that out by accident, of course, not by testing. Actually, the lethal range is probably much farther."

"How much is it?" Norma asked.

"A hundred and twenty-five handfuls of money."

Well, that was just plain too much. Norma gave the guy a dirty look, and the stripes fell off his suit. He started to give them the pump for free, but they turned around and walked out. Remember, they wanted to do everything on the up-and-up in case there was an investigation.

Driving home, they spotted the air compressor on Goliath's porch. "There! There's a water pump we can get for free!" Nancy said. "We can grab it real quick, and the people who live there will never know what happened."

"Are you sure that's what it is?"

"It looks like the water pumps in that store, doesn't it?"

"Uh, well, I guess it sorta does, in a way, maybe, if you were looking at it in dim lighting and had no eye for detail."

"Then that must be what it is."

Norma stopped the car, and they went up to the porch. "I'll get this end, and you get the other, okay?"

"Yeah. Count of three. One, two, three, LIFT!" The air compressor didn't budge.

"We're going to need help," Nancy said.

They drove to Hamburger Sty to have lunch and think about stuff. They needed just the right person to help because the helper had to be big and strong, and not only that but dumb because he would have to go along with whatever they told him without question. He'd have to be gullible.

And what do you know! Just the right person was there in the restaurant. A big, goofy-looking kid, and he had—oh my gosh!—Mr. Schurk's briefcase, the one they had thrown out the window, but what was he doing? Eating an Atomic Burger and squirting packets of mustard into the bags of Extra Smarts. Geez, what a dumb kid! All those smarts right there in front of him, and he was ruining them with mustard. On purpose! Jeepers creepers! Yeah, he *must* be dumb.

Norma and Nancy went over to him. "Hey, kid," Norma said.

Billy-Bob looked up. "Hi," he said. "Har har." He was acting dumb because he was getting evil vibrations from these women, evil vibrations he would never have noticed before. He knew something bad was going on, and he figured that if he acted dumb, they might let their guard down and he could find out what they were up to. "Har har," he said, hoping he sounded convincingly dumb.

"You want to make some spending money?" Nancy said.

"Uh…sure, har har. I mean, how much?"

"How about a tenth of a handful of money?"

"Is that very much?"

"Okay, kid, you drive a hard bargain. We'll give you a hundredth of a handful. But no more."

"Gosh, har har. A hundred is bigger than ten. I'll

be rich." If he wasn't sure that he was outwitting these women, he would be losing all his self-respect with this act.

"Now here's what we want you to do. We have something we want to move, but it's too heavy for us. We need a big, strong guy like you to move it for us. Understand?"

"Sure. I'm too heavy for you to move, but..." and he started looking confused. He hoped he wasn't overdoing it.

"No, no, you stupid kid," Nancy said, and Norma gave her a dirty look. "I mean, kid. We have a thing that we want you to move for us. Okay?"

"Okay. You want me to move you. Where to?"

"No," Norma said. "We want you to move a thing."

Billy-Bob decided to catch on here because he didn't want this part of the story to drag on and get boring, even though he was starting to have fun. "Oh, you want me to move a *thing*," he said.

The Neuralgia Sisters were happy. They'd gotten through to him.

"Sure. I'll do it." He stood up and grabbed the briefcase. Norma snatched it from him. She didn't believe for a millisecond of an instant that it would be dangerous to let him have it—no, not at all. He had ruined the Extra Smarts (she thought), and besides that, she and Nancy could outsmart anyone at any time, anywhere and anyhow in any way, no matter what. The thing was, Norma was convinced that Billy-Bob would make a mess in her car if he brought those bags of goo along. They looked all icky and sticky, and he would undoubtedly want to play with them. She had no clue what, if anything, would clean that stuff out of her upholstery.

"Why don't you leave that here," she said.

"But...but it's pretty," he said.

"It'll be here when you get back."

Billy-Bob considered. He had eaten a bag of the new, upgraded, mustard-enhanced Extra Smarts, so he was already as smart as he was going to get and he was going to stay that way. He could sacrifice the rest of the bags, if he had to, in order to...what did he expect to do? Get mixed up with these women so he could... what? Foil their plot to take over the world? Uh, yeah, sure. Some pretty far-fetched stuff had happened already, but *that* was *too* far out there. But still, something told him he had better stick with them.

And maybe it would be good not to have any more Extra Smarts with him. These women might decide to eat them, and *that* would lead to greater trouble. Yeah, best to leave them behind. "Promise?" he said.

"Cross my heart," Norma said. "It'll be right here when you get back."

They got into Norma and Nancy's car and drove to Goliath's house. When Billy-Bob saw where they were stopping, he knew for sure they were up to no good.

Nancy pointed toward Goliath's house. "See that big grey thing on the front porch?"

Billy-Bob tried to swallow his surprise. "Yup." He knew now that that thing was an air compressor, and further, that the Neuralgia Sisters had no business being interested in it. His mind raced, considering all the possibilities. But he couldn't figure out an explanation that made sense. So as not to look too thoughtful, he drooled on himself and asked, "What is it?"

"It's just a thing we need. Get it and bring it here."

Well, the best thing to do, at least for the time

being, was to keep playing along. "Okay," he sang, and jumped out of the car and ran up to the porch. He picked up the air compressor and lugged it back to the car. Nancy had the trunk open.

"Put it in here," she said.

Billy-Bob dumped the air compressor into the trunk.

"I think we're going to have a problem," Nancy said. "The trunk lid isn't going to close. It'll stick up and block the view out the rearview mirror."

Norma regarded the trunk lid. "Maybe we should break it off. We can get it fixed easily enough when we're rich and in charge of everything."

Nancy had a different idea, though, a rare instance of showing a capacity for abstract thought. "Let's leave it sticking up," she said. "It's, like, symbolic. This is no time for looking back."

Norma was charmed with the idea. "Yes," she agreed. "We should be looking *forward*."

Nancy nodded. "But now we need to figure out how this daggone water pump works."

***

Goliath was stuck with one piece of charcoal. It had been an almost perfect day; he sold the first ninety-five pounds in a mere hour! But after that, it got really slow. He sold a few more chunks, but now it seemed as if no one wanted any charcoal. Goliath sat on his stool, watching for prospects, waiting for somebody to come along and buy the last piece. "Hey, mister. Wanna buy a piece of charcoal?"

"No, kid. Go away."

"Hey, cat. Wanna buy a piece of charcoal?"

"Meow."

And so it went. He had to get finished soon. He figured on going back to Hrobigothr's place under the bridge to spend the night, but it was all the way across town and it would take a long time to get there. He still wasn't sure whether he would get in trouble with his mom if he stayed up past his bedtime.

In an abandoned building across the street, Miss Cranberry sat watching Goliath through a second-floor window. She had some freeze-dried muskrat ears to munch on and a pair of binoculars to watch with. She was sitting back from the window, with the lights off so Goliath wouldn't notice her. Actually, the lights were off because the building had no electricity, not because Miss Cranberry had turned them off, but she would have turned them off if she could have turned them on. It was a good thing her pupils weren't there because their bright faces would have lit up the room.

Anyway, she was watching over him with a loving eye. And she had noticed that he seemed much better rested in school that day than he had the day before. Maybe things were starting to go better for him.

At the opposite corner of the intersection, in another abandoned building, Dexter Kroger sat at a third-floor window keeping an eye on Miss Cranberry. He had followed her there. His room, too, was dark, mainly because it had no light fixture. But that suited Dexter just fine.

(Why was Goliath selling charcoal at an intersection surrounded by abandoned buildings? Well, they weren't abandoned when he started working there. But then, one day the mysterious brain disease we talked about earlier struck all the people who worked in those buildings, and you can guess the rest. Goliath was safe, though. He was wearing a hat that day.)

Dexter had a camera and a pack of cigarettes. The camera was to take pictures to use as evidence in case Miss Cranberry did something she shouldn't. The cigarettes were for atmosphere. Dexter didn't smoke, but it kind of seemed necessary under the circumstances to have the pack lying out on the table next to him.

Down on the street, Goliath sighed. He looked up as a car drove by, and he saw Billy-Bob in the backseat—and, of all things, Othello's tongue depressor sticking out of the trunk! Gosh, that was strange. Something must be going on that he should know about.

Goliath jumped off his stool and started jumping up and down, waving. "HEY! HEY!" he shouted. Then he added, "HEY!"

Up ahead, Norma heard the shouting and stopped the car. She leaned out the window, twisted around, and saw Goliath. "There's a kid back there shouting at us, waving a piece of charcoal."

Nancy said, "I bet he's Mr. Antwerp's vendor for this neighborhood."

The Neuralgia Sisters talked. They talked about how if they went back and got the kid, they'd have Mr. Antwerp's last charcoal vendor out of the way. But then they realized they didn't need to worry about piddly little stuff like that, now that they were embarking on their plan for world domination. After all, the whole world was much bigger than the city's charcoal business.

Goliath started running toward them.

Up at her window, Miss Cranberry got interested.

Charcoal vendors didn't normally chase down cars.

After all that talk about charcoal vending, Billy-Bob leaned out of his window and looked. "That's Goliath," Billy-Bob said, and then he decided to add, "Har har."

"You know him?" Nancy asked.

"He lives next door," Billy-Bob said. And now that he was smart, smarter even than the person who came up with the idea of putting five blades on one razor, he was able to think about a whole bunch of different things all at once. He, Billy-Bob, was thinking about what to do with the rest of the Extra Smarts, like whom he could give them to, assuming they were still at Hamburger Sty when he got back to them—if, that is, he was able to get back to Hamburger Sty at all. But he was using only a small part of his brain for that. With another part, he was developing a diet that would make him good-looking. So far, the diet included pretzel tree leaves and french-fried smoke rings. That would give him an attractive chin, but of course he needed more. He would figure it out, though. Another part of his brain was working on a process for synthesizing a good thirty-weight motor oil from the remnants of old people's unrealized dreams. And yet another part of his mighty brain was working on a rebuttal to Whitehead and Russell's *Principia Mathematica*. In addition to having all that churning around in his head, he was carefully analyzing everything that was going on around him so he could thwart the sisters' plans. And he was considering the wiring scheme he had noticed in the air compressor when he was carrying it to the car. Part of the housing was gone, leaving the wiring exposed, and for some reason, it didn't seem quite right.

"He lives in the house where we got that big, heavy thing," Billy-Bob said. He had an idea that it would be good if he could get the Neuralgia Sisters to take Goliath along, too, because he, Billy-Bob, might need help. It might endanger little Goliath to be involved in this, but then again, Billy Bob was starting to believe there might be a terrible, terrible danger regardless.

"Then he would know how to work it, wouldn't he?" Nancy said.

They were falling for it! "Yup, sure would, har har."

Goliath came up to the car.

"What do you want, kid?" Nancy asked.

"Uh..." Goliath didn't know what to say. He didn't know how to accuse these women of stealing his sister's tongue depressor. "Uh, do you want to buy a chunk of charcoal?"

"Why would we want to buy a chunk of charcoal?"

"Gosh, ma'am. I need to sell this last piece so I can quit work tonight and go find the bridge where the troll lives. My mom kicked me out of the house."

This caught Billy-Bob by surprise. He felt bad for Goliath, but then again, it might be good for his, Billy-Bob's, plan.

"You're staying under a bridge?" Norma asked.

"Yes, ma'am. With a troll."

"We have a better place for you to stay," Nancy said.

"Yeah, come on in the car," Norma said.

"Gosh, I don't know. My mom told me not to go with strangers." And she had. One day about a year before, Othello had told him, "Don't go with strangers. You'll get in trouble." Well, these women, although they seemed nice enough, were strangers. On the other hand, since his mother had kicked him out of the house, maybe he didn't have to do what she said any-more. It was a tricky question, and he still wasn't sure about the bedtime thing.

"But Billy-Bob's here. He's not a stranger. He's your friend," Nancy said.

"Yeah, Goliath. That's right, har har."

"I don't think Billy-Bob likes me," Goliath said.

"Sure I do, Goliath," Billy-Bob said. "We're good pals, har har."

Well, there it was. He wasn't sure whether he could trust these women because they had stolen Othello's tongue depressor, but then again, this could be a differ-ent one. And if Billy-Bob liked him now, fine. He proba-bly didn't remember the commotion on the front porch or their scuffle at the shopping mall. After all, Goliath had noticed that Billy-Bob didn't seem to be too bright. But he was mostly harmless, at least when he wasn't punching someone in the knee. Goliath got into the car.

***

Mr. Sigmoid had decided it was time for a raise. After all, he had been working as a vendor for Schurk Enter-prises, a job far below his abilities—below his dignity—for almost a week, and he'd already sold a whole half pound of charcoal. Okay, so it wasn't much, but that only showed how far beneath him this job was, how he really belonged in a job—no, not merely a job, but rather a position, a *career*—with greater responsibility and authority. Mr. Sigmoid selling charcoal? Ha! That was like expecting the president of the United States to wash the dishes at the White House. Okay, yeah, right, he would do it—Mr. Sigmoid would sell charcoal, that is—for a little while longer if it was necessary. However, it was beyond question that he needed more money.

So Mr. Sigmoid left his corner in the middle of his shift and walked to the Intolerance Building. He took the elevator up to the thirteenth floor, and there was Miss Spikenhammer reading *Spider Flambé*. She had tried to get lost when the Neuralgia Sisters told her to, but she wasn't very good at it. So here she was, back in the office again even though, unknown to her, her boss was, like, in jail and out of action, so there was no point to her being there.

"Hello, Miss Spikenhammer," Mr. Sigmoid said. "How's everything?"

She didn't know how to answer that; she had no clue how most things were. So she said, "Say, I thought you were in your office. All those people came in to see you. What happened to everyone?"

The first time she had thought he was Mr. Schurk, it caught him unaware. This time, he decided to have some fun with it.

"That was my twin brother, Mr. Sigmoid," he said. "We look just alike."

"Oh."

"Miss Spikenhammer, could you do me a favor?"

"Why certainly, Mr. Schurk."

Mr. Sigmoid giggled to himself. Gosh, but this was fun! "Could you run down to the hardware store and pick up some light bulb fluid for me? The bulb in my desk lamp is low."

"Yes, sir." Miss Spikenhammer got up and left.

Mr. Sigmoid hadn't expected her to fall for it. He had noticed, when he was there earlier for the job interview, that Mr. Schurk had a whole daggone *case* of the stuff in his office. He watched the door swing shut behind her, and then he giggled out loud.

After he got finished giggling, Mr. Sigmoid knocked on the door to Mr. Schurk's office. No answer. He opened the door and peeked in. Nobody there. Well, he could wait. He went into Mr. Schurk's office and looked around. The bookcase was pulled out from the wall, revealing an opening to a sliding board that went down. Jeepers, *that* looked like fun. He would have to try it sometime, but right now, he had to sit tight and wait.

Mr. Sigmoid sat at the desk. Nice. Actually, the whole office was great. There was a bar in one corner, an exercise bicycle in another corner, a stack of *Modern Bad Guy* magazines in another, a three-bedroom apartment in another, and a dead roach in the last corner. Well, maybe the dead roach wasn't all that great. But the rest of it was. And to top it all off, in the pulled-out bookcase, there was a TV set. Yeah, the perfect way to pass the time while he was waiting.

Mr. Sigmoid got up and turned it on. A news anchor was talking. "This afternoon, police arrested that slimy dog Dexter Kroger on suspicion of the murder of young, innocent, helpless George Baklava, whose demise was a great loss to our community. Kroger was apprehended following a wild car chase that went all the way across the city. In fact, you probably saw it in person, so I'm not really sure why we're bothering to put it on the news."

They showed a film clip of Mr. Schurk, in handcuffs, being taken into the police station.

Gosh, Mr. Sigmoid thought. That's me! No, wait. That's not me; I'm here. So that must be Mr. Schurk. What do you know about that? But if that's Mr. Schurk on TV there, being arrested, then what about Dexter Kroger?

Mr. Sigmoid knew Dexter Kroger. They went to a lot of the same parties, and Mr. Sigmoid knew Dexter well enough to know that he wasn't Mr. Schurk. But why would the police think Mr. Schurk was Dexter?

The news anchor was continuing. "Kroger, a collection truck driver for the Midwest Stagnant Air Company, was identified as Baklava's murderer by the Old Codger who lives in the house next to the vacant lot where Baklava and his friend Cato Kierkegaard were found."

It still didn't make sense to Mr. Sigmoid.

"If this still doesn't make sense," the anchor said, "it might help if I mentioned that Kroger was located by police officers who saw him drive by in his collection truck, chased by an angry mob. The officers were able to identify him as Dexter Kroger by the license plate number on the truck. After his arrest, Kroger claimed to be Mr. Schurk, president of Schurk Enterprises. However, when police called the Neuralgia Sisters, upstanding, civic-minded citizens who are two of Mr. Schurk's best employees, they identified the man not as Mr. Schurk, but as Dexter Kroger. Serves you right, Dexter."

Ah, Mr. Sigmoid thought. That explains it all.

"I think that should explain it all," the news anchor said. "In other news, police are trying to catch a thief in the rich people's neighborhood..."

Of course! For some reason—never mind why—Mr. Schurk was being chased by an angry mob. And for some other reason—again, never mind why—he was driving Dexter Kroger's truck, which led the police to believe he was Dexter, who, for some reason—never mind why—was wanted for murder. And the Neuralgia Sisters, who could have gotten him off the hook by identifying him as Mr. Schurk, turned out not to be such loyal employees after all. They left him hanging out to dry. And if they told the police he was Dexter Kroger, he would most likely be convicted.

So what?

Well, suppose you have a businessman who's in jail, Mr. Sigmoid was thinking, and no one knows he's in jail because they arrested the wrong man in a case of mistaken identity. And further, suppose he's probably not going to be able to clear up the misidentification because a couple of people who are deemed trustworthy have (for whatever reason) maliciously confirmed that he is this other person.

And suppose there's another guy who's a dead ringer for this businessman.

Okay, so, suppose all that, and then suppose the dead ringer were to wander innocently into the businessman's office, as he himself had just done, sit in his chair, and...well, allow everyone to believe he, the dead ringer, was actually the businessman. The dead ringer could take over his identity.

Would the guy, the dead ringer, have any chance of getting away with it? Well, what if the dead ringer himself had been fired from his previous job in disgrace and cast out into the world to fend for himself? No one would question what had become of him, would they?

Mr. Sigmoid began going through the desk drawers.

17. Interesting Travel

Oh, gosh, Miss Cranberry thought when she saw Goliath get into the Neuralgia Sisters' car, I'd better follow along. That Billy-Bob kid was in the car, and the last time she'd seen him, he was causing trouble for Goliath, punching that sweet little boy in the knee and everything. She ran down the stairs and outside.

Oh, gosh, Dexter thought. I'd better follow along. That Billy-Bob kid was in the car, and the last time Dexter had seen him, the kid had to pee really bad. Then Dexter saw Miss Cranberry, of all people, run out of another building and into the street. He stopped thinking about Billy-Bob having to pee, which he didn't really want to think about anyway, and ran downstairs to follow her.

The Neuralgia Sisters drove through town, and Miss Cranberry ran along behind them. She was able to keep up because she was wholesome, and physical fitness and good health are part of wholesomeness. Dexter ran along behind her, and he was able to keep up, too, because he had been an all-pro athlete in college. The Neuralgia Sisters didn't see them with the trunk lid blocking their view through the rear window. If they had broken it off, as Norma had wanted, they would have been able to see both Miss Cranberry and Dexter following. They would have become suspicious and taken evasive action.

Ah, "would have." As fun as it is to talk about, it doesn't really matter.

They came to Don Quixote International Airport. Norma and Nancy and Goliath and Billy-Bob got out of the car. Billy-Bob took the air compressor out of the trunk, and they went into the terminal, their merry little band. Miss Cranberry snuck in and hid behind a post. Dexter snuck in and hid behind another post. Both of them wondered what was up with that thing that looked like an air compressor. It seemed like a strange thing to carry into an airport, and Billy-Bob seemed like a strange person to be carrying it.

And outside, near the runway of the plane Goliath and his little group were going to take, off to one side, a guy was hiding behind a dumpster with a vial of Stur-D-Glu in his devious little hand. His name was Fritz, and he had been studying the take-off routine of the airline for weeks. His studying had shown him that as soon as the baggage guys loaded all the baggage on and went away, there would be a seven-minute period when the plane would be sitting still with no one watching. If he were to run up to the plane during that time, the only people who might see him would be passengers looking out the window, but—heh, heh—they'd think he belonged there.

Fritz was going to get up under the plane with his vial of Stur-D-Glu and glue the tires to the runway, thus preventing it, the plane, from taking off.

Why? Because it would be hilarious. Fritz giggled to himself like a little girl as he watched the baggage guys loading suitcases.

Inside, Norma and Nancy went to the ticket counter. "We want four tickets," Norma said.

"*Airplane* tickets," Nancy added. This was important; she didn't want to leave any chance for a misunderstanding.

"To the equator," Norma said.

The woman at the ticket counter gave them four tickets. It was nice, the airline lady thought, this family outing to the equator. "That'll be eighty handfuls of money," she said.

"We're not going down there to commit the biggest crime in history," Norma said.

"That's right," Nancy said. "We're not going to use this water pump in a fiendishly clever plot to extort sixty-four pavillion handfuls of money from the UN."

"It never entered our mind," Norma said.

No, they didn't want anyone to be suspicious.

And Dexter, behind his post, commenced wondering about stuff again. He wondered why Miss Cranberry, if she was really a bad guy, was following these people who had Goliath. Did that, then, mean that these twin sisters, whoever they were, were good guys? Probably so, or she wouldn't be hiding from them. But then how did Billy-Bob, who was indisputably a bad guy, fit in? Had they captured him? Was he being brought to justice? Was he a spy? Maybe he wasn't as dumb as he looked.

Actually, he couldn't be. And it looked as if he was being friendly toward Goliath.

Hmmmm...This was going to require more study.

Outside, Fritz watched the baggage guys wrestle a large statue of a pair of tweezers onto the plane. He held his vial of Stur-D-Glu in one hand and stroked it lovingly with the other.

Norma and Nancy finished buying their tickets and went to the departure gate. Miss Cranberry frowned and stroked her chin so that anyone who saw her would know she was thinking. She was trying to figure out how to continue following Goliath, little Goliath. It was out of the question to get on the plane with them. Those two women wouldn't know who she was, but Goliath... as soon as he saw her, he would say something, and then the situation would get hairy. She, Miss Cranberry, couldn't have that.

"Collision Airlines flight number thirty-four to the Equator now boarding," a woman said over the PA.

The Neuralgia Sisters and Billy-Bob and Goliath got in line. Billy-Bob was carrying the air compressor. The Neuralgia Sisters and Goliath weren't carrying anything.

The baggage guys finished loading. Fritz watched them drive their baggage truck back toward the terminal. As soon as they were out of sight, he would be ready to make his move.

Miss Cranberry, still behind her post, began thinking more rapidly. Holy smoke, she thought, I'm going to lose them! And then she had a flash of inspiration, a flash brighter than the faces of the pupils in her class. She ran outside.

Dexter didn't need a flash of inspiration. It was clear that if he didn't follow, he would lose track of her quickly. In fact, immediately.

Miss Cranberry, with Dexter following, ran around the corner of the terminal and toward the plane.

And Fritz, who was about to dash out to his target,

saw a man and a woman run out onto the runway. Holy smoke! He couldn't glue the plane down if they were out there to see him. His mouth dropped open, and then he started grinding his teeth. Curses!

In frustration, Fritz whammed the vial down on the ground. Then, as those two people ran across the runway, he stepped forward to get a better view around the corner of the dumpster. His foot came crunching down on the vial of Stur-D-Glu, which broke open and oozed out a generous amount of glue under his shoe.

The plane started taking off. Miss Cranberry ran along behind it, with Dexter behind her. Fritz watched.

The plane quit being on the ground and took off into the sky. Miss Cranberry kept chasing it, and Dexter kept chasing her. It was strenuous, but as we have seen, Miss Cranberry and Dexter were both physically fit and athletic.

Dejected, Fritz tried to walk away, but he couldn't. He started grinding his teeth even harder. Then he bent down to try to untie his shoe so he could step out of it. Unfortunately, that didn't do him any good. He had a hole in the sole of his shoe, and his foot was glued directly to the ground.

Everybody (except Fritz) went south. It was difficult for Miss Cranberry and Dexter because on the ground, they had to cross streets—some of them busy—and climb fences and run around buildings and such. The airplane didn't have any of those problems. It could fly right over all that stuff.

And inside the plane, the Neuralgia Sisters were talking about how neat it was going to be to rule the world.

"It's going to be neat to rule the world," Nancy said.

"You can say that again," Norma said.

"I don't have to. You heard me the first time, and besides, you already knew it."

"I'm going to buy a flying dog."

"Why?"

"To ride around on."

"No, you need a bigger animal for that, like a flying horse."

"Don't be silly. There's no such thing as a flying horse."

"I'm going to have a house built, a house that covers the whole state of Iowa."

"Is that a state now?"

"I think so. And as soon as we get that cute little kid to show us how the water pump works, we can show the UN we mean business."

"Yes, and the business we mean is mean business."

Goliath, sitting behind them, didn't hear any of this. He was reading, intently, the January issue of the *World Muffin Review,* which he had found in the pocket on the back of Norma's seat. But Billy-Bob, next to Goliath, was listening, and he was glad to hear they thought the machine was a water pump because it gave him an idea. He elbowed Goliath gently to get his attention, took the magazine, and wrote a note in the margin. "Goliath, don't say anything. Just write notes so no one can hear us. I'm smart now," Billy-Bob wrote. He passed the magazine and the pen over to Goliath.

"Gosh, Billy-Bob, that's keen," Goliath wrote. "Congratulations. You have nice penmanship, too. But how come we don't want anyone to hear us talk?"

"Because we don't want the Neuralgia Sisters to hear what we're going to say, and we don't want them to find out I'm smart."

"Oh. Who are the Neuralgia Sisters?"

"The women we're traveling with. They're the Neuralgia Sisters."

"They're nice, aren't they?"

"No, they're not. They're up to no-good, rotten, awful things."

"You mean like crime?"

"Yes, exactly like crime. I don't know what their
plan is, but for some reason it involves getting you to
operate the air compressor for them. They think it's a
water pump."

"What air compressor?"

"The machine we have with us. It's an air compressor."

"So if they're up to no good, I shouldn't operate it for
them."

"You can't. You don't know how it works, remember?"

"Oh, yeah. So, like, then, what's the problem?"

"The problem is that they think you can operate it,
and they'll expect you to. Another problem is that it
can't do what they want it to do. It can't shoot water."

"They're dumb, aren't they?"

"No, not really. But they're not as smart as they
think. And here's something else: I noticed that someone has tampered with the wiring. The way it's rigged
up now, if they try to turn it on, it'll cause a series of
electrical reactions in the air that'll destroy the planet within a matter of minutes. The whole Earth will
crumble into tiny pieces about the size of toenail clippings. But I have a plan. We need to let them keep
thinking it's really a water pump and you know how to

work it. Okay?"

"Sure. But they'll figure out I can't work it when the time comes to use it and I don't know what to do."

"I have it all figured out." Billy-Bob cracked his knuckles and rolled up his sleeves. He flipped through the magazine and found a new page with blank space. "When we get to our destination and it's time for you to show them how to work the machine, tell them it's broken, but you can fix it—which is true, but you're not going to fix it the way they're expecting. Have them get you a couple of screwdrivers, a small flathead and a Phillips, and a pair of pliers. Then arrange the wires like this."

And then Billy-Bob drew a diagram. It was a good diagram, an excellent diagram. It was a diagram for the ages. After all, Billy-Bob was smart.

"There's a switch on each end of the machine," Billy-Bob continued in writing. "They look just like light switches. Tell the Neuralgia Sisters that the switches have to be flipped at the same time. Exactly the same instant. And make sure they do it themselves."

Goliath looked at the diagram. Gosh, but it was complex. It was also complicated and intricate. And elaborate. And difficult to understand.

"I don't understand it," Goliath wrote.

"All you have to do is memorize what it looks like. When you start looking at the wires, it'll make sense."

Goliath looked doubtfully at Billy-Bob. Billy-Bob smiled and nodded reassuringly. "Trust me," he wrote.

Well, trusting Billy-Bob wasn't the problem. Trusting his own ability to learn the diagram was. "I don't think I can memorize it," Goliath wrote. "Can't we tell them the machine doesn't work, and they'll forget the whole thing?"

"I don't think so. If you tell them that, they'll have to see for themselves. They'll try to turn the machine on, and then, well..."

"Toenail clippings?"

"Exactly. The fate of the whole world depends on us."

Goliath began studying his little fingers to the bone. After a few minutes, he noticed a small arrow coming from the diagram. It pointed to a mathematical formula at the bottom of the page.

"What's this?" Goliath wrote.

"There are several variations on this particular model of air compressor. The only way to tell which one we have is to look at the pressure gauge. That's the round thing with the pointy needle in the middle and numbers around the edge."

"Okay."

"I didn't get a good enough look to determine which variation we have, but it's simple to figure out. Look at the biggest number on the gauge. Different variations of this model have different biggest numbers. Okay, so, then, you see where we have 'X' in this formula, right?"

"Sure."

"All you have to do is plug the number you see on the pressure gauge, the biggest number, into the formula where the 'X' is. Then solve the equation, and that'll tell you the number of terminals you need to move the yellow wire to the right. Understand?"

"Sure. But I don't understand the equation."

"You don't have to. Just memorize it."

Gadzooks!

Arithmetic!

And the fate of the world depended on it, too. This plan was kinda cool, in a way, like sabotage and stuff, with him as the saboteur, but still...it required arithmetic.

"Would you like something to drink?" The stewardess was beside his seat with a cart of drinks. Milk, juice, coffee, etc. Goliath took milk. Billy-Bob took acorn juice.

Goliath went back to studying. Okay, he could learn the formula. But using it would be a song of a different color.

He was scared.

Eventually, they came to the Gulf of Mexico. Down below, without any hesitation, Miss Cranberry ran out into the water and began swimming. So did Dexter. The airplane flew above the water. Fritz kept on standing there at the airport off to one side of the runway, glued to the ground, trying to figure out whether there was some way he could blame his misfortune on his brother.

On they went (except for Fritz), southward.

Billy-Bob watched Goliath study the diagram, trying his best to memorize it. Gosh, the poor little fella was breaking out in a sweat from the exertion. He was trembling. Billy-Bob wished he could have brought his Extra Smarts with him so he could give Goliath some. Since Goliath was already pretty smart, it wouldn't give him much of a boost, but any little bit would help. Well, they would have to hope for the best.

The airplane flew over some more land and finally arrived at Equator International Airport. Billy-Bob took the air compressor from the overhead luggage rack and got off the plane with the Neuralgia Sisters and Goliath. The four of them went out to the front of the terminal and hailed a cab.

Oh, gosh, Miss Cranberry thought. I hope they're not going far. She was tired.

Oh, gosh, Dexter Kroger thought. I hope they're going someplace close. He was tired.

Oh, gosh, Goliath thought. I hope I can remember how to fix that air compressor. He was anxious.

Oh, gosh, Billy-Bob thought. I hope Goliath can remember how to fix that air compressor. He was worried.

Yes, indeed, the Neuralgia Sisters thought. Things are going great. They were smug.

Oh, boy, the cab driver thought. Tourists with an air compressor. I can gouge them for an outrageous fare! He felt greedy.

The cab driver opened the trunk, and Billy-Bob put the air compressor in. Then everybody—everybody except Miss Cranberry and Dexter, that is—got into the cab and drove away. Miss Cranberry and Dexter followed on foot.

They went out into the countryside. Open fields, cows, sheep, deer, turkeys, chickens, horses, dogs, cats, rabbits, goldfish, gerbils, zebras, camels, bears, lost mailmen, unicorns. It was enjoyable for Miss Cranberry and Dexter, running out there in the fresh air, out there where it was healthy. Dexter felt his blood pressure going down. Miss Cranberry felt her lung capacity increasing. Both felt their skin clearing up.

And way out there, way out in the countryside, mountains appeared in the distance, away from the road. Nancy noticed them first. "Hey, there's some mountains," she said.

They drove close to the mountains, and Norma told the driver to stop.

"How much do we owe you?" Nancy asked.

"Six handfuls of money," the driver said.

"SIX?" Nancy shouted. The driver's freckles crawled up inside his skin. He cringed.

"That's perfectly all right," Norma said, handing over seven handfuls of money. "Keep the change." They could afford to be extravagant. After all, they were soon to have sixty-four pavillion handfuls of money.

"Th-thank you," the driver quivered. The Neuralgia Sisters told Billy-Bob to get the air compressor, and they sent the driver on his way.

"That looks like the highest one," Nancy said, pointing. Everybody set out toward the mountain. Eagle-eyed Billy-Bob spotted a cloud that looked like Othello. He took that as a good omen.

Walk walk walk, climb climb climb. By the time they reached the top, it was night. "Okay, you can put the water pump down now," Nancy told Billy-Bob. "We're stopping here."

Goliath looked around. He gazed at the stars for a few moments, feeling small.

"We'll get a good night's sleep," Norma said. "Then in the morning," she looked over at Goliath, "you can show us how to work the water pump."

"Yeah," Nancy said. "It'll be great."

Goliath's eyes got as big around as the Empire State Building. Oh, wait. The Empire State Building isn't round. But it's big, so you get the idea. Billy-Bob, off in the background, made motions at Goliath. He, Billy-Bob, motioned toward the air compressor and then acted out using a screwdriver and a pair of pliers.

He finished it off by pantomiming walking against a strong wind.

"It's, uh, it's broken," Goliath said. "That is, the, uh, water pump. It's broken. But I can fix it. I'll need a couple of screwdrivers and a pair of pliers."

"Oh, for heaven's sake," the Neuralgia Sisters said in unison. Then Nancy said, "You should have told us earlier."

"Well," Norma said, "we have to go to the hardware store in the morning anyway, to get the special steel-belted radial hose. We can pick up the tools while we're there."

"Let's go to bed now," Nancy said.

Goliath looked at his watch. It was past his bedtime. He hoped he wouldn't get in trouble.

And a short distance away, in their separate hiding places in the woods, Miss Cranberry and Dexter Kroger made beds out of twigs and leaves. They were grateful for the chance to get some shut-eye after all that running and swimming and climbing over stuff at top speed.

***

The next morning, back home, Cleopatra and Othello had run out of money. Little Goliath had been gone only two days, and already things were getting bad.

"Aren't you going to cook supper?" Cleopatra asked.

"I can't," Othello said. "We don't have any food. We'll have to go out to eat."

"We can't. We don't have any money."

"Then how are we going to eat?" Othello asked.

"Oh, my gosh!" Cleopatra screamed. "We're going

to starve to death!" She began running around all over the house in a panic. "It's awful! Oh, starvation! Oh, no!"

Othello grabbed Cleopatra and slapped her. "Calm down," Othello said. Cleopatra calmed down. "Thanks, I needed that," she said.

"We can go to Goliath's corner and get some money from him," Othello said.

"Yes, we can, can't we?"

So off they went, off to Goliath's charcoal-selling corner. Both of them needed to go because Othello was the one who could remember where they were going long enough to get there, and Cleopatra was the one who could see. But when they got to the corner, Cleopatra couldn't see Goliath. He was at the equator, and she couldn't see that far. His stool was still there on the sidewalk, but that didn't do them any good. The stool didn't have any money.

"He's not here," Cleopatra said. "We're going to starve!"

"Maybe we can go to Goliath's boss and ask him for some of Goliath's money," Othello said.

Then, as if on cue, a bus with a sign on the front that said, "INTOLERANCE BUILDING" drove up. The driver stopped and opened the door.

"Is this the bus that goes to the office of the charcoal company?" Cleopatra asked.

And since the fabulous Intolerance Building was the home of Schurk Enterprises, the bus driver said, with a great big smile in his voice, "Sure thing, lady."

They stepped into the bus. Not having any money for bus fare, Cleopatra put her hand up to the coin slot and said "Clink!" The bus driver was fooled.

The bus went on, and when they got to the Intolerance Building, the driver turned around to Cleopatra. "Hey lady," he said. "This building here is where the charcoal company is."

In the lobby, Cleopatra looked at the building's directory on the wall. Right in the middle, it said, "Schurk Enterprises—Purveyors of Fine Charcoal and Charcoal Accessories since 1983." Well, Cleopatra didn't know what purveyors were, or what the "accessories" might be, but she knew the word "charcoal."

"Thirteenth floor," she told Othello, and up they went, up in the elevator.

Mr. Sigmoid, of course, was in the office. He was sitting at the desk being in charge, watching *The Martin Hogwash Show* on TV. The guests were some people who lived on a diet of shirt buttons, had gotten crabgrass transplanted to their scalps in place of hair, and believed the world was secretly ruled by the ghost of Charles Dickens. Mr. Sigmoid was disappointed. He wanted Hogwash to have weird guests. But he watched anyway because it was television and that was what you were supposed to do with television.

And right in the middle of the show, who should walk in but the Most Beautiful Woman on Earth? Mr. Sigmoid was amazed. He was spellbound. He was giddy and lightheaded. He was in love. He knew they were soul mates, he and this woman. Their essences would unite and gel—nay, they would coagulate—or maybe congeal—into a nebulous, eternal holocaust of universal emotion and passion...

Mr. Sigmoid ran over to the escape chute, which was still open, and (gagging over all that overly poetic prose) threw up into it. Then he turned to Cleopatra. Yeah, this was one fine-looking' hunk-o-woman.

"What can I do for you?" he asked.

18. Hrobigothr's Lesson

At the equator, Nancy stayed with Goliath and Billy-Bob while Norma went off to get the special steel-belted radial hose, the tools Goliath had asked for, and breakfast. When she came back, they ate some big greasy things from a bag. Hiding in the woods, Miss Cranberry and Dexter ate whatever they could find. Dexter pulled leaves off of nearby trees and stuffed them raw into his mouth. Miss Cranberry prepared a delicious serving of anteater and butterfly leg stew, using a recipe she had learned from the *Outdoors with Marla Stibbert* show.

"Okay, kid," Nancy said. "Fix this bad daddy up and we'll get started."

Bad daddy? What bad daddy? Gosh, Goliath thought. Everything was getting weird. He didn't understand anything, and he didn't like it. He sniffed.

"The water pump. Get the water pump fixed up so we can use it," Norma said.

Okay, the water pump/air compressor. Goliath walked over to the machine and looked at it. Could he fix it? He wasn't sure how well he remembered the diagram. On the other hand, he definitely couldn't do it by standing around not doing anything. At any rate, he had to do something—*something*—or these two women would get mad at him. He didn't want that because, well, because they seemed mean. Besides that, the fate of the whole entire world depended on him.

Goliath looked at the biggest number on the gauge. It was five hundred. Okay, good.

He picked up a screwdriver and unscrewed a couple of wires. No, wait. That wasn't on the diagram. He screwed them back in place. Hold on. The one wire over there, the one twisted around like one of those big, thick pretzels, was on the diagram. No, they were both on the diagram, but he had to change only one, the puce one. He unscrewed it and looked for the new place to fasten it. Gosh, it wasn't there.

And Billy-Bob couldn't help him, either. If he did, the Neurosurgeon Sisters, or whoever they were, would catch on that he was smart, and they would figure out that he had a plan to use against them.

What Billy-Bob didn't know, what no one knew, was that if the Neuralgia Sisters had decided to buy Trudy's imagination at the pawnshop, they would have been able to figure out that Billy-Bob was smart and that the water pump was really an air compressor. Yeah, Trudy's imagination would have enabled them to pick up on all the subtle, telltale signs they had missed, such as the intelligent sparkle in Billy-Bob's eyes (a sparkle he couldn't hide), the fact that little Goliath kept looking nervously toward Billy-Bob and Billy-Bob always nodded reassuringly at him, and the words "air compressor" embossed on the tin plaque riveted to the side of the machine. Yes, they would have noticed all that and figured they had better give up on this attempt, go home, and start over. Then they would have found a real water pump and carried out their plan successfully.

But that didn't happen. What happened was that Billy-Bob watched Goliath carefully. Goliath looked nervous, and this worried Billy-Bob.

Goliath looked for the place to screw in the puce wire. It wasn't there! He sat down on the ground. His pants would get dirty, but he didn't care.

"Are you finished, kid?" Norma asked.

Goliath started crying. "I want to go home," he wailed.

And Miss Cranberry, hiding behind a bush, heard him. Her wholesome heart broke. It was obvious now that Goliath needed to be rescued. She jumped up without thinking and ran from her hiding place.

"I'm here, Goliath!" Miss Cranberry shouted, teardrops dripping from her words. She scooped Goliath up and tried to make away with him.

"Stop!" Nancy and Norma said. It was easy for them to chase Miss Cranberry down; she couldn't run very fast carrying Goliath.

"Let go of us!" Miss Cranberry yelled.

"We need the kid!"

Dexter Kroger, of course, saw all this. Miss Cranberry must be a good guy after all, he realized, since she was trying to rescue Goliath. He still wasn't sure whether she had been a bad guy before, but it didn't matter because she was doing something good now. Or trying to.

And that meant the Neuralgia Sisters were bad guys.

Dexter watched the situation develop, looking for an opening to jump in. The Neuralgia Sisters were subduing Miss Cranberry. Goliath was sitting on the ground crying. Billy-Bob was standing off to one side, looking dumb. He, Billy-Bob, didn't want to jump into the fracas yet because the Neuralgia Sisters might have guns. If things got too much out of control, someone could get shot.

Sure enough, just as Dexter ran forward and tackled Norma Neuralgia—his football training was really paying off—Nancy pulled a gun. "Hold it right there," she said.

Miss Cranberry didn't recognize him for an instant, what with the new 'stache and all. And then she did. "Dexter!" she cried.

"I was…uh, keeping an eye on you," Dexter said. And then, to make sure she didn't get the right idea, he added, "To make sure you were okay."

Goliath kept on crying. Billy-Bob wondered whether anyone else was going to appear.

Norma got up and grabbed some vines. She tied Dexter and Miss Cranberry up, and then Billy-Bob, too, for good measure.

Billy-Bob squirmed around to test the knots. They were solid. Didn't give a smidge. If the Neuralgia Sisters knew how to do one thing well, it was how to tie people up. Yeah, maybe he should have jumped into the fracas a minute ago. Now it was too late.

"I think we have everything under control," Nancy said. "Kid, you better get back to fixing that water pump."

Goliath cried louder.

"I'll shoot your friends if you don't."

Well, he couldn't let Miss Cranberry or Dexter Kroger or Billy-Bob get shot. He would have to be brave, Goliath would. If he could get this machine fixed up the way Billy-Bob had told him, everything would be all right.

He dried off his face on his shirttail, picked up the screwdriver, and went to work, trying his best to be brave, concentrating as hard as he could. Wires here, wires there; he was remembering the diagram.

***

Mr. Sigmoid invited Cleopatra and Othello to lunch. He invited Cleopatra because, of course, she was the love of his life. He invited Othello because...well, because it would be rude to leave her out. But really, she seemed like a nice girl. He would prefer it, though, if she were to find her own boyfriend who could take her to lunch.

They went to Hamburger Sty. And as they walked in, Mr. Sigmoid noticed a briefcase on a table. "Hello, what's this?" he said. He opened the briefcase and saw three large Seal-O-Matic food storage bags with brown, ooey-gooey-looking stuff in them. The bags had yellow labels that said, "Extra Smarts."

"We should try these," he said.

***

At the equator, Dexter whispered to Miss Cranberry, "If we get out of this alive, will you marry me?"

Miss Cranberry was ecstatic, especially since she liked his new mustache. "Oh, yes, Dexter. Yes." She tried to lean over and kiss him, but she couldn't move that far. "Consider yourself kissed," she said, gushing.

Goliath kept working. Soon, all he had left was the yellow wire—with its formula. He began shaking.

Then he stepped back from the machine and began thinking about nothing at all, and then about fermentation. He dropped his screwdriver. It hit the ground with a "plumph" sound, and a tiny cloud of dirt poofed up. He blinked at the Neuralgia Sisters.

"What's wrong, kid?" Nancy Neuralgia asked.

"My, uh...I got a cramp in my finger." He held his finger up and flexed it. "I think it's okay now."

"Well, hurry up and get this thing working."

"Yes, ma'am."

Goliath stepped back up to the air compressor. Five hundred divided by one hundred is...he took a deep breath. Okay, it was five. Now, top left corner. One, two, three, four terminals to the yellow wire. Multiply by five. Good gosh, this was awful. Four times five was...sixteen. Sixteen? Yes, it had to be.

"Are you almost finished?" Norma demanded.

"Uh, yes, ma'am." Now, what was that number? Wait. One, two, three, four. Times five. And that was twenty? Yes, twenty. Divide that by two...ten. He was doing it! And finally, subtract five, and you get...

He counted down on his fingers. Luckily, he had five fingers on each hand. Ten, nine, eight, seven, six. Five numbers down, you get six. Yeah, Hoobabloobus had shown him how to do that. Unfortunately, Goliath didn't realize that his friend was showing him an old joke.

Goliath pulled the yellow wire out of its terminal, counted six to the right, and slipped the wire in.

"It's ready now, ma'am."

"It's about daggone time," Nancy said. She and Norma walked over to the air compressor and shoved Goliath out of the way. They began rolling up their sleeves and cracking their knuckles.

Off to the side, Miss Cranberry was planning the wedding. "Miss Fluorine will be my maid of honor, and Goliath will be the ring bearer. I'll invite Ernest Hemingway, Eleanor Roosevelt, Ayn Rand, Leadbelly..."

"Miss Cranberry, all those people are dead."

"Oh, Dexter, you should have proposed sooner. But I love you anyway."

And at the machine, Norma and Nancy were finished rolling and cracking. Nancy turned to the special steel-belted radial hose. It was all rolled up on the ground, making a huge, rolled-up roll, and one end was connected to the air compressor. They had another piece of hose, about three feet long. One end of this piece was connected to the air compressor, and the other end had a nozzle attached.

Nancy took the long, rolled-up piece of hose and tossed it down the mountain. It unrolled as it fell. The hose unrolled, that is, not the mountain. The mountain had not been rolled up to begin with.

Off to the side, Billy-Bob looked satisfied with the way things were going. But he hadn't been close enough to see what Goliath had done with the wires.

It was nagging at Goliath, though—the idea that he might have made a mistake. He tried to think about what he had done, to mentally retrace his steps, but he couldn't remember clearly. The whole world was in danger of crumbling into tiny little pieces the size of toenail clippings, and his brain wouldn't work.

A few moments later, they heard a faint splash as the end of the hose went into the ocean, way far downhill at the shoreline.

"How do we turn this thing on?" Norma asked. She

sounded fiendish. She sounded eager. She sounded fiendishly eager.

Goliath tried to think. What had he done wrong? He didn't have a clue, but he knew he couldn't let them turn the machine on until he was sure about the wires. "Well, you, uh...uh... Is that the model 610?"

Nancy looked at the air compressor. "No, it's the model 56X. Now, c'mon, kid—"

"Oh, okay. It, uh, it makes a difference, you know." Goliath was doing his best to stall while he tried to think of what to do, but he was so busy thinking about how to stall that he couldn't think about what to *do*.

"We don't care. Just tell us how to turn this thing on, whatever model it is."

"Well, we have to plug it in."

Norma and Nancy looked at each other. Then Nancy picked up the power cord and plugged it into an outlet on a nearby tree. A little light on top of the machine blinked on.

Goliath gritted his teeth. The Neuralgia Sisters were getting ever closer to turning this machine on, but he was getting no closer at all to figuring out his mistake. He looked at Dexter Kroger and Miss Cranberry. They were making goo-goo eyes at each other, being in love and stuff. Miss Cranberry, his teacher who cared about him. Dexter Kroger, who...well, Goliath didn't know whether Dexter cared about him, but he had broken up the fight when Billy-Bob attacked him on the porch that one night.

"Now what?" Norma demanded.

He had to fix this, Goliath did. He had to do it for them, for Miss Cranberry and Dexter. And for Billy-Bob. And for his mother, and for Othello, and for

Hoobabloobus. And for that nice Ann Onimous lady and for Mr. and Mrs. Neuralgia, those nice people. And for Eunice Mae. And for Hrobigothr.

"Listen, kid, I'm getting ready to shoot somebody," Nancy said.

And thinking of Hrobigothr made Goliath remember something the troll had taught him that night under the bridge. "Hey, little guy," Hrobigothr had said, "if your problems ever seem too big, if the stress is too great to bear, here's how you can deal with it." And then Hrobigothr showed Goliath a relaxation technique, a sort of meditative thing that would make the universe drain into Goliath's own being-of-self. Or something.

"I'm trying to remember," Goliath said.

He took some slow, deep breaths and rolled his eyes back into his head, as Hrobigothr had taught him. He concentrated on Nothingness. Internally, he recited a little mantra the troll had taught him.

And then, after how much time he didn't know, Goliath was stricken with a sudden burst of inspiration, a burst of inspiration originating from a time before the beginning of the universe. No, forget that. He simply realized what the mistake was that he had made. You don't count five down from ten and end up at six. You subtract five from ten and get five. It was really the fifth terminal! "I…uh…" Goliath said.

"What's the matter, kid?" Nancy snarled.

"That yellow wire," Goliath said, feeling his voice shake, "that yellow wire should be one place over to the left."

"Oh, for crying out loud," Norma said. She yanked the wire out and plugged it back into the correct place. "Is that it?"

"Yes, ma'am."

"Now what do we do?"

Sure now that the air compressor was fixed correctly, Goliath began to feel more confident. "There's a switch at each end," he said in a steady voice. He felt a quick pang of concern that with this change in his attitude, the Neuralgia Sisters might catch on that that he and Billy-Bob had some kind of plan. And if they had bought Trudy's imagination, they would have suspected exactly that very thing. Instead, they suspected nothing at all. "You have to flip both of them on at exactly the same time," Goliath said.

"Good," Norma said. "One for each of us."

Nancy, with one hand, picked up the short piece of hose and pointed the nozzle up at the sun. She put her other hand on one of the switches. "Ready?" she asked Norma.

"Yeah," Norma said. "Remember, we want only a little squirt, just enough to make it flicker."

"Right. One, two, three."

The Neuralgia Sisters flipped the switches. A whole bunch of special polarized, magnetic, ionized electricity generated by Billy-Bob's clever wiring scheme shot into the sisters, Norma and Nancy. A surprised look washed over their faces, a look much like the one you would get if you suddenly found out you had been shooting pool with Grendel. They began glowing.

Goliath was surprised, too. He hadn't known what would happen. Billy-Bob hadn't told him because Goliath might have lost his nerve. But Billy-Bob, he knew what to expect, and things were going perfectly. He smiled. And Dexter and Miss Cranberry—well, they didn't see any of this because they were busy being lovebirds.

But that wasn't all. After lots of humming and clinking and all kinds of noise from the machine, the Neuralgia Sisters started floating up into the air!

"Hey, what's going on?" Nancy shouted.

"Get us down!" Norma added.

But up they went. The atoms in their bodies had been anticharged with subneutral quarkons, which made the pull of gravity on them so weak that they were to spend the rest of their lives floating two hundred feet up in the air, drifting around at the mercy of the wind and the birds and the clouds and airplanes.

Way to go, Billy-Bob!

Way to go, Goliath!

***

The equatorial police came to investigate, and each of our good guys told his or her part of the story. The Neuralgia Sisters tried to yell their version down to the officers, claiming they were victims of these vicious people who had tried to put out the sun. But the equatorial police didn't believe them because the vote was four to two against them. Also besides that, Dexter and Miss Cranberry were so aglow with love that the police couldn't help but believe them.

(Remember the police sergeant Nancy flirted with earlier in the story? If she had let him cook dinner for her, he would have been happy—nay, *eager*—to help them out. He could have, too. He was friends with the equatorial police. But what really happened was that when he saw the story on the news, he chuckled and sipped on his tea.)

Everybody went back home. Everybody except the Neuralgia Sisters, that is. They kept on floating around overhead and became kind of a...well, a joke. Yes, Norma and Nancy Neuralgia had finally gotten their comeuppance.

19. The Big Ceremony

Foreign correspondents had reached the scene at the mountaintop even before the police were finished questioning everyone. Consequently, the story got back home ahead of our heroes. A crowd, a huge crowd, met Goliath and the gang at the airport. Eunice Mae was there, and she came running up to Goliath and gave him a great big hug and a kiss on the cheek. He was embarrassed because people were watching. Othello and Cleopatra were there, and they forgave Goliath. After what he had done, they realized that he was a pretty good kid after all.

Dexter was able to go back to work; Mr. Midwest believed that the police had arrested the real killer. Why not? Dexter hadn't killed anyone, anyway.

Goliath was able to go back to work and to school, too. Mr. Antwerp was so proud of his little protégé that he promoted Goliath and made him his personal chauffeur.

And by the time Billy-Bob got back home, he had formulated treatments that would restore all of Cleopatra and Othello's brain functions, as well as Othello's eyesight, and he had finished developing the diet that would make him, Billy-Bob, good looking. Now he looked like a member of Duran Duran, svelte and graceful and fashionable, wearing a stylish tux and a tasteful Genius Association of America medallion on a gold chain around his neck. And being the great guy that he was, he also gave the brain treatment to all the people who had worked in those abandoned buildings around Goliath's street corner. Now that intersection was the most active, thrivingest area of the city for business and stuff.

Having eaten a bag of the enhanced Extra Smarts he found at Hamburger Sty, Mr. Sigmoid figured out how to assume Mr. Schurk's identity and run the charcoal business at such a high level of ethics that he sometimes got dizzy. And even with being so preposterously ethical, even after giving the redneck and suburban neighborhoods back to Mr. Antwerp, he was able to make millions of handfuls of money a year, pay his vendors extravagantly, and peacefully and harmoniously coexist with Mr. Antwerp. Wow.

Cleopatra ended up with the ability to operate a highly successful tattoo business on the Internet. She didn't like dealing with people, so having the business on the Internet meant she could tattoo people without ever having to meet them in person. She, too, made millions and starred in her own reality show!

And Othello's Extra Smarts enabled her to embark on a glamorous career in fake fossil restoration (which made quite heavy use of her color-matching abilities) and to rewrite her opera, the one she had written by accident, so that it actually turned out to be good. Or, well, sorta good, anyway.

Billy-Bob was disappointed because although he knew the recipe, he was unable to make any more Extra

Smarts. He couldn't get any more sodium cogitate.

***

The president, the president of the United States, was happy about the heroic deeds of Goliath and Billy-Bob and Dexter and Miss Cranberry. So happy, in fact, that he decided to have a special award ceremony on the White House lawn, with a big, special stage set up with all kinds of decorations and elaborate sound and lighting equipment. And TV people were there covering the event.

"I'm very happy about the heroic deeds of these fellow Americans," the president said at the ceremony. "The earth itself was in danger of getting crumbled into little pieces the size of toenail clippings, and none of us would have wanted that. I would never have seen my favorite show, *Bowling for Penicillin*, again." He paused, and the crowd applauded. "A new episode is going to be on tonight, and they say it's the best one yet." He paused and took a sip of water. More applause. "I think this shows why the United States is the greatest nation on earth."

More applause. The president frowned. "Well, okay. So the villains were Americans, too." He scratched his chin. "But you'll notice that we have four heroes to two villains. That's what America's all about. Four heroes for every two villains."

He sighed and then frowned. "Of course, I don't want to make it sound as if it takes four heroes to take care of two villains. That would be unflattering. What I mean is that America has the greatest number of heroes of any country on Earth."

The president was getting flustered. "But other countries have heroes, too," he added quickly. "But we have the best ones." More cheering.

"I don't mean, though," he said, sweating, "that heroes from other countries couldn't have done what these people did. I mean that—"

The first lady nudged him in the arm and whispered something to him. "Yes, well, let me introduce them," the president said.

Then he introduced Goliath and Billy-Bob and Dexter and Miss Cranberry. They blushed. None of them was used to this kind of attention. Dexter kinda was because he had been an all-pro athlete in college, and those guys get lots of adoring attention. But he wasn't used to it from the whole country, including the president his own self.

"And now," the president said, "for the awards. Goliath, will you please step forward?"

Goliath felt a little bit of stage fright, but he didn't have to do anything except step forward and stand there. "Goliath, I now bestow upon you the Special Presidential Award for Accomplishing Impressive Accomplishments." And with that, the president patted Goliath on the head.

There was more cheering and applause. The TV newsmen analyzed the event. Goliath, feeling like a good citizen, blushed more deeply, and then he stepped back as quickly as he could.

The president gave the rest of them pats on the head—Billy-Bob, Dexter, and Miss Cranberry. Each blushed. Newsmen analyzed.

"That's not all," the president said. "I would now like to introduce Father Willis O'Grotten."

Father O'Grotten stepped forward. "Good afternoon," he said. "I understand we have a wedding—several weddings—to perform here. Will the lucky couples please step forward?"

The lucky couples stepped forward. Dexter Kroger and Miss Cranberry. Cato and Miss Fluorine. Mr. Sigmoid and Cleopatra. Billy-Bob and Othello. Goliath and Eunice Mae. Phil Dogbladder and Mary Viscera (not previously in our story or known to any of our characters in any way, but they happened to have planned their wedding for that day). Now, of course, Goliath and Eunice Mae were children, too young to get married. And Billy-Bob and Othello were, like, just barely legally old enough, but they wanted to wait longer before taking such a big step. So their part of the ceremony was sorta, like, pretend-like, or fake. It didn't count. But they, the ceremony-organizing people, wanted to include them so as to make the occasion bigger and more festive.

Father O'Grotten cleared his throat. Newsmen analyzed it. "All right," Father O'Grotten said. "Marriage is sacred. You folks shouldn't be rushing into it just because you have the hots for each other. That's not why you're doing this, is it?"

Everyone said, "No."

"Good. Because I'll tell you right now, it really burns me up when people get married just to have sex. I hate people who get married just to have sex worse than almost anything. Well, except for communist vampires from Saturn. But if sex is all you want, you shouldn't get married. Understand?"

Everyone said, "Yes."

Father O'Grotten didn't seem convinced. In

particular, he eyeballed Cato suspiciously and muttered, in a low voice, "I've got my eye on you, young man." Then he continued the ceremony. "All right. Now, does everyone promise to love, honor, and cherish the person he or she is marrying?"

Everyone said, "Yes."

"Does everyone promise to be faithful to the person he or she is marrying?"

"Yes."

"That's good. Because I hate unfaithful spouses. An unfaithful spouse deserves to have his or her head shoved into a bucket of rancid pus. Understand?"

"Yes."

"Good. Does everyone promise not to change the channel in the middle of your spouse's favorite TV show, even if you can't stand it?"

"Yes."

"Promise not to smack your spouse in the face with a shovel?"

"Yes."

"Do you women promise to stay married even if all your husband's extremities fall off, and you men promise to stay married even if your wife's bodily openings grow shut?"

"Yes."

That last promise wasn't part of the official ceremony. Father O'Grotten slipped it in to make sure about the sex. Now he was satisfied, except maybe in the case of Cato. He paused and gave Cato a hard stare, and Cato tried to look innocent.

"Promise to send me half of all the money you make for the rest of your lives?" Father O'Grotten said.

"No."

That wasn't part of the ceremony either. He liked to see what he could get couples to agree to. Sometimes it worked. "Okay," he said, "first couple. Do you, Dexter Kroger, take Miss Cranberry to be your lawful wedded wife?"

"I do."

"And do you, Miss Cranberry, take Dexter Kroger to be your lawful wedded husband?"

"I do."

"Good for you. Next couple. Do you, Mr. Sigmoid, take Cleopatra to be your lawful wedded wife?"

"Absolutely and unconditionally."

"And do you, Cleopatra, take Mr. Sigmoid to be your lawful wedded husband?"

"Okay."

"All right. Do you, Billy-Bob, pretend to take Othello to be your lawful wedded wife?"

"I most certainly do," Billy-Bob said. Cato looked over at his brother and beamed with pride.

"And do you, Othello, pretend to take Billy-Bob to be your lawful wedded husband?"

"I suppose so."

"Do you, Cato, take Miss Fluorine to be your lawful wedded wife?"

"I might as well."

"Do you, Miss Fluorine, take Cato to be your lawful wedded husband?"

"You bet! He's cute, even in a body cast."

"Yeah, right," Father O'Grotten said. "Somebody wheel this boy out of the way. Do you, Goliath, pretend to take Eunice Mae to be your lawful wedded wife?"

"Sure thing, Mr. O'Grotten."

"That's *Father* O'Grotten."

"Sorry."

"Do you, Eunice Mae, pretend to take Goliath to be your lawful wedded husband?"

"I do."

"Do you, Phil Dogbladder, take Mary Viscera to be your lawful wedded wife?"

"Uh, yes, sir, yes, I do."

"Do you, Mary Viscera, take Phil Dogbladder to be your lawful wedded husband?"

"To be honest, father, I'm having second thoughts—"

Father O'Grotten, not paying the tiniest bit of attention, plowed onward. "Okay, you're all husbands and wives now, or pretend husbands and wives, or whatever. Swap rings with whomever you're marrying and kiss each other."

All the couples kissed, including Phil and Mary, although Mary's heart wasn't in it, and the crowd at the White House lawn and the TV audience got so carried away with the sheer romance of this massive wedding that three-quarters of the people in the United States ended up kissing all at once. Mr. Schurk, watching on the jailhouse TV, growled. "Shut up, murderer, I want to watch this," a guard said.

And Fritz, still glued to the ground at the airport, could hear a loud, sentimental-sounding "Aaawwww..." from the nearest house, which was a quarter mile away. The people who lived there were having a big party to watch the ceremony. But he, Fritz, didn't know what was going on. All he knew was that he wanted to go home. He looked up into the sky and hoped it wouldn't start raining.

And at that moment, the Neuralgia Sisters drifted over the White House lawn, cursing and wailing.

"Help!" Norma screamed.

"Get us down," Nancy shouted.

Father O'Grotten shook his fist at them. "Shut up! Can't you see there's a damn wedding going on here? Have some respect, why don'tcha?" He snorted wetly and turned his attention back to the task at hand. "I understand," he said, "that Othello has written a special poem for the occasion. Would you like to step forward and read it?"

"Yes, Father." Othello pulled a sheet of paper from inside the front of her dress and unfolded it. She stepped up to the microphone and cleared her throat. Newsmen analyzed.

"Hey, buttheads, help us! We're stuck up here!" Norma screamed. What made her more frustrated was that among the notes from her project to figure out how to boil water without heat was a formula that would show how to get them back down. It was right there on a three-by-five index card on her workbench. And try as they might, they were never able to get anyone to go look for it. They would shout at people and tell them about it, but the people just snickered at them. Later, their parents moved into the house, and they, Mr. and Mrs. Neuralgia, kept the furniture and threw out all of Norma and Nancy's other stuff. The card ended up in a landfill, buried under tons of food waste. The girls drifted over the landfill once every 7.3 months.

Back at the wedding, Father O'Grotten looked up at the Neuralgia Sisters. "Shut the hell up," he shouted. Then he turned to Othello. "Go ahead, dear," he told her in a sweet voice.

She began reading:

I love you, Billy-Bob.
The other girls said you were a slob.
But I know that's not true,
Oh, yes, I do.
Oh, Billy-Bob, I love you.
The other girls said you were full of icky goo.
But I know that's not so;
Yes, that's what I know.
And now we're pretending to get married today.
I'm so happy I don't know what to say.
So I'll write this poem
And then we'll go home.

As the crowd was popping open bottles of champagne, a guy was standing all by himself backstage among the wires and scaffolding and whatnot, listening to the poem. He had black hair and a bushy beard, and he was stuck in the nineteenth century. This guy's name was Bob, and he had a chainsaw. He had the chainsaw because the organizers of the ceremony were afraid it would be invaded by zombies, and Bob was the world-champion zombie killer. The chainsaw was his weapon of choice, and he could cut the heads off zombies like you wouldn't believe. And most important, he did it with *style*.

And Bob hated bad poetry. He hated it worse than just about anything, communist vampires from Saturn included. He didn't know that until she fell in love, Othello had been a pretty good poet. But then, well, that's what love does to a person's brain. Bob didn't know that, though. All he knew was that he hated bad poetry.

His eyes took on a faraway look. His face twitched. His fingers closed slowly around the rubber handle at the end of the starter rope. His jaw tightened. He yanked the rope.

Nothing happened. He gave it a couple more tugs. Still nothing. The chainsaw was out of gas.

"Come on," Mr. Sigmoid shouted from the podium. "Party at my house! Everyone's invited!"

— THE END —

PS: Because he was a true humanitarian, Billy-Bob arranged to have cheeseburgers catapulted up to the Neuralgia Sisters every day so they wouldn't starve up there.

Also, shortly after that, Billy-Bob published his rebuttal to *Principia Mathematica*, which, unlike previous, less-sophisticated critiques, believe it or not, had the effect of making arithmetic easier. But it didn't matter to Goliath. The switch had been flipped, exactly as Dexter had said, and Goliath was able to understand it at any level of difficulty.

Thanks to members of a couple of Sena Naslund's University of Louisville creative writing classes some years ago, who critiqued the first draft of this novel. Other thanks go to Linda Harris, Bob Maples, and Carol Lauer, each of whom, in his or her own way, helped shape this work into the awesome hunk of literature you see before you. Please don't hold it against them.

—RH

If you liked *Goliath*, try these other books by Ray Holland:

The Hermit: A dedicated career hermit becomes mixed up with a promiscuous young lady from a nearby village in this kinda-sorta parable-fairy-tale-type story. Who, if anyone, lives happily ever after?

Open Stage: A mysterious, alluring woman, a hyperactive, funny little man, and a very strange business deal leads Gilbert Ragwater to learn a few things about himself. It's a coming-of-age story for those of us with arrested development.

The Hookie-Pookie Man: His mother was from Earth, and his father was from another planet. He doesn't fit in anywhere, but he knows a woman of similar origin is out there somewhere—and he's determined to find her.

Soft White Underbelly: Join Thor and his friends as they overthrow the government from the comfort of Thor's home, go to a yard sale and find a weapon so powerful that it can't be used, encounter a soul-stealing snack machine at the airport, take inventory of everything on the planet, circulate a petition for a Better America, embark on a plot to assassinate Satan...and more. Much, much more!

www.ingramcontent.com/pod-product-compliance
Lightning Source LLC
Chambersburg PA
CBHW031303170626
46807CB00001B/293